James Craig has worked … and consultant for almost thirt… …den with his family. His first … …*don Calling*, is also available fr…

For more information visit www.james-craig.co.uk, or follow him on Twitter: @byjamescraig.

Also by James Craig

London Calling

NEVER APOLOGISE, NEVER EXPLAIN

JAMES CRAIG

Constable & Robinson Ltd
55–56 Russell Square
London WC1B 4HP
www.constablerobinson.com

First published in the UK by Robinson,
an imprint of Constable & Robinson Ltd, 2012

This is a work of fiction. Names, characters, places and incidents are either the product of the author's imagination or are used fictitiously, and any resemblance to real persons, living or dead, or to actual events or locales is entirely coincidental

A copy of the British Library Cataloguing in Publication data is available from the British Library

ISBN 978-1-84901-584-4 (paperback)
ISBN 978-1-84901-782-4 (ebook)

Typeset by TW Typesetting, Plymouth, Devon

Printed and bound in the UK

1 3 5 7 9 10 8 6 4 2

ACKNOWLEDGEMENTS

This is the second Carlyle novel. After publishing the first (*London Calling*), I started paying more attention to Acknowledgements pages in other books. Having looked through more than a few now, I have to conclude that I am getting a lot more help than other writers. Either that or they are being rather parsimonious with their thanks.

For my part, I have to say a sincere 'thank you' to many people. They include: Polly James, Paul Ridley, Michael Doggart, Luke Speed, Andrea von Schilling, Celso F. Lopez and Peter Lavery. Thanks as well go to crime fiction guru Richard Jacques and everyone at Brunswick, and to Mary Dubberly and all the staff at Waterstone's in Covent Garden.

Particular mention has to go to Chris McVeigh and Beth McFarland, digital media experts at 451 for all their help in promoting John Carlyle online. And, of course, nothing would have come of any of this without the efforts of Krystyna Green, Rob Nichols, Martin Palmer, Eryl Humphrey Jones, Emily Burns and all of the team at Constable.

Above all, however, I thank Catherine and Cate who continue to put up with all of this book stuff when I should have been doing other things. This book, and all the others, is for them.

ONE

Finding himself once again locked out of the Parker House hostel, Walter Poonoosamy, the drunk known as 'Dog', walked round the corner, into Drury Lane and headed north. His destination was the warren of streets around the British Museum. A tourist magnet, the area boasted plenty of all-you-can-eat restaurants, so the pickings were usually good.

Big Ben could just be heard chiming one o'clock as Dog turned into Great Russell Street. At this time of night the street was empty, just the way he liked it. He eyed the black refuse sacks that had been left out on the pavement, waiting for collection by Camden's heroic bin men. The morning's first collection truck would be along at around 7 a.m.; by then, most of the sacks would have been opened, and the rubbish strewn up and down the street. Dog knew from bitter experience that it was the early dosser that got the leftovers. Hunger was poking through his inebriation and he had to get in quick before the competition for the street buffet – the dossers from Tottenham Court Road and Russell Square – turned up. Now was the prime time to forage for leftover food, clothes and whatever other useful bits and pieces the locals had thrown away.

After considering various options, Dog stepped up to a collection of refuse sacks piled by a street lamp on the east side of the street, outside an Indian restaurant called Sitaaray. Pulling a Stanley knife out of his jacket pocket, he bent down and carefully slit open the nearest bag. A couple of minutes of careful rummaging yielded some decent leftovers: lamb shaami and chicken masala, as well as a couple of peshwari naan. As a meal, it was better than anything that he would have got at the hostel, and would go perfectly with the remains of the two-litre bottle of Diamond White cider that he had saved from earlier in the day. Checking up and down the road to make sure that no one had spied upon his good fortune, Dog gave a silent prayer of thanks for the city's endless bounty before retreating into the darkness of a nearby alleyway at the rear of a huge block of mansion flats to set about his feast.

TWO

Still dressed, unable to sleep, Agatha Mills stood at her living-room window and gazed out at the floodlit splendour of the British Museum. The view was the best thing about the flat, especially at night; she often spent time contemplating its Ionic columns and the sculptures on the pediment over the main entrance, depicting *The Progress of Civilisation*.

Progress indeed, Agatha thought sadly, shaking her head.

This view had been the thing that had made her fall in love with the flat when they had first seen it, almost forty years ago. She had badgered Henry to pay the asking price immediately, even though they couldn't afford it. He had been very grumpy about it at the time, something that still made her smile, even now. Over the years, however, as it became clear that the flat was the one sound financial investment they'd made in their entire lives, her husband had relented and graciously accepted that she had been right.

For Agatha, however, their joy in Great Russell Street had always been tinged with sadness. From that first visit, she had dreamed of taking her own children down the stairs, across the road and into the Museum. She had daydreamed of picnics in the courtyard, lost afternoons spent among the Egyptian mummies or the Roman treasures. If, at the time, she had known that there would be no children, she would have felt utterly crushed. Even now, there was a sharp stab of regret that she knew would never go away.

However, a stoical pragmatism ruled the Mills household: you have to live with your regrets – and they had done so. Life went on. They had found other things to occupy their time and their emotions. Sometimes she wondered if Henry was as disappointed as she was – being a man, after all – but ultimately that didn't matter. They weren't having some kind of competition to see who could wear more of their heart on their sleeve.

She thought of him now, asleep in their double bed and smiled. He was a good man who had taken on her struggles and made them his own. Over the years she had realised that he was a truly remarkable companion and she was lucky to have him.

A movement in the street below caught her eye. Stepping closer to the window, she gazed down on a tramp going through the rubbish, looking for something to eat, or maybe some discarded clothing. For Agatha, at her window at this time of night, it was a fairly common sight and no longer elicited much of a response other than the gentle voyeuristic thrill of spying on another human being going about their business. Having spent much of her life working in poorer countries, she was used to human scavenging. Indeed, she had seen much worse than London had to offer. Here, however, Agatha had found that she was less sympathetic to the plight of others. Maybe it was just that she was getting older, but she wondered if it was the city making her harder.

Like the other residents of Ridgemount Mansions, Agatha was infuriated by the rubbish that was strewn across the pavement most mornings, once their carefully sorted and bagged waste had been methodically dissected by the homeless ghosts who stalked the empty streets in the middle of the night. Occasionally, someone would call the police but it was a complete waste of time; if they ever turned up at all, the officers invariably failed to hide their disinterest in such a minor matter and made only the most perfunctory attempts to move the miscreants on.

She watched as the man collected a selection of items from one of the bags put out by the restaurant situated a couple of doors down the street, before disappearing into the shadows to enjoy his meal. A gust of wind sent some empty foil containers spinning into the road. Otherwise, nothing moved on the street below.

Stepping away from the window, Agatha heard a noise from the kitchen. Henry was clearly having trouble sleeping again. Until recently, it had been unusual for him to get up in the night but now, it was an increasingly frequent occurrence. As he got older, he was becoming more restless.

'Henry?' She padded out of the living room and peered along the hall. The kitchen light was on. 'Are you all right?' The noise in the kitchen stopped, but there was no reply. He's becoming deafer by the day, she reflected. We're both getting on. That was another thing about not having kids: who would look after them when things got too much? Agatha's mother had ended up in a home; not much of a home, more a kind of modern-day bedlam. For Agatha the guilt and the shame of leaving her there was bad enough, but it was as nothing compared to her steely determination that the same thing would not happen to herself, nor to her husband. Her father had keeled over from a heart attack while out buying a loaf of bread one day. At the time, it had been a terrible shock but, on reflection, that was a far better way to go than wasting away in a loony-bin.

'Henry?' she repeated sharply, annoyed by her own morbid musings. 'What are you doing? It's really rather late.' Agatha stepped into the kitchen and frowned. There was no one there. Sighing, she turned for the light switch, before catching a movement out of the corner of her eye.

'What the devil?'

The first blow caught her on the shoulder rather than on the head, but it was enough to send her crashing to the floor.

'Henry!' Agatha whimpered, trying to use a nearby chair to pull herself up. She had just managed to get herself into a kneeling position, when the second blow came. This time it did catch her squarely on the back of the head, sending her down for good.

THREE

Police in Chile have arrested a dancer who performed a series of striptease dances on the Santiago underground, the metro. Montserrat Morilles has been dubbed 'La Diosa del Metro', the Metro Goddess. She told reporters: 'Chile is still a pretty timid country. People aren't very extroverted and we want to take aim at that and make Chile a happier country.'

Carlyle stuck his head out from under the duvet and switched off the clock radio. He rubbed the sleep from his eyes and watched his wife get dressed. Standing at the bottom of the bed, with her back to him, Helen tossed her T-shirt on to the floor and reached over for a pearl bra that had been left hanging on a nearby chair. She slipped it on casually and checked herself in the wardrobe mirror. Carlyle watched her buttocks twitch and felt a twitch of his own.

One of the many things he loved about his wife was her beautiful arse. It was a very fine arse; pert, smooth and not quite symmetrical. A wave of enthusiasm crept over him; he wanted to jump out of bed and grab it. Another twitch. He gave himself a vigorous scratch in order to confirm what he already knew – his morning erection was quite spectacular.

How much time did they have? He heard the television spring into life in the living room. Alice would be grabbing fifteen minutes of crap while eating her breakfast, before going to school. That would be more than enough time. First, however, he needed to piss. He was just about to swing his feet out of the bed when Helen turned to him and gave him one of her worrying smiles. Apart from the bra, which showed a generous amount of areola, she was still naked. Apparently oblivious to her provocative appearance, she asked casually, 'Did you ever accept a freebie?'

'Good morning to you too.' Carlyle shrank back inside the duvet. The last thing he wanted to do now was to resume the previous night's conversation. Helen had picked up on a story in one of the Sunday newspapers about an inspector from the Harrow station who had been arrested on a raid in a local brothel. The paper had speculated that the officer had provided security for the establishment, known as Auntie Jayne's, *in return for payments of cash and services*. This had led Helen to loudly speculate about the inability of police officers to resist the temptations that The Job had to offer. Rather than keeping his own counsel, Carlyle had foolishly attempted to mount a defence of both his colleagues and, by extension, himself.

Glancing in the direction of his crotch, she raised her eyebrows. 'Well?'

'Define "freebie".'

'You know,' Helen put her hands on her hips, provocatively challenging him, teasing him. 'Did you ever go with a . . . whore?'

Whore. The word was carefully chosen: both derogatory and accusing.

Carlyle blinked twice and stared at the ceiling. His erection was beginning to wane. What a way to start a Monday morning, being quizzed by his wife on his sexual history and his ethical standards. It was like being at work: you didn't have to *be* guilty to *feel* guilty.

He gave his situation as much thought as he could, knowing that he didn't have much time. Sitting up in bed, he put on his most dispassionate expression, which proved not to be too difficult at that time of the morning.

'No.'

Helen stepped into a pair of faded panties that did not match the bra. 'Are you sure? Most men have, you know. It's not a big deal.'

Carlyle didn't believe that last comment for a second. He knew a 'big deal' when he saw one. Scratching his head, he faked a yawn, playing for time. A light touch was needed here. Discarding dispassionate, he stuck on his face the most relaxed grin he could manage and ploughed on. 'Which do you mean? Could I have forgotten banging a hooker? Or am I telling you the truth?'

'Either.' Helen pulled a light brown jumper over her head and picked up a pair of black jeans. 'Both.'

Deciding that attack was the best form of defence, Carlyle tossed aside the duvet with a flourish and slid out of bed. He had nothing to declare but his semi-erection. Scratching his balls, he stepped forward and gently kissed his wife on the forehead. 'I don't think so . . . I mean, I would have remembered.'

Stepping away from him, Helen quickly buttoned up her jeans. Involuntarily, Carlyle grabbed his cock and squeezed it gently before giving his balls another pleasurable scratch. Now he really needed to piss, but he couldn't duck out of the bedroom too quickly, it would look like he was running away.

'So you're sure?'

Yesterday's boxers lay on the floor next to his own jeans. He picked them up and gave them a quick sniff – not too bad . . . they would do for another day. 'Look,' he said, struggling into the underpants, careful to revert to her choice of language, 'there are whores and there are *whores*. Your average crackhead is not, in my experience, much like Julia Roberts in *Pretty Woman*.'

Helen looked him up and down, reminding him – not that he needed reminding – that married life really was a continuous assessment. 'So, if they had been prettier, or cleaner . . .'

There was no going back now. He tried another grin. 'Julia Roberts isn't really my type anyway.'

'But what if they looked like, I don't know – the girl in that Bond film – Eva Green?'

Eva Green? 'They don't.'

Helen started brushing her hair. 'But if they did? And if all you had to do was hand over the money?'

This time he did grin. 'Policemen don't have to pay. We get *freebies*, remember? Which is just as well, given the cash – or rather the lack of cash – in my pocket.'

Helen now smiled her checkmate smile. 'So you would? Or you did?'

So much for humour. Carlyle's grin vanished, as his heart sank. 'I need to piss,' he said quietly.

FOUR

The inspector sat outside Il Buffone, enjoying the gentle morning sunshine. The tiny 1950s-style Italian café sat just across the road from his flat on Macklin Street, on the corner of Drury Lane in the north-east section of Covent Garden. Inside, there was just enough room for the counter and two tattered booths, each of which could seat four people, or six at a squeeze. It was a case of risk a random dining companion inside or take one of the small tables outside on the street, where you were more likely to be left alone. Besides, the exhaust fumes were free.

Although he didn't appreciate any company at breakfast, Carlyle's preference was to eat inside where he could sit under the poster of the 1984 Juventus scudetto-winning squad. The poster was torn and faded, curling at the edges and held together with Sellotape. Marcello had tried to replace it several times, most recently with the Italian World Cup-winning team of 2006. Always, however, the protests of Carlyle, and a few other regulars who knew their football, forced him to return the team of Trapattoni and Platini to their rightful place.

Today, however, Carlyle had hit the morning rush-hour and both inside booths were full. Sticking his head through the door, Carlyle didn't spot anyone who seemed like they were about to leave. Hovering in the doorway, he looked pleadingly at Marcello, the owner, who just nodded and said: 'I'll bring it out.'

The inspector had barely sat down when Marcello appeared at his table, dropping a double macchiato in front of him, along with an extremely impressive-looking cherry Danish that positively begged to be eaten. Carlyle looked down at the pastry and felt the drool building up inside his cheeks. He then gave Marcello what he hoped was an expression of humble gratitude.

'I thought you'd like that,' Marcello grinned, already heading back inside. 'See? It's gonna be a great day.'

Carlyle took a sip of the macchiato, letting it scald his throat, finishing his coffee before taking a knife and carefully cutting the pastry into quarters. Picking up the largest piece, he closed his eyes and contemplated the imminent sugar rush.

'*Hey!*'

The first slice of Danish was just about to reach his mouth when he heard the blast of a horn, followed by the screech of brakes. A woman started to scream. Looking up, he saw an old man in a cream raincoat on the ground in front of a white fruit-and-veg delivery van, by the zebra crossing in front of the Sun pub on Drury Lane, less than twenty yards away. Carlyle looked at the slice sadly and dropped it back on his plate. Ignoring the growling of his stomach, he got up from his table and strolled towards the scene of the accident while signalling to Marcello – who showed no interest at all in the mini-drama unfolding outside his door – that he would be needing another coffee.

Drury Lane was a relatively uncongested single-lane, one-way street, heading south to north. It could get you all the way from the Aldwych to High Holborn while avoiding the busier streets nearby. In order to get to the traffic lights at the north end that little bit quicker, drivers of all descriptions liked to put their foot to the floor and race up the thoroughfare as quickly as possible. The whole exercise was completely pointless since average traffic speeds in Central London remained a stately ten miles an hour, essentially the same as for the horse-drawn carriages more than a century earlier. Carlyle, who didn't own a car, could never understand the common urge to hurtle 200 yards only to spend longer at the next stop. Maybe it was a genetic condition; more likely these drivers were just tossers. Either way, it was a miracle that there weren't more accidents.

In this case, the front wheels of the van had stopped on the zebra crossing itself but it wasn't clear if it had actually hit the old man. Leaning out of his window, the van driver was remonstrating with the woman bystander who had now stopped screaming.

'It's a zebra crossing!' the woman shouted, seemingly oblivious to Carlyle's arrival.

'The silly old fucker just walked straight out,' the driver snarled, looking like he wanted to reach out of the window and grab her by the throat. He revved the engine, but couldn't move with the man still sprawling out in front of him. A taxi now pulled up behind the van, the cabbie giving an extended blast on his horn, just in case anyone had missed the fact that he was there.

'If you hadn't been going so fast,' the woman replied, 'this wouldn't have happened.'

'Mind your own fucking business, you stupid bitch,' the man shot back, his attention now focusing on Carlyle, who was writing down his registration number.

'Oi! Fuckface!' The driver stuck his head further out of the window of the van. 'What do you think *you're* doing?' Sweat was beading on his shaven head. He was wearing a replica of the new Spurs away strip for next season, a fetching mocha and brown number in a retro style. Carlyle thought about arresting him just for that. Instead, he showed the driver his ID and told him to switch off his engine. That prompted the taxi driver behind to let loose with another long blast on his horn. Carlyle ignored him. Already the traffic was backing up towards Great Queen Street and beyond, but that wasn't his problem. They could wait. He turned back to the old man and helped him up.

'Are you okay, Harry?' Carlyle asked.

Harry Ripley dusted himself down and fiddled with a button on his coat. He smiled sadly, like a man who fully expected to find himself dumped in the middle of the road every now and again. 'Hello, Inspector.'

'Did he hit you?'

The old man gazed at the tarmac. 'No. I'm all right.'

'Was it his fault?'

'I'd say fifty-fifty.'

Carlyle nodded back in the direction of the café. 'I'm just having a coffee in Il Buffone, so why don't you come and join me?' The old man nodded and shuffled back on to the pavement, before heading slowly towards Carlyle's table. The driver took this as his cue to restart his engine. Carlyle stepped back in front of the van, holding up his hand as if he was a traffic cop. 'Not so fast, sunshine. Hold your horses.'

The queue of traffic was now well into double figures and the cacophony of complaints was growing. The woman who had remonstrated with the driver was hovering on the pavement outside the Sun, as if unsure whether to stay or go. Carlyle turned to her and smiled, which only seemed to make her more uncomfortable. 'Don't worry. It's all right now, I can sort this.'

'Don't you want a statement or something?' the woman asked.

No, I bloody don't, thought Carlyle. The paperwork would be the kiss of death; his day would be over before it had even started. How come members of the public only wanted to be helpful when it wasn't necessary? 'No, it's fine.' He tried to sound grateful. 'I'll be able to handle it. Thanks for stopping.'

'Are you sure?'

'Well . . .' Carlyle looked down at his shoes, trying not to smile. *Are you sure?* How many times over the years had he been asked that question? He was a policeman. Of course he was sure. 'I'm sure.'

'Well, if you change your mind,' the woman said, 'I work at the launderette at the far end of Betterton Street.' She gestured over her shoulder. 'You can get me in there.'

'I know it,' Carlyle said, which was true. When the Carlyle family washing-machine had exploded earlier in the year, he had been a regular customer. 'Thanks.'

Reluctantly, the woman turned and walked away, leaving Carlyle to return his attention to the van driver. He moved to the driver's door. 'Name?'

The man couldn't have looked any more pained if someone was poised to stick a red-hot poker up his arse. 'Smith.'

Carlyle raised an eyebrow.

'No, really,' the man said, pulling his wallet from the back pocket of his jeans, 'it is Smith. Dennis Smith.' He fished out his driver's licence and flashed it through the window.

Ignoring the card, Carlyle leaned towards the window. 'Okay, Dennis, you seem to have violated various traffic laws here, as well as behaving in a way that could easily have led to a breach of the peace.' Talking bollocks, of course, but getting his attention. 'And that's before we talk about any actual injury to the victim's person. Or about you calling me "fuckface".'

'But,' Smith complained, 'you just sent him off to get a coffee. He's not hurt at all. Anyway, it was his fault.'

Carlyle let his gaze wander round the inside of the van. 'Are you up here often?'

Smith shifted in his seat. 'A bit.'

'Well, I'm round here all the time and I don't want to see any more boy-racer shit from . . .' he stood up to look at the name on the side of the van '. . . *Fred's Fabulous Fruit 'n' Veg*.'

'But—'

'But nothing. If I see this van doing more than twenty miles an hour up Drury Lane, you'll be nicked and I'll make sure that your boss knows about it. Now fuck off and drive carefully. Try not to knock over any more pensioners today.'

Scowling and muttering under his breath, Smith rammed the van into first gear, revving the engine as he pulled away. Stepping back on to the pavement, Carlyle heard the jeers of the other drivers who had been caught up behind this spat. As he walked back towards the café, he caught a couple of basic hand gestures reflected in the window of the William Hill betting shop, but chose to ignore them. As he reached the table, Marcello appeared with Carlyle's second macchiato and a mug of tea for Harry Ripley. Without saying a word, Carlyle sat down, drained the cup and methodically ate the quarter slices of his Danish, one after another.

Harry lived three floors below the Carlyles, in Winter Garden House. He had been a close friend of Carlyle's late father-in-law for many years and had known Helen since she had been born. Now in his late seventies, Harry had served in Korea in 1952 as part of the City of London Regiment of the Royal Fusiliers, for which he had received both UK and UN Korea medals. Although he didn't have a clue what Harry had been doing in Korea, Carlyle had admired both honours on several occasions. Harry had followed his twenty years in the military with another twenty as a postman, working out of the Mount Pleasant sorting office on Farringdon Road, near King's Cross. He had been retired almost fifteen years now and a widower for more than a decade. He had no kids and, as far as Carlyle knew, no other family. Now all he wanted to do was die – 'while I still have my health' as he put it. His fantasy, articulated many times over a pint of Chiswick Bitter in the Sun, was to keel over while watching Arsenal win the Premier League, which was how he had come by the moniker 'Heart Attack Harry'.

Carlyle fought a powerful urge to demolish another Danish. 'What was that all about, Harry?' he asked casually.

The old man slurped his tea and gazed into the middle distance. 'The bloke should have stopped. He was going too fast.'

'You should be grateful he wasn't going any faster,' Carlyle sighed. 'Anyway, that guy was a Spurs supporter. You should have known he was going to miss.'

Harry chuckled.

'It's not funny, mate. Have you ever tried anything like that before?'

'No.'

'Well, don't do it again, or I'll bloody kill you.'

Harry looked at him soulfully. 'It was an accident.'

'Bollocks, Harry, you did it on purpose. You gave that bloke a hell of a scare, even if he was a prize twat. You just can't behave like that.' He gazed up at the blue sky. It was already pushing 70 degrees; not London weather at all. Clearly, the day was going to be an absolute scorcher. 'And what's with the raincoat?'

Harry shrugged. 'You never know when it might rain.'

Carlyle glanced at his watch. He really should be on his way to the station. 'For fuck's sake, it's supposed to be more than eighty degrees today; the hottest day of the year. And knock it off with this morbid shit. There's nothing wrong with you. I'll probably kick the bucket before you do. In fact, I'll bet you twenty quid that you get to a hundred, no problem at all. Your telegram from the Queen is guaranteed.' Did they still do the telegrams? Carlyle wondered. He hoped so. Harry was as much a Royalist as he himself was a Republican, and if the thought of a 'Well done' message from Buckingham Palace couldn't cheer him up, nothing would.

Somehow, Harry managed to slip an even more downbeat expression on his battered mug. 'It doesn't just turn up, you know.'

'What?'

'The telegram from Her Majesty.'

'Oh?' Carlyle realised he shouldn't have gone there.

'Someone has got to ask her for it.'

The grumpy old sod was making the inspector feel like the world's biggest optimist. Taking a deep breath, he made a determined effort to remain cheery. 'At least they don't charge you for the privilege,' he said, wondering if they did.

'And you've got to prove your age.'

'Give Helen a copy of your bloody birth certificate then,' Carlyle snapped, his patience gone. 'She'll send it off to the powers-that-be, when the time comes.'

'She'll be dead by then.'

'Who?' said Carlyle, unsure whether to be concerned. 'Helen?'

'No,' said Harry, 'the Queen. She's older than me, you know.'

Carlyle felt irritated and relieved at the same time. 'Whatever. Anyway, you'll be fine.'

'Come on, Inspector,' said Harry, a slight tinge of anger appearing in his voice, 'don't try and kid me. I've had a decent innings and I don't need to drag it out. "Quit while you're ahead", my old dad always used to say, and he was right. I don't want to leave it too late and turn into a vegetable in some horrible care home. Or be left forgotten and starving on a trolley in a hospital corridor. I've no family and it should be my choice. Assisted suicide, they call it. It's all the rage these days. They had a guy die on the telly the other night.'

Carlyle grunted. He knew about the programme that Harry was referring to. The thought of it made his squeamishness flare up like an ulcer and also depressed the hell out of him. When Helen had insisted on watching it, he'd gone off to bed with a book. Even now, he shivered at the ghoulishness of it all. 'The bloke on the telly had some incurable disease. And he spent three grand to go to Switzerland to have it done in some Alpine clinic.' He looked directly at Harry. 'Then there's another seven grand, at least, to come home again and get buried. Do you have ten grand?'

'No.'

'Well, you can't bloody die, then,' Carlyle grinned, 'can you?'

'There are other ways,' Harry said evenly. 'You don't have to go to Switzerland. Didn't some copper in Wales walk up a mountain with a bottle of Scotch and freeze to death?'

Carlyle remembered it well, as it had been the talk of the station for days. 'Yeah, I should imagine Wales is a good place for that. They have plenty of mountains.'

Out of the glare, came merciful relief in the form of an angel. A pretty blonde girl in a very short skirt turned off Drury Lane and began sauntering down the other side of Macklin Street, talking into her mobile phone as she did so. Her toned legs were very long and tanned and she had a portfolio stuck under one arm. He guessed she was looking for the model agency a block away on Parker Street. Like Keats once said: *a thing of beauty is a joy forever*. It was the best cure for depression he knew.

Harry caught him staring and smirked. 'Too young for me.'

Carlyle said nothing as the girl did a U-turn and disappeared back down Drury Lane.

'Too young for you too.'

'Harry . . .'

'I read about it in the paper,' said Harry, returning to his theme, all thoughts of playing chicken with the traffic abandoned.

'Huh?'

'The policeman who walked up a mountain to kill himself.'

'Oh, yeah.' If Keats was alive today, a thing of beauty would be a joy for about ten seconds, Carlyle thought sourly.

'He had a complicated love-life, or something.'

'It must have been bloody complicated.' Carlyle reached inside his jacket for his wallet. 'For him to want to top himself.' He groaned when he realised how little cash he was carrying, barely enough to pay the bill. 'Anyway, I really have to go.'

'You didn't know him, did you?'

'No, funnily enough, he's one of the one hundred and forty thousand police officers in this country that I don't know personally.' As if by magic, Marcello appeared to clear away their cups. Carlyle handed him a tenner, signalled that he didn't need any change, and stood up.

'According to the papers, he had serious women trouble.' Harry struggled out of his chair.

'Don't we all?' Carlyle grinned, delighted to have finally got the conversation on to something other than death.

'Nah,' Harry said absent-mindedly. 'He wasn't henpecked like you. His problem was that he was shagging too many of them – way too many of them. Couldn't keep it in his trousers.'

Carlyle looked at the cheeky old codger. *Henpecked*? He thought about saying something, but let it go. Waving goodbye to Marcello, he stepped into the road. 'I'll see you soon. Pop in on Helen and Alice – they'd love to see you. In the meantime, don't cause any more trouble. That's an order.'

'Or I could get arrested?'

'Yeah.'

The old man's face lit up. 'I could die in custody. Fall down some stairs.'

Carlyle laughed as he started down the road. 'You never know, Harry. You never know.'

FIVE

'Where the bloody hell have you been?'

Leaning back in his chair, Carlyle looked blankly at his sergeant.

'I called you on the mobile,' Joe complained, the exasperation clear in his voice.

Carlyle fished his phone out of the breast-pocket of his jacket. The screen said he had missed four calls. Four bloody calls. That was about par for the course with Carlyle and his mobile phones. He looked up and tried to appear apologetic. 'Sorry.'

Having just returned from a week's holiday in Portugal, Sergeant Joseph Szyszkowski was tanned and, despite his current irritation with his boss, extremely relaxed. He looks like he's lost a bit of weight, Carlyle thought idly. And caught up on his sleep.

Lucky bugger.

Carlyle was glad to have his sergeant back. Joe was not your average copper. He was second-generation Polish and somewhat unworldly. But they had been working together for more than five years, and he was one of the few people – the *very* few – on the Force with whom Carlyle enjoyed working and, more importantly, trusted.

'Well, now that you're here, we have to go.' Joe casually dropped a piece of paper on Carlyle's desk.

Carlyle picked up the sheet of paper but he didn't read it, and didn't move from his seat. 'What's this?'

'Agatha Mills.'

'Who's she then?'

'She,' Joe grinned, 'is the little old lady who was brained last night in her flat up by the British Museum.'

'Nice place to live,' Carlyle sniffed.

'Not for her. Not any more. The husband called it in earlier.'

Carlyle glanced at the sheet of A4. 'Serious?'

'Dead.'

Carlyle felt a wave of indifference sweep over him. He held the paper up to the light, as if he was checking a twenty-pound note for its watermark. 'And it's come to us? Shouldn't it be for one of the geniuses at the Holborn station? They're closer to the British Museum than we are.'

'Well, it's come to us.' Joe was used to Carlyle's initial lack of interest. His boss often took his time to get warmed up and become involved in a case. By the time he did, the matter was often either solved or the inspector was off on a mission, with his sergeant in tow. Either way, Joe knew that he would buck up eventually.

Carlyle exhaled dramatically. 'Okay then,' he said, bouncing out of his chair with mock enthusiasm. 'Let's go and take a look.'

Coming out of the police station, Carlyle sidestepped a couple of winos sitting on the pavement and took a left turn, heading north. After cutting down Henrietta Street, he led Joe at a brisk pace through Covent Garden piazza and up Endell Street in the direction of Bloomsbury. A little more than five minutes later, they arrived at Ridgemount Mansions, a solid, six-storey apartment block facing the British Museum on Great Russell Street.

Agatha Mills had lived – and died – in flat number 8, on the first floor. After being buzzed into the building, Carlyle nodded to a couple of uniforms who were canvassing the neighbours, before ignoring a rickety-looking lift and climbing the stairs. He reached the front door of the flat just as a couple of forensic technicians, laden down with bags and the tools of their trade, came struggling out. Carlyle recognised one of them, but couldn't remember his name.

'The body's in the kitchen,' the techie explained. 'Bassett's in there too.' Sylvester Bassett was a pathologist working out of the Charing Cross station so Carlyle knew him reasonably well. They had worked together three or four times during the last year.

'Thanks.' Stepping past the technicians and into the flat, Carlyle sniffed the air. There was the usual mix of cooking and people smells. There was no obvious scent of death, but that was not unusual. Death, in his experience, kept itself to itself.

The front door opened on to a hallway that ran the entire length of the apartment, leading to rooms on either side. Moving further inside, Carlyle noted a bathroom, a living room – where a big-boned WPC he didn't recognise was babysitting some older bloke, presumably the husband – and two bedrooms. At the far end of the hall, on the right, he came to the kitchen. His first thought was that it was surprisingly large, easily twice the size of his own kitchen at home. There was a round dining table in the middle, surrounded by three chairs. Like the rest of the place, it had a wooden floor and the white tiles on the walls helped make the place feel clean and bright.

The man in the kitchen had his back turned towards him, but Carlyle instantly recognised Sylvester Bassett from his mop of curly golden hair (from this distance, you couldn't see the grey), as much as his unfortunate dress sense which today meant a natty brown corduroy suit, pink socks and what looked like a pair of plum suede loafers. Carlyle could never understand why a middle-aged man would spend so much time and effort just to look so fey. Bassett had his head poking out of the kitchen window, which gave on to a fire escape at the back of the building. He was humming to himself and smoking a cigarette.

'What have we got?' Carlyle asked.

Startled, Bassett took a step backwards, banging his head on the window frame. Cursing, he rubbed his head with one hand, while stubbing his cigarette out with the other. Tossing the dog end out of the window, he turned to Carlyle and gestured at the body. It lay face down, half under the table, with a pool of dried blood surrounding the head and shoulders. Agatha Mills was – or had been – maybe 5 feet 1 or 2 inches tall, with grey hair. She was dressed in a blouse which had once been white, with a blue skirt that almost reached her ankles and a grey cardigan. 'Smacked over the head with a blunt object,' Bassett explained, 'maybe a pot or a rolling pin.' He glanced around the room. 'Plenty of suitable things to choose from in a kitchen.'

'Have we found the murder weapon?' Carlyle asked.

Bassett pulled a packet of Benson & Hedges cigarettes out of his jacket pocket and started fiddling with it. 'Not yet.'

'Who's the guy in the living room?'

'That's the husband.' Bassett flicked open the cigarette packet's lid with his thumb, then closed it again. 'Mr Henry Mills. He's in a bit of a state.'

'I can imagine.'

'Been drinking.'

'That's understandable,' Carlyle said reasonably. 'But is he our man?'

Bassett smiled. 'You're the detective, Inspector.' He finally pulled another cigarette from the packet and pushed it between his lips.

Carlyle scanned the kitchen again. Apart from the corpse and the congealing blood, everything looked perfectly shipshape. 'Just asking your opinion.'

Bassett was now fumbling with his lighter. 'Looks likely,' he conceded.

Law of averages, Carlyle reckoned. Start with the most likely explanation and work outwards. Fucked-up families were what he did, after all. He took another look round. It was a well kitted-out kitchen with decent equipment: Miele and AEG machines rather than the buy-now, repair-later crap that most people usually bought. He clocked a fridge, washing machine, cooker, microwave and an expensive-looking coffee-maker almost as big as Marcello's Gaggia machine in Il Buffone, before his gaze paused at the dishwasher. A small orange light indicated that it was still switched on. Giving the body a wide berth, he stepped across the room. The machine had been set for an intensive 65-degree wash, rather than an economy bio 45-degree one, and it had obviously completed one cycle. Carefully, he brought the back of his hand close to the machine, staying just shy of touching it. The machine was lukewarm rather than hot, suggesting that it had last been in operation several hours previously.

He turned to Bassett, who was puffing on his latest cigarette as if it was his first one for many months, and pointed at the dishwasher. 'Has anyone looked inside this?'

Bassett thought about it for a second. 'I don't know. I don't think so.'

Carlyle turned to Joe, who had appeared from elsewhere in the flat and was hovering in the doorway. 'Make sure this has been checked for prints and then open it up.'

'Okay.' Joe went off to see if he could find any remaining forensic technicians.

'And see how the canvass of the neighbours is going,' Carlyle called after him.

'Will do.'

'Are you going to take her now?' Carlyle asked Bassett.

'Yes. I think we are more or less done here.'

'The report?'

'Shouldn't take too long. If there are any surprises, I'll give you a call straight away.'

'Thanks.'

In the living room, the WPC was sitting on the sofa, staring into space. Henry Mills was standing by the large bay window, contemplating the crowds entering the British Museum. A billboard in the courtyard advertised an exhibition devoted to

Babylon: Myth & Reality. Helen had been trying to get him to go with her to see it, but Carlyle knew it was just another one of those things they would never get round to doing. Not that this worried him; he could live without the Tower of Babel and the madness of King Nebuchadnezzar, so was happy to just let it slide.

After a few seconds, Mills half-turned in his direction. He was wearing jeans and a white shirt with a fine green check. His face was flushed. In one hand he held a glass of whisky, with the bottle in the other. The inspector clocked the label – Famous Grouse – and the fact that it was well on the way to being empty.

He gestured for the WPC to leave them. As she struggled out of the sofa, he experienced a ripple of disgust. 'Big-boned' wasn't the half of it. When did they start letting any fat slob join the force? he wondered glumly. Probably when most of the population started becoming obese, he told himself.

Carlyle let Mills look him up and down, while the widower sucked down another slug of Scotch. The look on his face suggested that it gave him neither comfort nor pleasure.

'I would lay off the drinking if I were you, sir,' Carlyle said stiffly.

'Oh, would you?' Henry Mills made a face. 'Well, it's my bloody house,' he drained his glass with a flourish, 'and it's my bloody wife.'

But you'll soon be at my bloody station, Carlyle thought. He was four feet from Mills and could clearly smell the drink already on his breath. Hopefully it would make him talkative or, just as good, forget to ask for a lawyer. 'That's an unfortunate form of words, sir,' he said, 'under the circumstances.'

Despite everything, Henry Mills grinned. 'Don't I know it, Mr . . .'

'Inspector.' Carlyle fumbled in a pocket for his warrant card. 'Inspector John Carlyle. I'm from the Charing Cross station.'

By the time Carlyle had managed to recover his warrant card, Mills had already turned his back on him and was pouring himself another drink. 'Want one?' he asked, over his shoulder.

Carlyle ignored the offer. 'Why don't you take a seat, sir?'

Assured that his glass was well on the way to being three-quarters full, Henry Mills plonked himself down in an over-stuffed armchair in one corner, beside the window, and then plonked the bottle on the floor beside him. Hoping she hadn't managed to break the sofa, Carlyle took the place vacated by the outsized WPC. Preliminaries over, he decided to jump straight in. Looking past Mills, out of the window, at a sky that could have been blue, could have been grey, he asked: 'Why did you kill your wife?'

Mills's brow furrowed and he gripped his glass more tightly. His mouth opened, but no words came out. Carlyle waited a moment. He was about to repeat the question when they were distracted by a noise coming from the hall. A second later, Bassett went past, followed by the body, bagged up, carried on a trolley. As Agatha Mills left home for the last time, her husband let out a low moan, sinking back into his chair. The next moment, Joe appeared in the doorway.

It's like trying to work in the middle of Piccadilly fucking Circus, Carlyle thought.

He signalled for his sergeant to come in, and Joe complied, perching on an arm of the sofa that was closest to the door and furthest from Mills, who was meanwhile staring morosely at the glass of Scotch now sitting precariously on the arm of his chair.

Still no one spoke.

Carlyle let himself enjoy the smell of the Scotch as he belatedly looked round the room. A large, empty fireplace took up much of one wall. There were a couple of photos on the mantelpiece; at first glance both appeared to be of Henry and Agatha on holiday. Above the fireplace was a massive poster depicting a clenched fist in front of a flag that Carlyle didn't recognise. In large text at the top it said *Venceremos*, and at the bottom *Unidad Popular*. Yellowed in places, with a tear in the bottom left-hand corner, it looked like the kind of thing you would have expected to adorn the wall of a student flat maybe thirty or forty years ago, but it had been placed in an expensive-looking aluminium frame that appeared to be worth many times more than the poster itself.

The other two walls were covered by shelves stuffed with books from floor to ceiling, mainly history and fiction as far as he could tell. Some of them were in English, but there were also many in foreign languages – Spanish, French and German. Most looked well-thumbed. There were also piles of books rising three feet high on either side of the armchair that Henry Mills was now sitting in. There was another stack in front of a small CRT television which was almost hidden in a corner by the window. A video machine sat on top of the TV, but Carlyle couldn't see any tapes. Neither machine was on standby and both were covered in a thick layer of dust. There was no sign of either a DVD player or a digibox.

Carlyle let his eyes skip across the spines of the books at random: *Pinochet in Piccadilly: Britain and Chile's Hidden History*; *Subversive Scriptures: Revolutionary Christian Readings of the Bible in Latin America*; *States, Ideologies, and Social Revolutions: A Comparative Analysis of Iran, Nicaragua, and the Philippines*. His eyes quickly glazed over as he worried that the titles alone could give him a headache. Carlyle liked a good read, but he couldn't imagine getting through the hundreds of books in this room alone. He got through maybe seven or eight books a year. If it wasn't a footballer's 'autobiography', it was the kind of thriller where someone had to be decapitated, dismembered or disappeared by page three – the kind of thing where a crazed serial killer believed he was channelling the spirits of vengeful Norse Gods, or some such. All good fun. In real life, of course, he'd never come across a serial killer and knew that he never would. This was London, after all, not some American urban hell.

He chuckled to himself. Mr and Mrs Mills were not the kind of people who read about serial killers, real or imagined. He could tell that they were a bit too high-brow for that. And maybe a little unworldly as well. The overall air of the room was one of comfortable mess; you got the impression that nice people lived here. Or, at least, had done until last night when one of them had brained the other, for whatever reason.

Closing his eyes, Carlyle counted up to thirty in his head. Opening them again, he slowly scanned the room once more. Noticing nothing new, he turned to Henry Mills, who had drained his glass but was making no effort to go for a refill. Carlyle was just about to resume his questioning when a young woman, one of the technicians, stuck her head through the door. 'Sir?' she asked, unsure which of the two policemen she should be addressing. 'Could you come to the kitchen for a minute?'

Carlyle sighed. 'Fine.' He got up and followed her back into the kitchen. It looked bigger with the body removed, but he was still careful to avoid the blood on the floor as he stepped towards the open dishwasher. Peering inside, he saw that it was largely empty apart from a couple of mugs and some cutlery. On top of a nearby work surface, however, was a steel skillet that had not been there before. It had been sealed in a plastic bag.

Carlyle looked at the woman expectantly, without feeling the need to expend the effort to either introduce himself, or to ask her name.

'This looks like it could be it,' she said, taking her cue.

Carlyle nodded. 'It must have been cleaned up pretty good in there.'

'Yes,' the woman said, 'and the outside of the dishwasher has been wiped clean of all prints. But we should still find some material in the filter or the pipes.'

'Good,' said Carlyle. Finally, he could feel his energy levels rising. They should have this sorted out by the end of the day, if not earlier. The thought of such an easy win put a spring in his step. 'That's very good,' he said. 'Very helpful.' He turned and walked back into the hallway. Checking his watch, he wondered idly if he could beat his previous record for closing a case. Seven or eight years ago, he'd had a homeless girl deliver up a full confession to the killing of her 'boyfriend' less than three and a half minutes from the start of her formal interview. Carlyle had been counting off the seconds from the clock in the interview room as she droned into the tape recorder. The boyfriend had been an evil, drunken bastard and had deserved everything he got, which in this case was more than a dozen stab wounds to the head and chest.

Carlyle had felt no real interest in the girl – a runaway from some provincial hellhole – or why she had done it. He couldn't even remember what had happened to her subsequently; if she had been sent to prison or placed into care. But he could still close his eyes and see her blank expression. And he recalled the fleeting satisfaction derived from closing a case almost before it had even been opened. Sometimes people couldn't get the words out quickly enough. Spilling your guts was an extremely commendable impulse, in the inspector's book. The question now was: would Mr Mills similarly oblige?

Standing in the middle of the living room, Carlyle looked Henry Mills up and down. He waited for Mills to make eye contact before speaking.

'What happened?'

'I don't know,' Mills replied.

'Did you kill her?' Carlyle asked evenly.

Mills looked at his empty glass. 'No.'

'Come on, Mr Mills, it looks very clear-cut to us.' He glanced at Joe, who responded with a vague gesture of agreement.

'No.' Mills shook his head. 'I didn't do it,' he said. He suddenly seemed completely sober.

Fuck, Carlyle thought. No confession means no record-breaking for me today. His energy levels started ebbing again. Time for our man to visit the station, he decided. Stick him in a cell for a while.

No more Famous Grouse.

No more armchairs.

No more comfortable untidiness.

No more options.

Wait a while and then charge him. Start making this thing feel real. But that would mean a lawyer, stretching things out even longer. He gave it one more push. 'You didn't do it?' He gestured at the glass. 'Or maybe you don't remember doing it?'

'No,' Mills said firmly, sounding clearer by the minute. 'I didn't do it. I haven't forgotten anything. I didn't even have one drink last night.'

Carlyle glanced at the bottle and decided that was not very likely. 'Okay,' he said, 'if you didn't do it, then who did?'

'I don't know,' Mills said again, as if it was an even more acceptable answer the second time around. 'She was like that when I found her.'

'Where were you when it happened?'

'In bed, asleep.'

'Did you hear any noise?'

'No. I wear earplugs because I'm a light sleeper.' He nodded in the direction of the window. 'The traffic . . .'

'If it wasn't you,' said Joe, 'do you know who *might* have done it?'

Carlyle folded his arms. This was the bit where they would be told that the victim was a modern-day saint who didn't have an enemy in the world.

Mills carefully placed his glass down on the floor next to the bottle and looked at the sergeant, hopeful that he might prove to be more reasonable than his rather snide boss. 'It had to be her enemies.'

'Her enemies?' parroted the inspector.

'Yes.' Henry Mills nodded. 'I'm sure it was them. No one else would have done this. Not to Agatha.'

Commander Carole Simpson eyed the large plate of sandwiches that had been placed on the table in front of her and groaned. Looking out across the river from the tenth floor of New Scotland Yard, she was suddenly struck by the thought that there must be millions of people out there who were actually having an enjoyable day. Not her. To say that being promoted had turned out to be something of a mixed blessing was an understatement. Meetings like this made Simpson feel that she had been transformed from a copper into a pen-pusher.

The Planning, Performance and Review Committee was almost three hours into its scheduled eight-hour session, and it was heavy going indeed. Sixteen people around the table, who either didn't know each other or didn't like each other, were reviewing the latest *Specialist Crime Directorate Management Information Report*, which presented the Directorate's 'key objectives and core performance indicators'.

The conference room was hot and stuffy. Simpson stifled a yawn as best she could. For her this was increasingly what modern policing looked like: number-crunching while hidden away in an airless room, as far away from the public as possible; as far away from the criminals as possible. It was enough to send anyone to sleep.

After everyone had carefully chosen their food, the committee turned to the Homicide section of the report. The overall homicide detection rate for the previous year was 85 per cent, slightly worse than the year before but still very satisfactory and – crucially – well within the performance target band.

As the discussion rambled on, Simpson recalled with some satisfaction how she had personally overseen the investigations regarding four of the murders in question. Her officers had enjoyed a 100 per cent success rate. And now she was putting all that effort to good use. Although technically not part of the SCD's efforts, she had made sure that the cases were included in the report, in order to boost the overall clean-up rate figures. After all, when you were locked in an endless battle with the politicians for money and resources, every little helped.

Having made the mistake of biting into a cheese sandwich, which was foul, she washed it quickly away with a mouthful of coffee while listening to someone raise the issue of the recently proposed changes in the murder law. The plan was to replace the existing partial defence of 'provocation' with one of 'fear of serious violence' or, in exceptional circumstances, 'seriously wronged'. Neither was much of a defence, Simpson reckoned. She was nervous at the constant attempts to fiddle with the laws of the land. Britain was a safe country; London was a safe city. Most people were good citizens or, at least, respectful subjects. The laws worked – they should be left alone.

Like any decent copper, the commander basically thought that the only successful defence against a serious charge should be 'I didn't do it'. Lots of people thought that they were 'seriously wronged' one way or another. In her book, that could never be any kind of excuse for murder.

'What is your opinion, Commander?' someone asked.

It was a question that neither expected nor deserved an answer. 'I think it is an interesting proposal,' she replied, letting her gaze move smoothly round the table. 'However, whatever happens, I am sure that we will maintain and build on our excellent performance record in this area.'

SIX

For the first time, Carlyle began to wonder if they were dealing with someone who wasn't quite all there.

'Which enemies?' he asked.

Henry Mills looked at him as if he was trying to decide something. 'The secret police,' he said finally.

Joe sat forward. 'We *are* the police, Mr Mills.'

'Not you lot,' Mills snapped. 'The *secret* police.'

'What "secret" police?' Carlyle asked. 'MI5?' Bored and frustrated, he was rapidly tuning out of this conversation. Mentally he was already back at the station, if not well on the way to going home for his dinner. He even wondered if there was going to be anything good on telly tonight before defaulting back to the matter in hand. 'Who do you mean?'

Mills stared at him blankly.

'MI6?' Carlyle tried again.

'No, no, no!' Mills pointed at the poster above the fireplace. 'Not our lot. Are you stupid?'

Joe sniggered. Carlyle gritted his teeth.

Henry Mills waved his arms about theatrically. 'I'm talking about the bloody Chileans.'

'Chileans?' Carlyle looked at the poster above the fireplace. He stuck his hands deep in his pockets.

'1973. The CIA-backed fascist coup d'état.' Mills gestured at the poster, saying, 'The overthrow of the government of President Salvador Allende. Didn't you learn about it in school?'

'I'm not interested in what happened in 1973,' Carlyle told him. 'I'm interested in what happened last night – here, in this flat.'

Now it was Mills's turn to grow annoyed. 'But I'm trying to explain . . .'

Fearing an extended history lesson, the inspector held up a hand. He wondered if maybe Henry Mills should have a lawyer, after all. The brief could try and talk some sense into his client. 'Why would someone from Chile want to kill Mrs Mills?' he asked.

'They were just fed up with her,' Mills said, a slight croak appearing in his voice. 'She never gave up.'

The two policemen looked at him quizzically.

'Agatha was finally getting to them. They wanted to shut her up.'

Closing his eyes, Inspector Carlyle saw a montage of all the bullshit stories that he'd had to listen to over the years flashing before him on fast-forward. Irritated beyond belief, he signalled to Joe and they went out into the hall.

'Can you believe this bollocks?' he said under his breath, still watching Mills through the doorway.

Joe leaned against the wall. 'The front door was locked, with no sign of forced entry. Same with the kitchen window. No fingerprints on the suspected murder weapon. We're checking the rest of the kitchen again right now, but nothing interesting so far. No unusual footprints, fibres or anything like that.'

'Mills has to be our man then,' said Carlyle, staring at the floor.

Joe nodded.

'At the very least, he'll have to come up with something better than this Chilean connection.'

'On the plus side for Mr Mills,' Joe observed, 'there was no blood on him or on any of his clothes, when we arrived. And there's no sign of him having tried to clean anything up.'

'He could easily have dropped any stained clothes in the rubbish,' Carlyle mused. 'The bin men have already been this morning. Better speak to Camden Council and find out where all the rubbish ends up.'

'Yes,' agreed Joe doubtfully.

'Don't worry,' Carlyle grinned. 'You can get a couple of PCs to sort through it all.'

'That'll make me popular.'

'It's tough at the top.'

Now it was Joe's turn to grin. 'How would *you* know, exactly?'

'Anyway,' said Carlyle, not rising to the bait, 'this looks fairly straightforward. Sometimes they are.'

'Hmm.' Joe scratched his head. 'Overall, it does look like a domestic.'

'I think it does,' Carlyle agreed. 'I don't know what he thinks he can achieve with this Chilean nonsense, but I suppose we should be grateful that at least he's not trying to blame little green men.'

The inspector stepped back into the room. Mills was still sitting calmly in his chair. He was like a blank page, if a bit grubby round the edges. Prepared to give it one last go, Carlyle rubbed his neck and consciously let a cloak of dispassionate formality descend over him.

'Did you and your wife have an argument, sir?' he asked.

'No!' Mills jerked out of the chair, accidentally kicking his empty glass across the floor. He watched it roll towards the inspector's shoes and stood up, as if mesmerized, unsure of what to do next.

Slowly, Carlyle bent down and picked up the glass. Stepping away from Mills, he placed it carefully on the mantelpiece. Happy Hour was over. The two men stood there silently for a few seconds, waiting for something to happen. Finally, Carlyle turned to his sergeant. 'Call a car, please, Joe, and take Mr Mills back to the station.'

SEVEN

Cerro Los Placeres, Valparaíso, Chile, September 1973

It was time.

His Term of Grace was over.

The dogs of the Lord were coming.

The dogs of the Lord were coming and he did not want them to find him naked. Tired but alert, William Pettigrew tugged a shirt over his head and pulled on a pair of torn Wrangler jeans. Stepping out of the bedroom, he counted the six steps to his front door, trying to ignore the tightening knot in his stomach. Hopping from foot to bare foot, he mumbled the lines of a prayer by a Trappist monk called Thomas Merton: 'My Lord God, I have no idea where I am going . . .'

The *Domini canes* arrived in a flurry of engine noise and exhaust smoke. There was the squeal of rubber on tarmac, the crunch of boots on gravel, angry shouts and fearful cries. When they finally stopped outside the house, Pettigrew felt a wave of serenity wash over him. 'There is no point,' he mumbled to himself, 'in hiding under the bed when a man with a machine-gun knocks on your door at two o'clock in the morning. Instead, you answer it.'

A soldier jogged towards him, rifle raised. He looked little more than a boy – seventeen, eighteen at most. Catching the youth's eye, Pettigrew acknowledged the sadistic twinkle in it, the almost pantomime menace in his voice. He breathed in the smell of body odour and refried beans mixed with Torobayo Ale.

Dropping his gun to his side, the boy jumped in front of the priest and spat in his face. Pettigrew flinched, but didn't wipe it off.

The first blow sent him crashing to the ground. He tried to breathe slowly, through his mouth, trying to ignore the fire alarm going off in his brain and the fire in his crotch as the pain raced round his body on a surge of adrenaline.

In the shadows, someone laughed. A callous voice cried: 'That's got to hurt!'

'*Bienvenido a la Caravana de la Meurte*,' the young soldier said grimly. Another gob of phlegm splattered on the ground in front of Pettigrew's face. He looked up. The slack grin on the soldier's face said it all.

Welcome to the Caravan of Death.

Enjoy the ride.

Pushing back his shoulders, Pettigrew stood up straight in front of the new Inquisition.

From his studies at the Catholic University in Santiago, he knew that, in these parts, the first Papal Inquisition officially ended only in 1834. It had lasted for more than 600 years.

Now it was back.

'It is time for me to die.'

Death, however, is not a specific moment. It is a process that begins when the heart stops beating, the lungs stop working and the brain ceases functioning. In this case, he knew that it was going to be a long, slow, painful process. He had shown the insolence and malapertness of the heretic, and now his false designs were to be crushed. The prophet, the dreamer, must be put to death and the execrableness of his false doctrines purged.

He didn't possess the apostolic humility, austerity, the holiness required for anything remotely approaching salvation.

It was too late for zealous preaching.

It was too late for voluntary confessions.

Now there was nothing to do but embrace the pain.

Instinctively, in their souls, the soldiers knew that no man must debase himself by showing toleration towards heretics of any kind. Pettigrew braced himself for another kick. He knelt forward, getting as close to the boy's boots as he could without making it look too obvious. If he didn't get much backlift, the boy wouldn't be able to get much force into the next assault and maybe it would just be a glancing blow. Rocking gently on his knees, he could smell the boot polish. It had been smeared across the toes of his scuffed boots, like make-up on a corpse. If he'd bothered to rub it in properly, he thought idly, I might have seen my face reflected back at me. Instead, there was just darkness.

The boots took a step back. He closed his eyes, took a deep breath and waited.

The kick never came.

After a few seconds, the soldier stepped away and turned towards a yelping noise that had started up somewhere to his right. It sounded like a dog hit by a car, but Pettigrew knew that it wasn't. Cursing and screaming, a woman he didn't recognise was being dragged down the street by her hair. The boy soldier jumped forward and, without breaking stride, let fly with a casual half-volley, like a kid kicking a stone along the street. His right boot landed somewhere near her mouth and Pettigrew watched her face explode in a mess of crimson, like something out of a Sam Peckinpah movie. The yelping and cursing stopped, replaced by a low, frothy moan.

The soldier studied the toe of his boot and carefully began cleaning it on the back of his left calf, smearing a mixture of blood, snot and nasal cartilage across his olive-green fatigues. Satisfied with the result, he turned back to face the priest, eyes glazed. Stepping closer, he pointed at a large puddle of green paint over to Pettigrew's right, which was spreading slowly across the scrub of the tiny front yard. The eight tins of Eden Green paint had been a birthday present from his sister. They had been stacked by the door for several months now, waiting for him to get round to painting the outside of his house, a three-room shack his friends and neighbours had helped him build two summers ago. The soldiers had clearly found them too much to resist, kicking them over as they'd jumped down from their trucks.

'Get down!'

William Pettigrew looked at him uncomprehendingly.

'Lie in it, fucker!'

The priest looked at the paint and hesitated.

'Get on with it,' the youth's face turned pink as he struggled to find the right words, 'motherfucker!'

Another boot caught Pettigrew in the small of the back. Forced down into the puddle, his shirt and trousers were immediately soaked in the cloying green paint. Lying still, he felt a small pulse of satisfaction that he had managed to get dressed before opening the door. To be both naked *and* green would have been a terrible embarrassment.

Of course, it was also a waste of good paint, but that seemed a total irrelevance now, since it wasn't as if he would be coming back to start the decorating.

A boot tickled his ear. 'Why didn't you stay away, dickhead?'

It was a good question.

William Pettigrew was well known locally as a so-called 'Red Priest', a liberation theologian and, therefore, a troublemaker. That meant that he was always likely to be on someone's list. When the coup began, his friends had warned him that he would be a target; that he should lie low, maybe even leave the country for a while. Pettigrew was lucky – he had that option; he had a passport and he had money. He could go back to Great Britain and leave this all behind. On several occasions, the Archdiocese and the ecclesiastical governors had made it clear to him that this was a course of action of which they would approve.

He had toyed with going to Scotland – his great-great-grandfather had been an innkeeper in Montrose – to see for himself where the Pettigrews had first come from. But, deep down, he knew that was just a fantasy. He would never run away.

In the event, he did leave Valparaíso . . . for a little while. After a couple of nights of listening to the shooting, he had headed for a village twenty kilometres up the coast, where he spent a couple of nights on a friend's floor. The whole thing quickly seemed melodramatic and self-indulgent – cowardly, even. By running from his fate, he had put himself in a prison of his own making. After all, Cerro Los Placeres was his home. There was nowhere else to go. There was nowhere else he wanted to be.

He knew that he had to suffer with the people here, share the suffering of the powerless, the impotent. He knew that he could offer his neighbours no solutions to this terrible situation. He didn't know the answers. But he could walk with them, search with them, stay with them. Die with them.

His only weapon was forgiveness. Forgiveness is fuelled by love; violence is fuelled by fear. Love is the antidote to fear. And he knew that love is what he would need in his heart when he arrived at the gates of Heaven.

So he came back.

For a couple more days, he went about his business in Valparaíso unmolested. It seemed that no one cared about William Pettigrew.

Until now.

Another kick brought him back to the present. More words were whispered in his ear:

'You are an idiot as well as a pervert.'

'Do you think God cares what happens to scum like you?'

'You should have fucked off back to England, while you had the chance.'

'The Church shrinks from blood but we do not.'

After a couple more kicks, and a few smacks around the head

with a rifle butt, Pettigrew's hands were tied firmly together in front of him. Careful to avoid getting any of the bright green paint on their fatigues, two soldiers hauled him towards the rear of a canvas-covered truck. Half-lifted, half-pushed, he was bundled inside. There were maybe ten or twelve other people already in there, but no one that he recognised in the gloom. They instinctively shied away from him, fearing any association that could make their situation worse. Righting himself, he found a space near the tailgate. Shouting and laughing came from outside the truck. Inside there was only a pensive silence, laced with a heavy dose of fear.

Five minutes later, the tailgate was closed and the canvas flaps at the back of the truck pulled down. Someone shouted to the driver that they were ready to go, and the truck rumbled into life. After a few more seconds they set off, travelling at a steady pace of not much more than twenty miles an hour. Out of the back, through the gaps in the canvas, Pettigrew could see that they were being closely followed by a group of three soldiers in a jeep. One was manning a machine-gun mounted on the back, just in case anyone decided to take their chances and jump. No one did.

It was clear that they were heading south, towards the port area. Pettigrew had been what they called a 'worker priest' in Valparaíso's Las Habas shipyards for almost a year, so he knew this route well. He also knew why they were going there. A couple of naval vessels had arrived in Valparaíso two days before the socialist government had been overthrown. With the President, Salvador Allende, dead, and 'leftists' of all descriptions being rounded up, rumours quickly began circulating that these ships were being used as overflow facilities for the prisons.

'A nice bit of sea air – and free board and lodging,' someone had joked at the time. 'A lot better than Londres Street,' the man had added, referring to the Communist Party headquarters in Santiago which, as everyone knew, was now being used as a torture centre.

Pettigrew had looked at him askance.

'Like a little vacation really.'

Really? Well, his vacation started here.

They moved slowly through the streets. The city seemed desolate even for the middle of the night. Lights were out. Windows were closed. Doors firmly bolted shut. People were curled up in their beds, worried that they might be next, wracking their brains for any behaviour, any words, that might lead to a midnight visit and a one-way trip to Las Habas.

Even the dogs that habitually prowled the dustbins looking for food had the sense to take the night off.

Inside the truck, someone started sobbing. Another began quietly reciting the Lord's Prayer. At the end, there were a couple of ragged *Améns*, followed by more silence. A woman close to Pettigrew squeezed her rosary so tightly that the string broke and the beads fell to the floor, scattering at their feet. She glanced at Pettigrew and shrugged. He said nothing. They both knew that it was far too late for God.

They made four more stops on the way. Pulling up outside houses that the priest didn't recognise; picking up men and women whom he didn't know. At each stop, two or three more people were shoved into the back of the truck. There was some shouting, a few screams but no real complaints and no resistance.

By the time they reached the dockside, the truck was full. The driver slowed his speed as he pulled onto one of the piers. Through the gap in the canvas, Pettigrew caught a glimpse of a distinctive four-mast schooner, the *Dama Blanca*. The *White Lady* was a familiar sight in Valparaíso, being the training ship for the cadets at the city's Arturo Prat Naval Academy. He had even been on board once himself, during an Open Day early in 1972. Visitors were given a tour of the bay, some free rum and a rather boring lecture on Arturo Prat and his good works.

This time, no doubt, the programme would be rather different.

Despite everything, Pettigrew managed a smile when he recalled Agustín Arturo Prat Chacón. Prat was a very Chilean kind of hero. He took a bullet between the eyes in 1879 while fighting the Peruvians.

Almost 100 years later, there were 162 streets named after the great man in Chile. In Valparaíso, there was an Arturo Prat statue as well. By all accounts, Prat was much taken by the liberalism of the times. His academy was supposed to teach future naval officers 'academic, moral, cultural and physical education'. Pettigrew wondered which part of the curriculum they were covering tonight.

Their truck trundled past a group of twenty or so people who had been rounded up by the military. Some were lying face-down on the quayside; others were kneeling. All had their hands clutched behind their heads. Half a dozen armed sailors stood around them, keeping guard, smoking, sharing the occasional joke. Above them all, a group of maybe thirty navy cadets stood at attention on the main deck of the ship itself, watching closely despite keeping their gaze fixed firmly on some invisible point in the inky sky.

The truck came to a gentle stop and the canvas covers at the back were thrown open. Without being told, people started getting off. 'I hope you know how to swim,' one of the soldiers joked as Pettigrew jumped down from the truck onto the cold cobbles.

As soon as it was empty, the truck headed off into the night, no doubt in search of its next passengers. Stretching, Pettigrew looked around. The pier was kept in darkness, the only light coming from the ship's portholes and from the orange street lights in the town above. He shivered as a chill breeze cut in from the sea. Without being told, he sank to his knees on the dockside, keen to fit in. Most of his fellow travellers followed suit. He bowed his head and was quickly rewarded by a blow to the neck with the stock of a sailor's rifle. Without complaining, he looked up and carefully studied his tormentor. The latter was tall and pale, with thin wrists, a small mouth and green eyes. His tunic was unbuttoned at the neck and an unlit cigarette dangled from his mouth. Avoiding the red priest's gaze, he recorded

Pettigrew's existence and silently moved on. Pettigrew watched him wandering through the kneeling group, casually offering the occasional blow, seemingly as engaged as a man pruning his roses.

It was another fifteen minutes or so before the detainees were formally handed over to the ship's commander. Even at times like this, we Chileans like our ceremony, Pettigrew mused. He was almost surprised that they didn't have a brass band on hand to provide a musical accompaniment. They were pushed up the gangplank under a hail of kicks, blows and curses.

On the deck of the ship, his hands were untied and he was told to crouch with his hands behind the back of his neck. As the final prisoners shuffled on board, he counted twenty-six men and twenty-two women. He guessed that their ages ranged from something like fifteen to sixty-five. They were arranged in eight rows of half a dozen each, facing away from the pier. Wandering between the rows came a dozen or so guards carrying lances, sticks with steel points. Overseeing the group, perched on a raised deck-hatch to Pettigrew's left, were two teenagers manning a machine-gun that looked as if it had come from the First World War. If they had opened up, they could have taken everyone out in about ten seconds.

Once everyone was on board, the order was given for the prisoners to strip. A few bemused glances were exchanged, but again no one complained. Not wishing to be hit again, Pettigrew quickly dropped his trousers and wriggled out of his underpants. Pulling his paint-covered shirt over his head, he folded his clothes neatly, out of habit, and placed the pile at his feet. A cadet quickly scuttled over and took his clothes away. Standing as straight as he could manage, with his arms folded, he tried not to watch the others get undressed. The near silence was occasionally broken by a burst of gunfire from somewhere in the city. At one point, he heard another truck on the jetty. It stopped near to the ship but no one else came on board the *White Lady*.

Finally, everyone was done. Naked and standing grimly to

attention, people tried to make themselves seem as small as possible, almost trying to will themselves somewhere else.

All except for one woman: standing in the row in front of Pettigrew, she stood defiant, back arched, legs planted apart, hands on hips, staring down any sailor who cared to take her on.

She was an amazing sight, hairy, with a backside you could eat your lunch off, large breasts and nipples like bullets. He was ashamed of himself, but it was impossible not to stare.

Forgive me, Father, he thought, for I have sinned in my head.

Pettigrew willed himself to look at his feet and think about . . . Montrose, about football, Jesus, the Church, agrarian reform . . . anything to keep his mind off his groin. Others clearly had the same problem. There was some mumbling among the ranks, and he turned to see that a youth standing next to the warrior woman was struggling with an enormous erection. The poor soul went beetroot red in the face as he tried – and failed – to hide it between his legs. The guards roared with laughter and took turns at trying to hit his penis with their sticks; one threatened to shoot it off. But they quickly grew bored with the game and, thanks to God, the errant member eventually subsided.

As dawn began to break, a new group of sailors appeared, carrying hoses. Someone shouted, 'It's time for a wash you dirty bastards!' With a flourish, they turned high-pressure jets of seawater on the prisoners. The ranks broke as everyone tried to get out of the line of fire, while the guards stabbed them with their sticks to keep them under the jets. Water immediately went up Pettigrew's nose and in his mouth, and he was constantly gagging, on the brink of drowning. A jet of water hit him directly on the head and the pain was terrible. His eyes and ears felt as if they were being stabbed.

After about twenty minutes, they finally turned off the hoses. That's when he really felt the cold. His hands and feet were numb and he could see one poor woman beginning to turn blue. Everyone was hopping from foot to foot to try and stay warm. He imagined they looked like lunatics dancing on a trip to Hell.

Some time later, they were taken down below and herded into a space maybe forty feet long and twenty feet wide, lit by three bare light bulbs. There were no portholes. At each end was a sliding metal door, with an armed guard stationed immediately outside. Each person was told to take one thin blanket. There were enough hammocks for maybe half of them, with a canvas dividing off the quarters for the women. Beside the doors were four large buckets to serve as their toilet. The lodgings had clearly been used before. The floor was still sticky with fluids that Pettigrew did not want to inspect too closely. There had been some attempt to clean the place up for the new arrivals but, at best, it had been half-hearted. The smell of disinfectant only partially covered the smell of piss, shit and body odour. No one wanted to think about what had happened to the previous guests.

EIGHT

The city hummed around him. Reassuringly familiar, it soothed his agitation. Too impatient to wait for a break in the traffic, Carlyle jumped in front of a small, red delivery van, studiously ignoring the exaggerated hand gestures of the driver as he skipped down Long Acre. Reaching Seven Dials, a mini-roundabout, with a pillar at its centre bearing six sundials (the seventh being the pillar itself, casting its shadow on the ground), he headed towards the north end of Mercer Street, close to Shaftesbury Avenue.

On the west side of the street was a small block of council flats known as Phoenix House. Built in the 1950s with the cheapest concrete available, the building would probably have been more robust if it had been constructed out of cardboard. Still, it looked clean and, from the outside at least, didn't smell too badly. Carlyle buzzed, waited for a few seconds, heard the door unlock, and went inside.

On the top floor of Phoenix House was Flat 8. For more than a year now, it had been used as a knocking shop by a young Birmingham girl called Sam Laidlaw. The place was tiny, no more than 500 square feet all told, but it had a small roof terrace which allowed Laidlaw's clients an al fresco option in the summer.

Laidlaw's maid, Amelia Jacobs, was a retired prostitute who had known Carlyle for more than twenty years. She was a reliable contact, who had built up a healthy balance in his favours book over the years. A few weeks earlier, when she had asked to make a rare withdrawal, Carlyle knew that he would have to go and pay her a visit. Having already put it off a couple of times, he now felt obliged to put in an appearance.

If not exactly the stereotypical hooker with a heart of gold, Jacobs was an impressive figure. She was a plain-looking black woman in her mid-to-late thirties, about 5 feet 4 inches with a no-nonsense short back and sides haircut and hard eyes that never focused on you. If you passed her on the street, you might imagine that Amelia was a teacher, or maybe even a lawyer. The reality was rather different, but Carlyle knew that Amelia was nonetheless worthy of considerable respect. Above all, she was a survivor. Local legend had it that she had once tried, with some success, to bite off the penis of an obnoxious punter. Carlyle knew a nurse working at UCLH on Gower Street who claimed to have been on duty when the unfortunate bloke arrived in A&E. He had asked Amelia about the incident once – she had just smiled and said matter-of-factly: 'Another few seconds and he would never have seen his thing again.'

Happily for visiting punters, and middle-aged policemen, reaching the top floor only meant three flights of stairs. There was a lift, but it rarely worked. Even when it did, Carlyle would rather take the stairs than risk getting stuck inside.

Jogging up the stairs, he felt only slightly winded.

Amelia met him at the door. 'Thanks for coming, Inspector,' she smiled.

'No problem,' Carlyle replied, trying to control his wheezing. 'Sorry it's taken me so long to get here.'

She made a non-committal gesture. 'Come inside.'

A couple of minutes later he was sitting on an orange sofa in a drab sitting room that surely would be depressing enough to dampen anyone's lust. He was nursing a dangerous-looking mug of coffee with a slick of what looked like washing-up liquid glistening on the top. Sam Laidlaw sat in a chair opposite him, staring at the floor like the naughty schoolgirl that she basically was. She was twenty-two or twenty-three going on fifteen. Her platinum-blond hair matched her sickly skin. It had grown out at the roots and badly needed redoing. In a grubby white T-shirt, grey jogging pants and no make-up, she looked a total mess. It would be like fucking a corpse, Carlyle thought. On the other hand, trying to be generous, it was relatively early. For her, the working week had yet to start.

Amelia explained the situation to Carlyle. The problem was a familiar one. His name was Michael Hagger, a local mini-gangster-turned-entrepreneur, occasional pimp and father to Sam Laidlaw's four-year-old son, Jake. Hagger, according to Jacobs, was threatening to take the boy away from his mother as part of a long-running dispute about money.

'Where is the boy now?' Carlyle asked, suddenly worried in case he had ignored this situation for too long.

'He's on a play date,' Amelia replied. 'And he's in nursery now too. We got him into Coram's Fields after Easter. Three days a week.'

'That's good,' Carlyle said limply. At least the boy was being looked after properly some of the time. The Coram's Fields Play Centre was fifteen minutes up the road, on the way to King's Cross. It was run by Camden Council, and the staff there did a fantastic job with a broad range of kids from different backgrounds. His daughter Alice had gone there for a couple of years before starting school, and her mother still visited now and again to drop off spare books for the library. He would mention Jake to Helen and see if she could make some discreet enquiries.

Laidlaw remained mute. She had lifted her gaze far enough off the floor to stare intently at a blank 32-inch television screen in the corner. Carlyle followed her gaze and checked out the pile of DVDs on the floor by the TV. *Postman Pat* and *Duck Dodgers* cartoons peeked out from underneath a pile of generic porno titles. Carlyle had to resist the urge to gag. Apart from anything else, he was a big fan of Duck Dodgers, Daffy Duck's Space Protectoret hero, having watched many episodes alongside Alice when she was younger. Now he wanted to scream. Calming himself down, he knew that he really would have to call Children's Social Services.

'What do you want me to do?' he asked.

'Talk to Hagger,' Amelia replied. 'Let him know that you've got your eye on him.'

As if that would make any difference.

'Okay,' Carlyle sighed. 'Where will I find him?'

Again the girl said nothing.

'The usual places,' Amelia said.

That narrowed it down, thought Carlyle. 'I'll start at the Intrepid Fox,' he said, to no one in particular, mentioning a pub two minutes down the road in Soho where Hagger was known to hang out.

The doorbell rang. Without saying a word, the girl got up and slouched out of the room.

'That'll be the twelve-thirty.' Amelia signalled for him to get up. She glanced at her watch. 'He's early. The randy little sod obviously thinks he gets extra time that way.'

'When you're in the mood,' Carlyle grinned, 'you're in the mood.'

'I suppose so,' Amelia said, raising her eyes to the ceiling. She ushered him towards the door. 'Thanks, Mr Carlyle.'

'I'll let you know how I get on,' he replied, happily handing her back the untouched mug of coffee.

'Thanks.'

'But I'll need to speak to Social Services about Jake.'

She started to complain, but thought better of it.

He softened the blow. 'Just so that there's someone else keeping an eye out for him too.'

A pained expression crossed Amelia's face. 'Jake *is* loved, Inspector.'

'Maybe he is,' Carlyle shrugged. 'But that's not always enough. That girl's too young.'

'Sam does her best.'

'The kid is four already. Unless the situation here changes, and quickly, he is fucked for life.'

'What else can she do?'

'She can go on benefits,' Carlyle hissed, 'like everyone else.'

'What? And live on a hundred and twenty quid a week?'

'There are worse things than being poor. She needs to smarten up.'

'I know.'

'For the kid's sake.'

'Yes.'

'That's your side of the deal.'

The woman nodded. 'I understand.'

'It's a deal then.' Carlyle smiled with as much enthusiasm as he could muster. 'Expect me to hold you to it.'

On his way down, Carlyle passed a sheepish-looking man in his fifties who was trudging up the stairs while keeping his eyes firmly on the steps in front of him. Outside, in the sunshine, it felt even hotter than before, as if the temperature had been raised another five or ten degrees. The air was turning heavy and it seemed as if the forecast thunderstorms were now on the way. He had a nagging headache from too much caffeine, and his appetite for what was to come back at the station had dwindled to next to nothing. Needing to rehydrate, he went round the corner into Earlham Street and bought a bottle of water and a mango smoothie from the Big Banana Juice Bar next to Cambridge Circus. He stepped off the pavement and between a couple of parked cars, downing the water first and then the smoothie. The Fopp music store in Shaftesbury Avenue across the road was advertising *The Clash* by The Clash. He wasn't sure about the lurid pink cover and he wasn't going to spend thirty quid on a book, but he fancied a peek. For Carlyle, The Clash were, still, the greatest rock band ever. He had seen them a few times before their untimely demise, and he wanted to wallow in a little nostalgia for those days of his youth.

Dropping his empty bottles in a bin, he crossed the road and stepped inside, experiencing the usual mix of pleasure and guilt at bunking off, even if only for a short while.

* * *

When he finally returned to Charing Cross police station, Carlyle dawdled at his desk, still in no hurry to get into the interview room. If Mills was going to stick to his Chilean story, it was likely to be a long and painful afternoon. Carlyle had endured more than his share of domestics over the years, and it was always a struggle spending hours going round the houses just to get formal confirmation of what you already knew. The endless ability of people to delude themselves never ceased to amaze him. Numbers, on the other hand, never lied. Carlyle was a firm believer in statistics, and the statistics told you that most victims were killed by people they knew. It was common sense, of course: usually, the only people you can annoy enough for them to want to kill you, *are* your nearest and dearest. Carlyle knew of several occasions when he himself might have been in serious trouble if Helen had been holding a skillet at the time – or vice versa. That was just a reality of everyday life . . . and death.

On his way to the basement he passed the front desk, eyeing the usual motley collection of supplicants waiting to be disappointed in one way or another. He nodded at Sergeant Dave Prentice, chewing on the end of a pencil while he contemplated some form that was lying in front of him.

'Dave.'

The desk sergeant pulled the pencil out of his mouth and looked up. 'John.' He had the exhausted look of a man who had spent too long on the front line, trying to keep the public at bay. Carlyle, like everyone else in the station, knew that he was counting down the days to his long-awaited retirement to Theydon Bois, a suburb at the eastern end of the Central Line.

'Anything interesting today?'

'Not really.' Prentice nodded towards a sickly-looking man in chinos and a white shirt, sitting on one of the benches. 'That bloke,' he whispered, smirking, 'says some schoolgirls tried to beat him up in the National Gallery.'

Carlyle looked at the guy. There wasn't a mark to be seen on him. 'Where are the schoolgirls?'

'They did a runner.'

'Stands to reason.'

'But the guy insists on making a complaint,' Prentice sighed. 'What a tosser. He can sit there for a while. Anyway, did you hear about Dog?'

'No. What's he done now?' Carlyle asked. Walter Poonoosamy was a regular nuisance in the neighbourhood. His nickname came from his preferred way of chiselling tourists, asking them for cash to support his fictitious pet Labrador which went by the name Lucky.

'He was found dead last night in a pew in the Actors' Church,' Prentice explained. 'The rector came across him there when he was closing up. Gave him quite a scare, apparently. They reckon it was a heart attack. He was only forty-four, which is amazing considering he looked well north of sixty.'

'I suppose so,' Carlyle conceded. 'But at least he beat the odds.'

Prentice looked at him quizzically. 'How do you mean?'

'I read somewhere that the life expectancy for homeless guys is forty-one. If he made it to forty-four, Dog beat that by almost ten per cent.'

Prentice shrugged. 'Tough old world.'

'Yes,' said Carlyle, 'it sure is.'

Upstairs, Joe was waiting for him. He was munching a chicken sandwich while watching a couple of men in suits record the space between the desks with metal tape measures.

Carlyle gave his sergeant a questioning look.

'Estate agents,' explained Joe softly, sticking the last of the sandwich in his mouth.

'What?' asked Carlyle. 'Are we selling the station?'

'Buying it.'

'Huh?'

'Apparently,' said Joe, 'the station building was sold to a

hedge fund or something as part of a job lot several years ago, in a sale and leaseback deal. The cash paid for a black hole in the pension fund. Anyway, now that the property market has collapsed we're going to buy it back. According to the *Police Review*, the Met is going to make a fifty million pound profit.'

Carlyle watched as the two men disappeared round a corner, in search of other things to measure. 'Better than the other way round, I suppose. But when did we become property developers rather than coppers?' He scratched his head. 'Is Henry Mills downstairs yet?'

'Yeah.' Joe had now turned his attention to a chocolate doughnut which then disappeared in three rapid bites. 'He's in interview room six. We're ready to go.'

Riddled with prevarication, Carlyle was more interested in food. 'I'm going to get a bite to eat,' he said. 'Then I'll go and have a chat with him. In the meantime, round up all the reports, so we can go through everything this afternoon.'

'Will do.'

'Anything from Bassett yet?'

'Yeah,' said Joe. 'He emailed through his preliminary findings. Nothing we don't already know. The force used in killing her was more than you might expect from an old guy like Henry Mills, but in these type of domestic situations you never know.'

'Quite.'

'It looks like the skillet was the murder weapon. They found some hair and skin in the dishwasher pipes.'

'Any fingerprints on the machine?'

'His and hers – some smudges. But no others.'

'Good. Nice and quick.'

'Yeah, looks like we caught Bassett on a good day.'

'Lucky old us. Anything else?'

'Not really,' Joe shrugged. 'They found some other unidentified prints in the kitchen, but that's about it.'

'You'd expect that,' Carlyle said.

'Yeah, but some of them were on the window frame.'

Carlyle thought about that for a second. 'Inside or outside?'

'Inside,' Joe replied. 'I don't know if they checked on the outside.'

'Ask Bassett. I wonder if they were Chilean fingerprints?'

Joe laughed. 'Even the mighty Sylvester Bassett won't be able to tell us that.'

'Shame. Anyway, see what he *can* tell us.' Another thought popped into his head. 'And see if you can find out anything about Agatha Mills on Google.'

Joe looked at him doubtfully.

'I know, I know,' Carlyle sighed, 'but it's worth five minutes. Just in case. Maybe there really is a Chilean connection of some sort.'

Joe's frown deepened.

'It we find anything it will help us understand where Mr Mills is coming from,' Carlyle persisted. 'See our way past the bullshit.'

Twenty minutes and a cheese sandwich and a double espresso later, Carlyle was sitting in interview room number six, across the desk from Henry Mills and his lawyer, a mousy, nervous-looking woman who looked and sounded Mediterranean. A police constable stood by the door to ensure fair play. Carlyle had never come across this lawyer before but he knew immediately that she wasn't going to cause him any trouble. Not with this case, at least. Focused on that thought, he had forgotten her name even before she had finished spelling it.

Under the harsh lighting of the windowless room and missing the comforting arm of the Famous Grouse, Mills seemed jumpy. He was well on the way to drying out and clearly wasn't too happy about it. He's probably as uninspired by his representative as I am, Carlyle thought. He dropped an A5 pad on the desk, carefully pulled the cap off his biro, and jotted *HM, 7/6* on the top of the page. The interview would be recorded but he liked to take his own notes. At least 99 per cent of what would get transcribed from the tapes would be rubbish – all ums, ahs and lawyerly equivocation – and he didn't want to waste time by having to wade through all that kind of crap later.

'We have been waiting here over an hour,' the lawyer whined.

You're paid by the minute, Carlyle thought, so what do you care? He tried to look sincere. 'My apologies,' he said, before switching on the tape-machine and running through the formalities. That done, he leaned forward and eyed Henry Mills as if the lawyer wasn't even there. The smell of whisky had faded from the man's breath, but he looked incredibly tired, as if his new surroundings had sucked some of the life out of him. The room was warm and stuffy. Even after a double espresso, Carlyle himself still felt a bit sleepy. 'Okay,' he proceeded casually, 'in your own words, tell me what happened.'

Mills looked at the lawyer, who nodded stiffly. Dropping his hands on to the table and avoiding eye contact, he launched into the monologue that Carlyle knew he would have been refining in his head since calling the police earlier that day. 'I really know nothing. I went to bed about nine thirty. Agatha was listening to a radio programme in the kitchen. I read a bit of the new Roberto Bolano book – do you know it?'

Roberto who? Carlyle shook his head.

'It's nine hundred pages long,' Mills continued, 'and I'm finding it a bit of a struggle to get into. After a few pages I felt sleepy, and I must have switched the light off before ten.' He stopped to grimace in a way that looked contrived to Carlyle. 'Agatha often stays up later than me, so there was nothing unusual about that. I woke up about seven forty-five and she wasn't there, and then I got up and I found her . . . dead . . . . and I called you.' He looked up and shrugged. 'That's it. I don't know what else to tell you.'

Carlyle let a few seconds elapse. The only sound inside the room was the low whirring of the tape-machine. He counted to thirty in his head, waiting to see if Mills would offer up anything else.

. . . 27, 28, 29, 30 . . .

Mills kept his eyes on the table and said nothing. Carlyle decided to give it thirty seconds more.

. . . 58, 59, 60 . . .

Still nothing. The lawyer meanwhile looked as if she had all the time in the world. Finally, Carlyle spoke: 'How does it feel?' For a second, he wondered if he'd actually asked such a soft question. He ignored the surprised look on the lawyer's face and instead stared firmly at Henry Mills.

Thrown by the question, Mills thought about it for a minute. Carlyle could see that he was wrestling with his thoughts, trying to work out an honest answer. For the first time, he felt a pang of empathy with the dishevelled man in front of him. It struck him that if Helen's skull had been smashed in – even if it had been Carlyle himself who had brained her – he would have been left distraught. Life without his wife, he imagined, would be like a living death. He would become a kind of zombie, just like the man in front of him.

'I don't know,' Mills said finally. 'If you're morbid enough to imagine these things, I suppose you expect it to be dramatic, gut-wrenching, a rollercoaster of emotions. In reality, it's been a very tedious and boring day. I should have laid off the Scotch, like you told me, Inspector .'

Carlyle gave him a small bow.

'I know I should say something like *the reality hasn't hit me yet*, but what the "reality" is, remains to be seen. Agatha and I have been married for almost forty years, we don't have any children, and our lives could be considered fairly,' he thought about the right word, 'self-contained.'

Carlyle nodded, trying to look thoughtful, inviting him to continue.

'That's not to say we had separate lives – we didn't. What we had was a very comfortable combined existence where neither of us felt compromised.' His eyes welled up and he struggled to keep his voice even: 'Seeing her lying there on the floor – it wasn't her. It wasn't real. It wasn't *us*.'

Carlyle waited for more but nothing was forthcoming. He glanced at the lawyer, who seemed to be confused by her client's opening gambit. Was that a confession or not?

Switching off the tape-machine, Carlyle turned back to Henry Mills. 'I want you to take a break,' he said gently, 'and then we can have another go. Talk to your lawyer here. She will know the kind of detailed questions that I'm going to ask. If you've basically given me your full statement, then it is going to take a while for us to go through the evidence. If you can think of anything – anything at all – that might help your case, now is the time to tell me. Then, if you want to change your story, we can get this thing sorted out quickly and you can have a rest.'

He had almost got back to his desk on the third floor when he felt his phone vibrating in the back pocket of his jeans. Seeing that it was his wife, he hit the receive button.

'Hi.'

'John. You have to get to the school.' Helen's tone was verging on fraught.

'There's been a bomb scare . . .'

NINE

By the time he got to the Barbican, the place looked like a scene out of some straight-to-video cop movie. The whole arts complex surrounding the school had been cordoned off. Outside the tape, tourists and office workers mingled, sharing a mixture of concern and curiosity, while resisting the best attempts of a dozen or so uniformed officers to move them along. As he approached the Silk Street entrance, Carlyle counted more than a dozen police vehicles, including two large Bomb Squad vans. He wondered how long it would take them to search the entire site – several hours at least. There would certainly be no more chance of school today. He pulled up Alice's number on his mobile, and cursed when he got a 'network busy' message.

'Fuck!'

Ending the call, he redialled immediately. And got the same message.

'Bastard fucking phone!'

And again.

And again.

At the fifth or six attempt, he got through. After barely two rings, his daughter's voicemail kicked in. *Hi! This is Alice. Leave a message and I'll get back to you. Bye!*

'Alice,' he said as calmly as he could manage, 'it's Dad. Call me when you get this.'

Keeping the phone in his hand, he walked up to a sergeant standing by the police tape. Flashing his ID, he got a nod of recognition.

'Where are the schoolkids?' Carlyle asked.

'Gone to the RV points, sir,' the sergeant said in a practised manner.

'And where are the RV points?'

'Er . . .' The officer shrugged.

Carlyle was just about to slap him, when they were interrupted by a middle-aged woman with a clipboard. 'Which class?' she asked Carlyle briskly.

'Er . . .' Now it was Carlyle's turn to show his ignorance.

The woman hid her frown behind her clipboard. 'Teacher?'

'A man, I think,' was as much as Carlyle could manage.

This time the woman made no attempt to hide her contempt for his ignorance.

Summoning up the patience of a saint, she gave him one last try. 'Upper or Lower school?'

'Lower,' Carlyle said decisively. He knew he had to have a fifty-fifty chance of being right on that one at least.

'They will have gone to Monkwell Square.'

Carlyle looked at her blankly.

'It's just next to the Ironmongers' Hall,' the woman said.

'Just back the way you came, sir,' the sergeant said helpfully. 'Head towards St Paul's – it's just before you get to London Wall. Should only take you about five minutes, maximum.'

'Thanks,' Carlyle replied through gritted teeth. Turning on his heels, he headed at a trot back through the gawkers and the randomly parked police cars.

It took him only a couple of minutes to find the Square. The place was full of girls in uniform gossiping in small groups, lounging about on the grass and generally looking quite pleased at the prospect of the afternoon off. Quite a few were smoking and he was shocked to see one girl, who looked to be even younger than Alice, taking a casual drag on a cigarette as she sat under a tree. How would he react if he found his own daughter smoking? He would cross that bridge if and when he came to it.

First he had to find her. It took him another few minutes to locate someone who looked like a teacher – a tall man in a suit, also brandishing a clipboard. Careful not to tread on any of the pupils, Carlyle stepped forward and introduced himself.

The man nodded. 'John Doherty, Deputy Head of the Lower School.' When Carlyle explained that he was looking for his daughter, he frowned. 'There's no need to overreact.'

Overreact?

'It's probably just a false alarm,' Doherty continued. He looked as if he was in his early thirties, but with his floppy straw hair and boyish features he managed to look younger than many of the girls. 'Everyone has been accounted for. We've told all the ones that don't normally get picked up that they can go home.'

Before Carlyle could respond, the phone started vibrating in his hand. It was a text message from Alice: *At home. All ok. x*

A mixture of relief and frustration washed over him. He looked up, but the teacher had already walked off. For a few seconds, Carlyle stood there, feeling like a spare part. Then he called his wife and left the Square, heading west.

The bell rang, shortly followed by a low rumble of excited chatter. Michael Hagger leaned against a pillar outside the entrance to Coram's Fields Nursery. Trying to look like the kind of bloke who would regularly pick his kid up from playschool, he watched the children start to stream out, still happily playing, stuffing their faces with snacks, or chatting about the day. Mostly it was women – mothers or childminders – doing the collecting, but there was the odd father here and there making the effort to be part of the post-school run.

Once he was sure that home-time was in full swing, Hagger slipped past a woman struggling with a buggy and went inside the building. Smiling at the girls in reception, he casually walked down the corridor towards Jake's classroom.

Wearing jeans, trainers and a *Thomas the Tank Engine* T-shirt, the boy sat at a desk, drawing on a piece of paper with a green crayon. He was concentrating hard, with his tongue poking out of one corner of his mouth. For the first time, it struck Hagger that he was a good-looking lad. Must get it from me, he thought. A teaching assistant stood at a sink in the far corner of the room, tidying away a selection of paints and brushes. She had her back to them and didn't turn round when he entered the room.

Jake saw him and made a face. 'What are *you* doing here?'

Hagger forced a small smile. 'I've come to pick you up.'

Jake looked confused. 'You never pick me up.'

'Well, I am today,' Hagger replied through gritted teeth.

'Where's Mum?'

Hagger reached over and patted him on the head.

'I'm picking you up today,' he repeated. 'I thought it would be nice.'

The teaching assistant was still busy putting caps back on tubes of paint.

'Mum always picks me up,' the boy said stubbornly. 'Or Amelia.'

A right pair of useless, lazy bitches, Hagger decided. 'They said I could come and get you today.'

'Mum says you're a complete bastard,' Jake said casually, lowering his gaze and pressing the crayon harder into the paper. 'And a total cunt,' he added, swapping his green crayon for a red one.

'Does she now?' Hagger bristled.

'What is a cunt, anyway?'

'Nothing.'

The boy looked up. 'It's a bad word, isn't it?'

'She's only joking.' Hagger grinned nervously. He glanced towards the back of the room but the teaching assistant clearly hadn't heard. She had the taps running now, washing out some pots.'

'Amelia too.'

'They love me really. Just like you, eh?'

Jake still didn't look up. 'I want to wait for Mum.'

Hagger had expected this reaction from the boy. He knew that he had to be quick. He couldn't afford a scene. Dropping a small bag of jelly babies on the desk, he whispered, 'I thought we could go and get an ice cream.'

The boy grabbed the sweets and stood up. 'Okay,' he said, tearing open the packet. He looked up at his father. 'Then can I go and see Mum?'

'Of course.'

Happy to be on his own for once, Dominic Silver relaxed on a couch in his house on Meard Street in Soho. Gideon Spanner, his eyes and ears on the street, was out on his rounds and so Silver had the place to himself. The room was silent apart from the hum of traffic outside, interrupted by the occasional burst of a police siren. He had muted the television, on which was playing a rerun of Evander Holyfield's 1989 fight with Michael Dokes, to focus on a report in the *Evening Standard*. It was the unremarkable story of two drug dealers who were due to be sent down for up to twenty-seven years after police found two holdalls containing 50 kilograms of heroin in the boot of their car. The report claimed that the 'haul' was worth almost £5 million 'on the street'. I'm not sure what street you're thinking about, mate, Dom sniffed. Off the top of his head, he estimated that anyone would do well to generate three and a half million from such a load in these straitened times. Still a tidy sum, but well below peak prices. The deepening recession was savaging all types of discretionary spending; even the drugs business, which had held up better than most for longer than most, was now seriously feeling the pinch. Austerity was the name of the game now, even when it came to getting wasted.

He turned back to the newspaper story. The dealers claimed to have been picking up leaflets that they had ordered from a printing business. According to this version of events, the leaflets were not ready for collection at the appointed hour. Meantime, the men were asked to deliver the holdalls instead in return for £250. The jury had taken less than fifteen minutes to find the cretins guilty. It was a surprise that its deliberations had taken that long. The police must have been pissing themselves.

'Idiots!' Silver studied the mugshots of the duo that accompanied the story and shook his head. He had mixed feelings about the police's success in this case. The drugs had belonged to a rival dealer and someone else's product being taken off the market was always good news. Without feeling too smug, Dominic felt that natural selection would always work to his advantage. At the same time, however, it showed that you could only push your luck so far. Disappointed customers would still want servicing and any gap in the market invited a free-for-all. There were plenty of people who would happily spill blood for the sake of market share. That was the capitalist way.

Dominic closed the paper and tossed it on the floor, thinking that it was getting ever closer to the time when he really should be calling it a day. He shut his eyes and tried to clear his mind of all its various distractions.

This, he knew, was a big test.

Could he live up to one of life's basic rules?

Could he quit while he was ahead?

TEN

A shower and a fried-egg sandwich went a little way to easing the frustrations of the day. Alice had retired to her bedroom to do her homework, and seemed completely unfazed by recent events. Picking up the evening paper, Carlyle flopped on to the sofa beside his wife. 'What a day!'

Helen finished sending a text message and dropped her phone on the coffee-table. 'Well, at least there was no bomb. Apparently a couple of the older girls called it in.'

Carlyle gave her one of his many bemused looks. 'Huh?'

'They were due to have a test. They didn't want to do the test, so . . .'

'So they said that there was a bomb in the bloody school?' he spluttered.

'Yes.' Helen grinned.

He half-laughed. 'Well, I suppose that's using your initiative, kind of.'

'But sadly for them,' Helen continued, 'one of the girls used her mobile to call it in. They are *soooo* busted.'

'Jesus. How do you know all this so quickly?'

Helen tapped her nose with a finger. 'The mothers' network is always first with the news.'

'Very impressive.'

'There's more.'

'There is?'

'Yes.' Helen's face darkened. 'The sniffer dogs didn't find any bombs, but they did come up with eight bags containing drugs.'

‘What kind of drugs?’ Carlyle asked.

‘I don’t know.’

‘Dope, presumably.’

‘What about that skunk stuff?’ Helen asked. ‘Isn’t that the new super-threat to the nation’s teens?’

‘Only if you’re a neurotic middle-class parent,’ Carlyle yawned, ‘happy to throw a bottle of Sauvignon Blanc down your throat every night while lecturing your kids about how they shouldn’t even look at a spliff.’

Helen regarded him thoughtfully. Normally she was the more liberal side of the relationship. When it came to drugs, however, her husband’s laissez-faire fatalism made her more than a little uncomfortable.

‘Basically,’ Carlyle continued, on a roll now, ‘it’s all the same stuff. You either use it or you abuse it. Some people can handle it; some people can’t. I’ll ask around in the morning, see what I can find out.’

‘Okay. That would be good. One of the bags belonged to a girl in Alice’s class.’

That stopped him in his tracks. ‘You’re kidding!’

His wife shot him a look that indicated that she most definitely wasn’t. ‘I don’t think she’s one of Alice’s friends but, still, we’ll have to keep a close eye on things.’

‘Yes,’ Carlyle agreed, moving swiftly from the realms of the theoretical to the pragmatic, ‘we will.’ He leaned across and pulled Helen towards him. For a while they just lay there, each of them thinking about their daughter and about the dangers ahead; each knowing also that there wasn’t really anything that they could do about it right now. You just had to wait and see how things turned out.

Finally Helen moved things on. ‘How was your day?’

‘Well . . .’ Carlyle sighed. He talked her through the story of Agatha and Henry Mills, or at least as much of it as he knew.

‘Will the case be closed tomorrow?’ she asked.

‘I hope so. We’ll see what Mr Mills has to say for himself in the morning.' Henry Mills had been left to stew in the cells overnight. While Carlyle had been chasing around after his daughter, Joe had seen the man later that afternoon. Mills had stuck to his story that he had been fast asleep when someone had been practising their forehand smash with a frying pan on the back of his wife's head. Exasperated, Carlyle had made it clear to the lawyer that they would charge him in the morning. Mills's passivity was curious, but people reacted to stressful situations in different ways. Carlyle thought he might just be shutting down, trying to keep the outside world at bay. He decided to send in a psychologist to see what they made of the man. If nothing else, it would give a clear sign to Mills, and his lawyer, that they were curious about the state of his mental health. If the lawyer was sufficiently switched on, she would realise that the police weren't buying her client's story, but that they would probably be willing to do a deal on the grounds of diminished responsibility or something similar.

The inspector didn't see the point of long sentences for domestic cases; it wasn't as if the killers were a threat to the wider public, and it cost a fortune to keep them in jail. Far better that Mills's lawyer got him to take a five-year deal, and the whole thing got wrapped up now. That way, he would probably be out in less than three. The alternative would be to go through the protracted, convoluted and hugely expensive legal process. If he did that, Mills would probably get eight to ten. There was a chance that he might get off on either a technicality or a jury's sympathy vote but, if they were doing their job, the lawyer would tell him that it wasn't worth the risk, or the hassle. Even if he won, he would still end up spending more than a year in custody, given the painfully slow speed at which the wheels of British justice manage to turn.

For Carlyle, the length of the sentence was an irrelevance. A win was a win. And a quick win was the best kind of all. Once guilt was confirmed, the case was closed. Nine times out of ten, he didn't really care what happened beyond that.

Trying to forget about Henry Mills for a while, Carlyle returned to the evening paper. As usual, he read the sports pages first. Finding nothing of interest, he turned to the front. On page four his eye caught a story about an advert that the British Humanist Association had placed on the side of some of London's red buses, proclaiming: *There's probably no God. Now stop worrying and enjoy your life.* Carlyle, a devout atheist, immediately took offence at the word 'probably'. 'These bloody lentil-sucking, sandal-wearing, liberal do-gooders,' he harrumphed to himself under his breath. 'Why can't they just tell it like it is? There *is* no bloody God. End of story. If people could just acknowledge that basic fact, everyone's life would become a lot easier.' Almost willing himself to get more annoyed, he read on: *A spokesman said: 'This campaign will make people think – and thinking is anathema to religion.'* Bollocks it will, thought Carlyle sourly. If you are stupid enough to believe in God, what good is a bloody slogan on the side of a sodding bus?

Feeling his cheeks colouring, he looked imploringly at Helen, who was still curled up on the other end of the sofa. Well aware of the warning signs whenever her husband started winding himself up, she studiously ignored him, saying nothing and keeping her eyes firmly fixed on the television. She was watching that show where various 'celebrities' are dropped into the Australian jungle and made to debase themselves for a couple of weeks to no apparent purpose.

A serious woman in most other respects, Helen was addicted to junk television, and it drove Carlyle mad. This programme had to be one of the worst. He felt the urge to flee the room, but lacked the energy to haul himself off the sofa. His eyes were drawn back to the screen where a mound of bamboo worms were wriggling on a large plate which had been placed in front of one of the contestants. There was a close-up of the man's disgusted face, as a worm was waved in front of him by one of the grinning presenters. Carlyle's mouth fell open. 'Christ!' he exclaimed. 'That's Luke Osgood!'

'*Sir* Luke Osgood,' Helen corrected him, reminding him of the former Metropolitan Police Chief's recent knighthood. The gong had helped to soften the blow of his very messy and very public sacking by the Mayor of London a year or so earlier.

'What the hell's he doing in the jungle?' Carlyle spluttered.

'He's got to eat all of those worms on the plate in three minutes or no one in the competition gets anything to eat tonight.'

'Yes, yes,' said Carlyle, hating it when Helen tried to be funny like this, 'but what's he doing there in the first place?'

'This is part of his reinvention as an all-round media performer,' Helen said, as if it was the most natural thing in the world for the man who had been Britain's top policeman for five years to be conducting himself in such an appalling manner.

Carlyle studied the screen intently. The man currently stuffing bamboo worms into his mouth bore only a limited resemblance to the haggard bureaucrat who had been last seen leaving New Scotland Yard by the back door, hounded by journalists, with the scorn of his political masters ringing in his ears. Osgood's previously messy hair had been cut short, bleached (to hide the grey) and spiked with gel. He sported a tan that bordered on orange and, although it was hard to tell on the television, Carlyle thought that there was a suggestion of some plastic surgery to remove the lines around his eyes and to make his lips fuller. 'His mid-life crisis just gets worse,' he sneered.

As Commissioner, Osgood had never impinged much on Carlyle's working life, but his subsequent behaviour had caused some surprise. Barely two months after getting the sack, he left his wife and kids, announced that he was bisexual, and set up home with a twenty-five-year-old ballroom dancer who had arrived in London from Bergamo. Now the 'pink policeman' had a weekly column in a Sunday newspaper, and seized every opportunity to go on television or the radio to criticise Christian Holyrod, the Mayor who had sacked him, or else his former colleagues and his successor, Sir Chester Forsyth-Walker, a self-proclaimed 'copper from the old school'.

Carlyle didn't know anyone on The Job who didn't think Osgood should have just taken his money, a pension pot of £3 million, and disappeared into the sunset with his mouth firmly shut and his newfound sexuality kept firmly hidden in the closet. How can anyone get to fifty and suddenly decide that they're gay? For once, Carlyle found that he was in step with the majority view of the rank and file across London's police stations, which was that Osgood could have no complaints if someone was to drag him down a dark alley and kick the living shit out of him for being such a pathetic, ego-crazed tosser.

'They've got his boyfriend waiting for him at a nearby hotel,' Helen replied. 'He's quite cute.'

Carlyle frowned. 'Luke Osgood? Cute?'

'No!' Helen giggled. 'The boyfriend. He's called Gianluca.' She arched her eyebrows theatrically. 'Quite the Italian stallion.'

Carlyle chose to ignore his wife's professed admiration for the hunky Gianluca, keeping his focus on Osgood, who was now well on the way to finishing his wormy snack. 'But why is he bothering with all this?' he asked. 'He can't need the money.'

'I think he's got a taste for it.'

Carlyle frowned again. 'For what? Worms?'

'No,' Helen gave him a firm poke with her foot, 'for being a celeb. His ego is finally being allowed to run free. He's unleashed his frivolous side after a lifetime of being submerged in the system.'

'I see,' said Carlyle. He made a grab for her foot, but she pulled it away. 'Just be happy that *I* manage to stay submerged in the system. Letting my ego run free wouldn't put any bread on the table.'

'If you could make as much money as Sir Luke,' Helen grinned, 'you have my permission to eat as many bugs as you like. You can even take an Italian boyfriend.'

Carlyle gave her a funny look.

'Only joking. But there's plenty of money in all this for Lucky Luke. Apparently, he's getting paid a hundred and twenty thousand to do this show. With all his other work, he's making something like three-quarters of a million a year now.'

'Jeez.' Carlyle let out a long, low whistle. Seven hundred and fifty thousand would be three times what Osgood was getting as Metropolitan Police Commissioner. What a world, he thought; what a fucking stupid world. You could earn £250,000 a year, be responsible for 50,000 people and a budget of £3.5 *billion*, not to mention having to deal with the politicians and all their crap – or, indeed, the safety of some 7 million Londoners. Alternatively, you could triple your money for sitting about talking rubbish and eating worms. He had to admit that it was not really such a difficult decision. 'But what about his dignity?' he asked lamely.

'What about it?' Helen snorted, tiring of the repeated interruptions. 'How much did he have left when the Mayor sacked him? Anyway, how much is *your* dignity worth?'

Carlyle didn't need to think about it for long to conclude that the answer was a lot less than £750,000. 'God, all that cash! Could you imagine?'

'Don't feel too bad about it,' Helen said. She gave him another poke with her toe, but this time it was gentler. 'Osgood's only got a limited window of opportunity.' She disengaged her foot from his ribs and waved it at the screen. 'How many times can he do stuff like this? It's downhill all the way from here.'

'I suppose you're right,' said Carlyle.

'Before you know it,' Helen said, 'he'll be reduced to selling security shutters on late-night TV.'

'And opening supermarkets in Croydon,' Carlyle laughed.

'Do they do that sort of thing any more?' Helen asked.

'I dunno,' said Carlyle. 'You would assume so. Opening supermarkets and churning out z-list celebrities are probably the only things that this country is good at any more.'

On the other side of the world, Luke Osgood swallowed the last worm and raised his arms in triumph. 'Will he win?' Carlyle asked.

'No,' Helen said with certainty. 'Gay ex-policeman is too *niche* to win. He's also too middle-class. People like him are the ones who get halfway on shows like this: not complete losers who get voted straight off, but not popular enough with the masses to get through to the very end. To do that, you either have to be a cheeky chappy soap star who gets the mums' vote or a model with big boobs and a tiny bikini who gets the lads' vote.' She mentioned the names of a couple of people that Carlyle had never heard of. 'One of those two will win.'

As they watched Osgood return to his jungle camp in triumph, Alice appeared in the doorway. She deftly tossed a mobile towards the sofa and retreated to her bedroom without saying a word. Carlyle caught the phone before it hit him on the head. He felt it vibrating in his hand and automatically hit the receive button. 'Hello?'

'Inspector, it's Amelia Jacobs.'

Shit. He could immediately tell from the tension in her voice that it wasn't good news. 'Hi.'

'That bastard's taken Jake.'

That bastard. Michael Hagger. The bloke he was supposed to talk to. The bloke he was supposed to sort out.

'He picked him up from the nursery.'

Fuck, fuck, fuck.

'I was ten minutes late,' her voice cracked slightly, 'and they were gone.'

'Uhuh.' The inspector kicked out at the coffee-table in frustration. You fucking idiot, he told himself, why didn't you just warn the guy off? They were depending on you.

'John?' Helen gave him a quizzical look but he just shook his head.

'It's been on the TV,' Amelia continued.

Not the kind of stuff we've been watching, Carlyle thought angrily.

'On the news,' she explained.

'Yes.'

'God knows what will happen to that poor boy. You've got to get him back.'

He took a moment to compose himself. 'Who's in charge of trying to find him?' Amelia gave him a name. 'Okay,' Carlyle sighed, 'I'll have a word and see what I can find out.'

'You were supposed to have a word with Michael,' she snapped.

'I know, I know, I know,' he said sharply. 'Let me see what I can do. I will get back to you asap. Sit tight. It will be okay.' Not waiting for a reply, he ended the call.

'What's the matter?' Helen asked.

'The matter is,' he groaned, 'I've fucked up.' As he said it, the mobile started vibrating again in his hand. 'Shit!' He lifted the handset to his ear. 'Amelia . . .' He tried not to sound too exasperated.

'Inspector Carlyle?'

Carlyle recognised the voice and his heart sank even further. For the second time in less than five minutes, he should have let the call go to voicemail. 'Yes?'

'It's Rosanna Snowdon.'

Snowdon was a presenter on the local BBC News in London. Their paths had crossed on a previous case and Carlyle owed her a favour, maybe more than one, after she had introduced him to the politician Edgar Carlton. Two years earlier, when he had still been the Leader of the Opposition, Carlton had been caught up in a nasty little case involving rape and murder. Snowdon, a family friend of the Carltons, had facilitated an introduction for Carlyle. Later, when the whole thing had come to a messy, inconclusive end, she had probably saved what remained of Edgar's career by stopping him from trying to air the story in the media.

Largely untouched by any hint of scandal, Carlton had gone on to become Prime Minister after a landslide election victory. Snowdon, meanwhile, was building her media career at a steady rate. As well as the local news, she now presented a weekly show called *London Crime*, which did reconstructions of unresolved cases around the capital and appealed to the public for help in solving them. A few months earlier, the show had featured one of Carlyle's cases, a particularly vicious mugging of a young mother in Lincoln's Inn Fields which had been linked to a series of other attacks in and around the Holborn area. Snowdon had asked Carlyle to come on the show, but he felt embarrassed about begging for people's help on television, and had sent Joe instead. The piece generated seventy phone calls and no sensible leads. The amount of police time that had been wasted as a result was too big for Carlyle to even think about trying to calculate it.

The case, of course, remained unsolved.

Carlyle was extremely uncomfortable about owing Snowdon a favour. As far as he was concerned, she was a user – a hustler who saw every item, every victim, as another step towards a celebrity presenter gig on national television, a rich banker husband and regular exposure in *Hello* magazine. But, however he felt about it, owe her he certainly did.

'How are you?' he asked, trying to inject some interest into his voice.

'I wondered if I could talk to you about something,' she said, not bothering with any preamble. 'Maybe we could have a coffee together?'

'This is not about the Mills case, is it?' Carlyle enquired cautiously. He hadn't seen it in the press yet, but it was only a matter of time.

'What?'

'Nothing. What's it about, then?'

'Don't worry,' she said rather brusquely, 'it's not about any of your cases. But I'd rather we talked face to face. Could you do nine o'clock tomorrow morning?'

Carlyle sucked in a breath. He was curious to find out what was causing Rosanna such concern. Whatever it was, it would doubtless be more diverting than his rather banal domestic slaying. On the other hand, she didn't pay his wages, and he did have to get Henry Mills processed. 'That would be tricky,' he said finally. 'Now is not a great time.'

'Please,' she said firmly, 'it's really quite important. It will only take half an hour and it would be a really big favour.' There was a genuine nervousness in her tone that he had never heard before. This was not the usual flirtatious Rosanna, the one that made him feel so uncomfortable. Stripped of its usual coating of ironic detachment, her voice sounded strained. Compared to the super-assured alpha female that he was used to, it was almost endearing.

'Well . . .' His interest was aroused. She might be playing him along, but he didn't think so. If nothing else, this could wipe the slate clean between them. Carlyle reflected for a moment. 'All right,' he said finally. 'Nine thirty.'

'Fantastic!' she said with obvious feeling. 'How about we go to Patisserie Valerie on Marylebone High Street?'

'Fine,' he said, heartened slightly by the prospect that he might at least get a good pastry out of it.

'Good, I'll see you there. Have a pleasant evening, Inspector.'

'You too.' Carlyle clicked off the phone and glanced at Helen, who was still engrossed in her television show. Luke Osgood was now dancing around his jungle clearing, wearing nothing but a yellow posing pouch and a red cowboy hat. He had a bottle of wine in one hand and a cigar in the other. Whatever else Luke has had done recently, Carlyle thought, he hasn't yet coughed up for any liposuction. Disgusted, he pushed himself off the sofa and fled the room.

For almost two hours, he lay in bed, racing through the final hundred or so pages of an excellent detective novel by an Italian writer, whose hero found himself fighting his way through the mire of 'corruption, fraud, rackets and villainy' with mixed success. Carlyle enjoyed it immensely. Finishing the last page, he closed the book and let it fall on the bedside table with a satisfying thud. Books like that should be required reading in schools, he thought. They should be thrust into the hands of the so-called literary experts who imagined that crime novels were just convoluted puzzles. Yawning, he stretched out under the duvet. For a short while, he enjoyed the luxury of letting his mind go blank, while staring at the ceiling. Then, giving up on any hope of his wife's imminent arrival, he switched off the light and prepared to dream of villains and villainy.

Draining the last dregs from his 750 ml bottle of Tiger beer, Jerome Sullivan nodded his head in time to the beat of T.I.'s 'Dead and Gone', grinning serenely, despite the music playing so loudly that the windows were shaking. No one within half a mile of his flat could possibly be getting any sleep, but the neighbours knew better than to complain. Jerome was not good with criticism. The last person to complain about his anti-social behaviour had ended up in the Royal Free Hospital with two broken legs.

Running his operations out of the bunker-like Goodwin House, the thirty-one year old was the biggest skunk and ecstasy dealer in the N5, N7, NW5 and NW1 postcodes. The 1980s four-storey, brown-brick building was perfectly designed for his business operations. It was almost as if Camden Council had built it to order. It even looked like a fortress. The windows were small and at least twenty feet off the ground. More importantly, there was only one way in; even that was on foot – there was no vehicle access. Seeing its potential, Jerome had appropriated the top two floors and set about strengthening the building's defences, so that if the police ever tried to raid it, it would take them at least two hours to get in. Short of bringing a Challenger tank down Marsden Street and pumping a couple of 120 mm rounds into the building, number 47 was impregnable.

Tossing the empty beer bottle onto the sofa, Jerome felt a sudden wave of boredom sweep over him. Reaching for his new toy lying on the coffee-table, he staggered to his feet and kicked at a couple of the bodies slumped on the floor. 'Get up!' he shouted over the music. 'Let's go up on the roof.'

Two minutes later, he was waving a Glock 17 above his head as he swayed to the music blasting through the asphalt below his bare feet. The 9 mm semi-automatic pistol had arrived earlier in the day, a present from a happy supplier; a reward for Jerome beating his sales targets for the first quarter of the year. The supplier – an Albanian people-trafficker who was diversifying into drugs – had thrown in a couple of clips of ammunition as well. Jerome hadn't realised that he had any sales targets, quarterly or otherwise, but he was delighted by the gift. He had never owned a gun before, and he wasn't sure what he was going to do with it.

But he knew he would do something.

By his standards, Jerome had been giving it some serious thought. The way he saw it, there was no point in having the gun, if you didn't use it to shoot someone. But who? For the moment, however, just holding it was enough. Wearing just a Nickelback T-shirt and a pair of ruby Adidas running shorts, he shivered in the night air. In the semi-darkness above the orange street lights he could see the goosebumps on his arms, but the cold was overridden by the overwhelming sense of power flowing from the Glock as he gripped it tightly in his hand. Sticking his free hand down his trousers, he gave his balls a vigorous scratch and felt a tingling in his groin. The Glock was giving him a chubby all right, and he hadn't even fired it yet. 'Oh man!' he groaned to himself. 'This has gotta happen, just gotta . . .'

Eric Christian, one of Jerome's key associates, a friend since their second year at nearby Gospel Oak Primary School, stumbled through the doorway and on to the roof. He was followed by a couple of hangers-on who didn't know the end of a party when they saw one. Eric looked at Jerome and grinned. 'Careful you don't walk right off the edge, man,' he drawled, trying – and failing – to light a large blunt with a Harley-Davidson lighter.

'No worries, dude,' Jerome grinned. He brought the gun down to eye level, gripped it double-handed and pointed it at Eric.

Eric's eyes widened as the blunt fell from his lips. 'Whoa, maaaan!' he drawled, trying to keep the nervous laugh out of his voice. 'Tell me that thing's not loaded.'

'Nah.' Jerome's eyes lost their focus. He pulled the gun to his chest and pointed the barrel skyward, like a man about to participate in an old-style duel. 'I took the clip out before. It's downstairs somewhere.'

The music beneath them reached a crescendo. Starting to dance again, Jerome pointed the Glock past Eric at the other two guys who had joined them. He remembered them now. They were pondlife: sometimes they did little jobs for him, sometimes they were customers. Both of them looked like they were going to shit themselves; one even stuck his hands up, like they did in the movies. Jerome thought this was hilarious and burst out laughing, thinking that if the gun were loaded, he might just pull the trigger. He turned back to Eric. 'We'll have to try it out soon, though.'

'Sure thing,' said Eric, laughing too. Pulling a mobile out of his back pocket, he began filming his friend. Panning across the roof, he zoomed in on Jerome before focusing on the Glock. 'Go for it, man. Let's make a movie!'

Jerome shrieked with delight. 'This one's for YouTube,' he shouted at the tiny camera. 'Comin' to get ya, baby!'

'You the man, Jerome,' shouted one of the losers.

'I'm a killer, man!' Jerome stepped closer to the camera and put the gun to his head, grinning like a maniac. 'This is how you muthafuckin' kill someone!' he screamed, eyes blazing. 'Just *sqeeeeeze*.' His index finger jerked back the trigger. There was a muffled crack and his eyes rolled back into his head. For a second, time stood still. Then, still holding the gun, he did a little sideways dance before stepping off the side of the building and disappearing from view.

Eric stood there, the background hum of the late-night traffic in his ears, trying to work out how his mate had done such a cool trick.

'Wow!' said a voice behind him. 'Did you get all that?'

ELEVEN

The number 25 bus travelled west along Oxford Street, bouncing past the clothes stores, mobile-phone booths, cafés and sex shops at an average speed of about three miles an hour. It would probably have been quicker just to walk all the way, but he couldn't be bothered. The top deck provided a dirty and depressing vista, an unappealing mix of third-world squalor and first-world weather. It was one of the few parts of his home city that made Carlyle feel ashamed, so he always did his best to ignore it.

This morning, on his way to his breakfast meeting with Rosanna Snowdon, he sat at the very front of the bus, with his head stuck firmly in *The Times*. On page three, he contemplated a story about a man in Wales who had spent thirty years in prison after having been wrongly convicted of the murder of a young woman. New DNA tests had shown that he could not have been the killer. The Criminal Cases Review Commission was rushing to have the guy freed.

Reading the article, Carlyle began to feel a physical pain in his chest. The whole thing was so depressingly familiar. The 'murderer' was described as being mentally ill. That was no big surprise – doubtless he had been an easy way of getting a serious case off someone's desk and a grieving family off someone's back. At the trial, the jury had returned a unanimous guilty verdict in double-quick time. The trial judge had thrown in his tuppenceworth as well, proclaiming: '*I have no doubt whatsoever that you were guilty of this appalling, horrible crime.*'

No doubt whatsoever. They just couldn't wait to throw away the key. How very satisfying. An appeal was refused. Only years later, when a new solicitor pushed for another look, did the Forensic Science Service test the bodily fluids collected from the crime scene.

In short, the case had been a total fucking mess, a serving policeman's worst nightmare. It also raised serious concerns about the integrity of dozens of other murder convictions which would now have to be similarly reviewed. The man's solicitor spelled it out for hopeful lags up and down the country: '*Anyone who believes that they've been wrongly convicted, and thinks DNA tests would help, should contact a lawyer immediately.*'

Carlyle wondered morosely how many of his own past cases could be undone by modern technology. It didn't bear thinking about. There but for the grace of God . . .

Slowly, slowly, slowly, the bus struggled another fifty yards up the road to stop at a red light. Carlyle closed the paper and stumbled out of his seat towards the stairs. The five-minute wait while the bus crawled to the next stop and the driver condescended to open the doors, did nothing to improve his mood. Not for the first time, he pined for one of the old Routemaster-style buses, where you could just jump on and off the open back platform whenever you liked. Finally back on the pavement, he got off Oxford Street as quickly as possible and headed north.

Ten minutes later, he was walking up Marylebone High Street. Still burdened by thoughts of what it must be like to be wrongly banged up for thirty years, he didn't pause to think about the purpose of his rendezvous with the alluring BBC journalist. Arriving at Patisserie Valerie, he found the place surprisingly empty for a weekday breakfast time. Deciding that he deserved a treat, Carlyle took a moment to inspect the cakes and pastries on offer, so that they could help lift his mood. Having paid for a large *pain au raisin* and a double macchiato, he repaired to a table by the window and set about cutting his pastry into quarters while contemplating a couple of minutes of undiluted pleasure before the hackette arrived. He had already earmarked a feature on the return of 1980s ska band The Specials for reading while munching. The lyric 'You've done too much, much too young' was bouncing happily around his brain. He smiled to himself, cheered by how much of the song he could still remember. Before he could reopen his newspaper, however, Rosanna Snowdon appeared from nowhere, gliding across his line of vision and pulling out the chair opposite.

Placing a glass of steaming peppermint tea carefully on the table in front of her, she sat down. 'Good morning, Inspector,' she began, shifting a large pair of sunglasses to the top of her head. 'Thank you for coming.'

Carlyle made a humble gesture. 'No problem.' Instinctively, he looked her up and down. As always, Rosanna was well turned out, looking sternly sexy in a rather sombre but expensive grey trouser suit and a pearl-coloured blouse which had just enough buttons undone to arouse one's interest. Looking tired and a little jumpy, she seemed to have lost quite a bit of weight since he'd seen her last, which was all to the good. On the other hand, even the inspector could see that her roots needed retouching, which was not so good. Overall, Carlyle thought, you're not looking great, but it's nothing that a couple of weeks in the Caribbean or The Priory, England's health farm to the stars, wouldn't put right.

She looked at his plate. 'Don't let me stop you.'

Carlyle smiled. 'If you insist.' He took a large bite out of one quarter of his Danish and washed it down with some coffee. For the next few minutes, they sat in amiable silence while he scoffed the rest of his pastry and she sipped demurely at her tea.

She waited until he had popped the last morsel into his mouth and was wiping his lips with a napkin before speaking again. 'I have a slight problem.'

Still chewing, he opened his eyes wide and waited.

'There's a man . . .'

More silent chewing.

Rosanna let out a large sigh and cut to the chase. 'I'm being stalked.' She took another sip of her tea and sat back in the chair, clasping her hands together as if preparing to launch into prayer.

'Isn't that normal?' He tried to present what he hoped was a cheeky grin.

She looked at him uncomprehendingly.

He kept digging. 'Aren't celebrities like you supposed to attract stalkers – the price of fame and all that?'

She gave him a hurt look that suggested his juvenile attempt at humour had overstepped the mark.

'Sorry.' He held up a hand, indicating a willingness to take her problem seriously. 'What's been going on? Give me the background.'

'He's a guy called Simon. I don't know his surname. I guess he's in his late thirties or early forties. He started hanging around outside my apartment building about two months ago. He's standing there when I leave the flat. Sometimes he even follows me to work.'

Carlyle reflexively glanced out of the window.

'Not today,' she continued. 'Not every day. Maybe once or twice a week. And there have been a couple of times when I've seen him hanging around in the evening, too.'

'Has he physically or verbally threatened you?' Carlyle asked in his best official tone.

Her brow furrowed. 'No, he's not threatening. It's more just . . . creepy. He always keeps his distance like he's too embarrassed to talk to me.'

Mentally ill, thought Carlyle. Another one. What must it be like, he wondered, to be a bit simple? Do you understand what kind of disadvantage you've been handed?

She noticed him drifting off into thought and started drumming her expensive-looking nails on the table. 'He sends me letters too.'

Letters? How old-school. 'What kind of letters?'

She almost blushed. 'Marriage proposals,' she said, staring into her lap. 'Six of them, so far.'

'Saying what?' he asked, his interest not really piqued by the thought of a harmless nutter with a crush.

'Saying just that: that he thinks we should get married and that he wants to look after me.'

If ever there was a girl who could look after herself . . . Carlyle thought. For once, he managed to keep his mouth shut and this thought to himself.

'My boyfriend reckons it's a joke,' she continued, 'but it's not like it's his problem. Anyway, he's rarely about.' She reached across the table and touched the back of Carlyle's hand. 'This is really stressing me out.'

Instinctively moving away, Carlyle sat back in his chair. Ignoring his feelings of discomfort, he concentrated on trying to empathise. 'I can understand.'

'Josh confronted the guy one morning, but he just kind of shuffled off. He disappeared for a few days, but then he came back.'

The boyfriend was Josh Harris, an England rugby player. One of those guys who was as broad as he was tall. He was a lock or a prop or something. Carlyle knew nothing about rugby, it being too middle-class for his tastes – just another one of those sad minority-interest sports that wasn't football. He had, however, seen the pair of them once or twice in the party pages of one of the free newspapers. Helen had teased him about his 'celebrity friend'. For some reason, he felt embarrassed about it.

'Have you spoken to the police?' he asked.

'You *are* the police,' she pouted.

'I mean formally.'

'Yes. I had a *formal* meeting with a Sergeant Singleton, a woman, at Fulham police station.'

'Fulham?' Carlyle repeated.

'That's where I live.'

'Okay.'

'I gave her copies of the letters.'

'Do you have them with you?' Carlyle asked.

'Of course.' Snowdon stuck a hand into her large tan shoulder bag, and pulled out a small bundle of envelopes held together with a red elastic band. She pulled off the band and handed the bunch of letters to Carlyle.

'Thanks.' He made a show of studying the envelopes. A couple of the postmarks were too smudged, but the rest had all clearly been sent via the same SW7 sorting office, suggesting, perhaps, that the guy was a local resident. Carefully removing each letter from its envelope, he laid everything out on the table. They were all written in blue biro on the same cheap, thin, white A5 paper. The handwriting was neat, but laboured, like that of a ten year old, making the sentiments seem all the more inappropriate. After what he hoped was a period of decent consideration, he replaced them all in their envelopes and handed them back to Snowdon.

'What did Sergeant . . .' His mind went blank.

'Singleton.'

'What did she say?'

'She said that they would act on any complaint.'

'So,' Carlyle asked, 'did you make one?'

'No.'

'Why not?'

'Two reasons.' She sat up in her chair, flicking a strand of loose hair from her eyes. 'First of all, I didn't think it would make much difference.'

It was a reasonable assumption. Information prised from the Metropolitan Police Force by journalists, using the Freedom of Information Act, suggested that half of reported crimes were 'screened out' (i.e. ignored) on the grounds that they were unlikely to be solved. Even someone like Rosanna Snowdon was unlikely to get much joy from the system when it came to such a low-key problem as this.

'And secondly,' she continued, 'I don't want the publicity.'

Carlyle stared at her and raised his eyebrows.

She made a face. 'Really. It would not be good for my image for this business to come out.'

'Why is that?'

She looked at him, as if not wanting to have to spell it out.

He waited.

'It would make me look weak,' she said finally, 'like a silly girl. Serious journalists don't get stalked by fans.' She thought about this last statement. 'Serious journalists don't have fans, full stop.'

Carlyle nodded as sympathetically as he could manage. Were there any 'serious' journalists any more? he wondered privately. Chained to a desk, churning out the same stories as everyone else, while anyone who could be bothered to read their stories could do it first, and for free, on the Internet; surely you were either just a hack drone or a celebrity 'face' these days? Both of them knew which one was the better option.

She reached back into her bag and pulled out a mobile. 'I have a couple of pictures of the guy that I took on my phone.' She hit a few buttons and handed it over to Carlyle.

There were three images showing a weary, unshaven and slightly overweight middle-aged bloke, wearing a jacket and a jumper. He looked pretty vacant and totally nondescript. 'Why don't you send me one of those?' he said, handing back the handset.

'Fine.' She hit a couple more keys and a few moments later, he felt a familiar buzzing in his pocket.

'Anything else?' he asked.

'Like what?'

'Emails, phone calls, threats . . . anything like that?'

'No. I've asked him myself to go away a couple of times. He kind of trudges off a little way down the road, and then stands hovering under a street light or something.'

Carlyle scratched his head, trying to think of what else she could tell him. 'Has he ever asked you for anything?'

'Like what?'

He made a face. 'Like . . . I dunno, an autograph?'

'He's never asked for anything,' she smiled weakly, 'other than my hand in marriage, that is.'

Carlyle changed tack. 'What else did the sergeant say?'

'Nothing really. She said that the guy was probably harmless but that I should be vigilant and call 999 if he ever threatened me.' For the first time this morning, she gave Carlyle some proper eye contact. 'It wasn't very reassuring, to be honest. I mean, it's not like it hasn't happened before.'

'This has happened before?' he asked, confused.

'Not to me,' Snowdon said. 'But I'm not the first presenter to be targeted.'

'Yes.' Carlyle remembered the case, a decade or so earlier, of a newsreader who had been shot dead on the street. That had been in Fulham too, if he remembered correctly. Maybe all newsreaders lived down there. The place had certainly risen in the world since the days when young Master Carlyle had grown up there.

'What a mess that was!' Rosanna exclaimed.

'The dark side of fame,' Carlyle mused. 'The thing is, Singleton's advice is basically sensible.' He knew that it wasn't what she wanted to hear, but it was all he had.

'Look,' she said, trying to press him further, 'I know you think that I am a bit of an autocutie airhead—'

'A what?'

'A pushy bimbo.'

'No.' He tried to put some conviction into his voice. 'Of course not.'

'All I want is to do my job and be left in peace, Inspector. That is reasonable enough, surely?'

'Of course.'

'It's a quality-of-life issue. I know this guy is probably not such a big deal, but he is beginning to get to me.'

'That's understandable,' Carlyle said. Reasonableness personified.

She traced the lip of her glass with her right index finger. 'And you owe me, remember?'

Here we go, Carlyle thought. He had been waiting for this moment and nodded in acknowledgement.

'Well,' she told him, 'if you can help me on this, it will make us even. More than even. You can come on *London Crime* any time you want, although not talking about this business, obviously. The new series starts next week and we could do with covering some decent cases for a change.'

'I will do what I can,' Carlyle smiled. 'Don't worry about the show – that's not my kind of thing.'

'God!' She rolled her eyes to the ceiling, and he watched her breasts swell inside her blouse. 'You must be the only cop in London who doesn't want to get himself on telly.'

He grimaced slightly, forcing his gaze back to eye level. 'The way I see it, having to go on your show – any show really – is an admission of failure.'

'Not really.' Rosanna half-lifted her mint tea to her lips and then returned it gently to the table. 'All you are trying to do is use the medium to good advantage.'

'But how often does it get results?'

That stopped her in her tracks. 'Well . . .'

He wondered if she'd ever really thought about it before. It was just some cheap entertainment. So who cared if it actually caught any criminals? But he pushed these thoughts to one side; he wasn't here to put her on the spot. 'I've become slightly involved in the Jake Hagger case,' he said, moving the discussion on. 'It's not one of mine, but I know the mother.'

'Ah yes,' she nodded, 'the little boy who was snatched from the nursery by his father.'

'Did you cover it?' Carlyle asked.

'No, we've been off air. But we could do it on the new series, if you wanted.'

'I think it's too late for that.'

'Why?' She looked at him carefully, happy to be talking now about someone else's problems. 'Do you think he's dead?'

Carlyle snorted. 'Sometimes I wonder if I *hope* he's dead.'

'But . . .' Slowly, a patina of understanding spread across her face 'Oh God, that is so horrible!'

Carlyle shrugged.

'Maybe you are being too negative,' Rosanna sniffed. 'After all, child protection is not really your thing. A lot of kids get found. They reckon around five hundred children are abducted in Britain each year. Almost all are taken by a disaffected parent who wants custody. Not nice, but a lot different from the kind of thing you're thinking about.'

Carlyle looked down at his empty cup. 'I'm no expert but, trust me, the last thing Michael Hagger wants is custody of his kid. He's either tried to sell him or he's used him in some other way in one of his business transactions.'

'Urgh!' She stuck a finger in her cold tea and stirred it aimlessly. 'That makes my problem look a little pathetic, doesn't it?'

Yes, it does, Carlyle thought. 'Not at all,' he said. 'But anything to do with kids is just the worst.' He smiled. 'When you become a mum, you'll realise.'

A rueful look passed over Rosanna's face. 'Josh would have kittens if he heard you talking about me having kids.'

'Well,' Carlyle said, feeling himself slip uneasily into father mode, 'if I was ever talking to Josh about it, I would tell him that, when the time comes, the only thing that he should be worrying about is doing what he is told, stepping up to the plate and performing.'

She blushed. 'Inspector!'

'It's true,' he grinned, pleased that he'd at least cheered her up a bit.

'He wouldn't be happy at all,' she protested.

He scanned the street outside and sat back in his chair. 'Alternatively, I could send round a couple of guys with baseball bats – threaten to break his legs.'

She laughed. 'I presume you know plenty of people like that.'

'I do,' he said, trying not to sound too pleased about it.

For a moment they sat in comfortable silence. Then she asked: 'Do you think there is any chance of finding Jake Hagger?'

Remember she's a journalist, a little voice piped up in the inspector's head. 'Off the record?'

'Of course.'

He thought about it for a moment. 'I think that there is as near to no chance as makes no difference.'

'I see.'

He glanced at his watch. It told him that he really should be getting back to the station and dealing with Henry Mills but, once again, for some reason the enthusiasm to do so just wasn't there. For her part, Rosanna didn't seem desperate to get off to work either. 'So,' he said finally, 'how are your political chums? Spend a lot of time in Number Ten?'

Spotting a woman acquaintance walking up the street, Rosanna waved to her, before returning her gaze to Carlyle. 'I have been to Downing Street twice, as it happens. It was nice, but not exactly life-changing. I know the Prime Minister's Director of Communications extremely well – I'm sure I could get you an invite there if you wanted.'

I wonder what Simpson would make of that? Carlyle reflected. 'Thanks. I'll bear it in mind.'

Rosanna leaned slightly over the table towards him. 'To be honest, I think that they're not finding it as much fun as they thought it was going to be.'

The poor dears, Carlyle thought.

'Edgar,' she continued, 'is finding it quite tough going. The poor chap is obsessed with the idea that he has been found out – as if you need to be a genius to be Prime Minister. Every time his poll ratings slip a bit further, he's waiting for Christian to come through the door and steal his job.'

'I would have thought the Mayor of London has enough on his plate as it is,' Carlyle mused, keen to hear more.

'Being the Mayor is not really a full-time job though, is it? Certainly not for a man of action like Christian. All you've really got any responsibility for is trying to stop the Tube drivers going on strike, which they do regardless, and implementing the congestion charge, which he wants to scrap anyway.'

'So what does he do, then?' Carlyle asked.

Rosanna gave him those big eyes. 'To be fair, Christian Holyrod *is* amazing. The job itself just isn't big enough for him. Apart from anything else, he needs his own foreign policy; he's a soldier right down to his DNA and he needs to operate on the biggest stage.'

This all sounded like gibberish to the inspector. 'I see.'

'Since he's got elected to City Hall, he really has achieved a lot.'

'Like what?'

'Well, he's successfully positioned himself as the number two politician in the country. He's also built up his portfolio of non-executive directorships.'

'Is that allowed?'

'Of course it is. It's vitally important that politicians keep in touch with the real world and see how business works. After all, that's how wealth gets created.'

I've often wondered about that, Carlyle said to himself.

'And,' Rosanna grinned, 'if they're earning good money outside, it makes it less necessary for them to have to fiddle their expenses.'

'Good point,' Carlyle laughed. 'What kind of directorships does Holyrod have?'

'Quite a range, I think. There's a media company, agribusiness, aerospace . . .'

'Interesting. Make sure you give Christian and Edgar my kind regards next time you see them.'

Rosanna put a gentle hand on his forearm. 'Inspector, don't take this the wrong way, but I think that if either of them ever see you or hear of you ever again, it will be way too soon.'

Recalling his previous run in with the politicians – an earlier case – Carlyle bowed modestly. 'I wouldn't have it any other way. I guess that means an invite to Downing Street is a non-starter.'

'Not necessarily,' she said.

'Oh?'

'I could probably swing something. It would have to be for one of Edgar's wife's charity events, some time when he was out of the country.'

Carlyle tried to look affronted. 'It wouldn't be the same, then.'

She shook her head. 'I think you just like causing trouble, Inspector.' The smile vanished from her face. 'Anyway, I must be going. Thank you for our talk.'

'I *will* do what I can to help with your stalker,' Carlyle promised. 'Let me speak to Singleton and we'll take it from there. Next time you see your guy, call me straight away.'

'He's not my guy,' she shot back.

He held up his hands in a conciliatory manner. 'You know what I mean. Just call me.'

'I'll do that.'

'The one thing that would be useful for me to have would be a surname. Maybe he's in care or has a medical history. Maybe he's not taking his medication. Maybe he just needs help.'

'Mmm . . .' She didn't sound too convinced. After all, this was supposed to be about *her* needs, not those of the man who was stalking her.

'Any further thoughts on that, or any other developments, let me know.' He pushed his chair away from the table and stood up, wiping some crumbs from his trousers as he did so. 'But don't approach him directly. Keep your distance and don't take any risks.'

'Yes, sir!' She gave him a mock salute and he was pleased to see a little of the old sparkle return to her eyes. Standing up, she hoisted the bag over her shoulder and dropped the sunglasses back on to her nose. Then she leaned over and kissed him on the cheek. 'Thank you for this. I am very grateful. Just knowing that you are on the case is a big help.'

On the case? Carlyle felt himself redden slightly. 'It will b-be fine,' he stammered as she turned for the door. 'Let's speak soon.'

TWELVE

A night in the cells had failed to encourage Henry Mills to change his story. He remained adamant that he had been soundly asleep while his wife was being brained in the kitchen of their flat. Neither disappointed nor particularly surprised by this answer, Carlyle formally charged him with murder and went back upstairs to sort out the paperwork. In a couple of hours, the Mills case would be off his desk and it would become someone else's problem.

He was waiting for his computer to start up when Joe Szyszkowski came by with a blue A4-sized folder under his arm.

'What have you got?' Carlyle asked, without preamble.

Joe perched on the edge of the desk, opened the file and flipped through some sheets of paper. 'It looks like he was telling the truth about the Chilean thing.'

'Yeah?' said Carlyle, looking at the somersaulting hourglass on his computer screen, not really caring any more.

'Agatha Mills had a brother,' Joe continued, ignoring his boss's off-hand mood, 'called William Pettigrew. They had a Chilean father and an English mother.'

'Pettigrew? Doesn't sound very Chilean to me.'

'There's a Scottish great-grandfather or great-great-grandfather in there somewhere,' Joe explained. 'There's a strong Celtic influence, apparently. A whole bunch of Scottish farmers went over in the 1840s and 1850s. And the Chilean navy was formed by a Scot, Lord Cochrane, when they were fighting for independence from the Spaniards.'

'Interesting,' said Carlyle, impressed.

'Wikipedia is a great thing.' Joe shrugged. 'We've always been tight with the Chileans, apparently. They've even had people fighting in Iraq.'

'Jesus!' Carlyle shook his head. 'What's it to them?'

'Dunno. Anyway, William became a Catholic priest in Valparaíso, a coastal town north of Santiago. He disappeared during the 1973 military coup, when the army overthrew the government.'

'That's what usually happens in a military coup,' Carlyle deadpanned.

Joe did not rise to the bait. 'The family,' he continued, 'were eventually told that William Pettigrew was dead, but no body has ever been found.'

'Again, not that uncommon.'

'Agatha Mills, however, spent the last thirty-five years going back and forth between London and Chile, trying to find out what precisely happened to her brother and who killed him. She never lost hope of bringing her brother's killers to justice.'

Carlyle sighed. 'Good luck on that one.'

'Well,' said Joe, 'you have to give the old girl some credit. She kept at it for decades, despite a history of threats from military types.'

'Death threats?' Carlyle perked up slightly.

'Yeah . . . at least, according to some of the press reports. Mainly low-level stuff, like having her laptop nicked or her car tyres slashed. But I read one story about her getting an envelope in the post with a couple of bullets in it.'

'The press are hardly reliable,' Carlyle snorted. 'I'm not going to start chasing my tail on the basis of a few clippings.'

'No,' Joe said, 'but still.'

The inspector grunted.

'You were the one who told me to check it out.'

'Okay,' Carlyle sniffed, 'so she pissed off some Chileans pining for the good old days under that general.' He groped for the name. 'Maggie Thatcher's mate.'

'Pinochet.'

'Yeah, right,' Carlyle nodded, 'General Pinochet.'

'I think he was arrested in London a few years ago,' Joe said, 'while enjoying our Great British hospitality.'

Carlyle raised an eyebrow. 'And?'

'And nothing. Storm in a teacup and then he went home.'

'Got away with it all,' Carlyle mused.

'I suppose so.'

'They always do.'

'To the victors the spoils.'

'Yes, indeed, Joseph.' Carlyle spent a moment contemplating life's endless unfairness. 'Isn't he dead now?'

'Pinochet?' Joe made a face. 'No idea.'

'Either way,' Carlyle mused, maybe just a little more interested now, 'it's all a long, long time ago. Why would anyone – apart from Agatha Mills, the loyal sister – still care about all this stuff now?'

'Because Chile has got a new President,' said Joe. 'A socialist – and a woman.'

'Interesting combination,' said Carlyle, still not seeing the relevance.

'She was a torture victim herself,' Joe explained. 'She ordered a fresh investigation into cases like William Pettigrew's.'

'Okay . . .'

'The Pettigrew case review was completed last year. It concluded that he was almost certainly tortured and then shot dead aboard a navy ship called,' he flicked through the papers again, 'the *White Lady*.'

'What did they do to him?'

'The usual stuff, I suppose,' said Joe. 'Electric shocks to the gonads, that sort of thing.'

'We could do with some of that downstairs,' Carlyle grinned.

'Different world back then.'

'Which *you* would know all about, I suppose,' Carlyle teased, 'having been what, about one year old at the time.'

'I bet *you* remember it well, though,' Joe said cheekily.

'Fuck off!' Carlyle laughed. 'I'm not that old.'

'You just look it.'

'That's a consequence of working with you, sunshine.' He thought back to 1973 – what did he remember? Not a lot. Certainly not what had been going on in a small country on the other side of the world.

'Anyway,' Joe continued, 'the investigating judge ordered the arrest of a couple of navy officers last year.'

'Names?'

'Dunno. But they are due to face trial for the murder of William Pettigrew in the autumn.'

'After all this time?'

'There are a couple of witnesses who say that they're now prepared to testify.'

'Okay, the family is finally going to have its day in court, so why bother bumping off Agatha Mills? It's not like she was there as a witness,' he looked at Joe, 'was she?'

'No, not as far as I know.'

'So she can't really testify. At least not to anything important.'

'She has been one of the driving forces behind this case getting to court, though.' Joe shrugged. 'Maybe the people who did it are still out there. Maybe they want to stop her; maybe they want to intimidate the other witnesses. Could be various things.'

They. Whenever you were dealing with *them*, you knew you were in trouble.

'Maybe.' Carlyle leaned back in his chair, placing his hands on his head. 'Maybe, maybe, maybe. An octogenarian fascist plot? It's all very thin.'

'I know.'

'So ultimately where does this little history lesson get us? Mrs Mills *née* Pettigrew had an interesting backstory.'

Joe nodded.

'A person or persons unknown, of a right-wing Chilean persuasion have a – what? Let's say a *possible*—'

'Theoretical,' the sergeant interjected.

'A *theoretical* motive for bumping her off. But do we have any evidence that anyone other than her old man was inside that flat of theirs the night she died?'

'No,' Joe replied.

'Do we have anyone reporting the sight of any foreign-looking gents acting suspiciously? Maybe mumbling a few words of Spanish? Doing the goose-step and clasping a photo of *El General* to their bosom?'

'No.'

'Anything on the CCTV?'

'No. The cameras at Ridgemount Mansions were there just for show,' Joe informed him. 'They aren't actually hooked up to any recording equipment. That would have added too much to the service charge, apparently.'

'What about cameras in the street itself? Thousands of bloody tourists walk along that street every day. Some of them must get mugged. And someone must film it.'

Joe shrugged. 'No one's looked at those, as far as I know. Do you want us to get on it?'

Carlyle thought about it for a moment then said, 'Nah. It would take too long. Got anything else?'

'No.' Joe stuck the documents back in the folder and placed it carefully on Carlyle's desk.

'Right, then,' said Carlyle, 'let's remember rule number one of this job. In the first instance, always stick with the blindingly obvious.' Sitting up straight, he turned towards his desk, getting ready to do battle with the Met's appalling IT system.

It was time to type up his report.

'Henry Mills has been charged. Justice will now take its course. In the meantime, my little Sancho Panza, we move on to the next thing.'

A look of bemusement passed across Joe's face. 'Eh?'

In the event, Carlyle managed only a couple of paragraphs of the report before he got bored and turned his attention to the latest football gossip on the BBC's web pages. After that, he decided that the paperwork could wait for twenty-four hours, whereas the gym could not. Intending to come in early to get it done, he promised himself that the necessary documentation would be on Commander Carole Simpson's desk before lunchtime.

On his way out of the station, he spied the colleague in charge of the Jake Hagger investigation. Detective Inspector Oliver Cutler was a twelve-year veteran on the Force who had been stationed at Charing Cross since the beginning of the year. Jacket on, heading towards the lift with a determined stride, he looked as if he was also leaving for the night. Carlyle quickened his step and caught up with him. 'Cutler!'

Cutler half-turned, but didn't stop walking. 'Yes?'

'Carlyle.'

'I know.'

Carlyle finally caught up with his man. Cutler pressed the lift button, saying nothing further.

'It's about Jake Hagger.'

'What's it to you, then?' Cutler asked defensively, keeping his eyes on the lift doors.

Carlyle had never really given Cutler the once-over before. A small bloke, he looked tired and distracted: a man who in the short term was being kept from the pint of London Pride that was waiting for him on the bar round the corner in the Sherlock Holmes pub and in the long term was winding down towards the earliest possible retirement on the best possible pension. Not the kind of guy you'd want if you needed to get a result, Carlyle thought sourly.

Cutler pushed the button again, hoping that the lift would save him from this conversation.

'I know the mother,' Carlyle said.

A knowing look washed over Cutler's face. 'Giving her one, then?'

'The father claimed he was going to sell the kid,' Carlyle said evenly, ignoring the jibe.

Cutler shrugged. 'Empty words.'

Carlyle took a position by the lift doors. 'I don't think so. Hagger wouldn't have kept Jake for this long. He couldn't look after a kid for ten minutes.'

'Maybe they left the country.'

'Neither of them had a passport.'

'It can still be done.'

'Hagger's just a local scumbag, not an international jet-setting scumbag. Camden High Street is about as far as he usually travels.'

Cutler scratched his nose absent-mindedly. 'Well, if he did sell him, then it's game over. I doubt it though – I don't suppose that he knows many couples who are desperate to adopt.'

'No.'

'Then some pervert will probably already have had their fun with the poor little bastard,' Cutler said without any obvious feeling. 'In that case, the most likely scenario is that the body's lying at the bottom of the West Reservoir.'

Carlyle nodded. More than once over the years he had fished bits of victims out of the decommissioned reservoir. A couple of miles away, in Stoke Newington, the reservoir was now used as a water sports centre. Carlyle had never seen its attraction; apart from anything else, the 'tranquil' setting attracted criminals and weirdos of various persuasions. It was widely assumed that there would be plenty more bodies and body parts discovered if the place was ever drained.

'There are so many of these cases,' Cutler continued, 'that people don't care any more. And even if they did, the public – as you know only too well – is no fucking use whatsoever. No one ever pays any attention to what's going on around them.'

'So, case closed?' Carlyle asked.

Cutler gazed at a spot beyond Carlyle's left shoulder. 'No, but it's as good as – unless you have anything for me?'

'No, but I told Sam Laidlaw that I'd ask around. If anything comes up, I'll let you know.'

'I knew it,' Cutler smiled. Finally, the lift arrived and he stepped inside. 'Give her one for me.' Rocking back on his heels, the inspector waited for the doors to close. Then, letting out a deep breath, he headed for the stairs.

THIRTEEN

Handcuffed, but still wearing his own clothes, Henry Mills moved into the courtyard in the middle of Charing Cross police station, flanked by two security guards. Behind him came two other prisoners, a nineteen-year-old glue-sniffing mugger and a fifty-two-year-old petty thief. The trio were being transported across London to Wormwood Scrubs, the Victorian prison, where they would await their respective trials at Her Majesty's Pleasure.

It was barely eight in the morning and a sharp chill lingered in the shade of the courtyard. Mills shivered, but breathed in deeply. It was the first time in almost two days that he'd enjoyed some fresh air, and he appreciated it. His night in the cells below his feet had been extremely unpleasant, the liberally applied disinfectant failing to cover the smell of innumerable bodily evacuations. He had spent the last twelve hours breathing through his mouth and failing to get any sleep. Equally, he hadn't been able to wash or shave in the last couple of days. Worst of all, he hadn't been able to brush his teeth, and his mouth felt as if a small animal had died in it.

Edging slowly forward with dainty baby steps, he tried to focus on nothing other than the small patch of tarmac immediately in front of his feet.

'Hold it!' One of the guards, an emaciated skinhead called Jeremy, with a tattoo of an angel on the back of his neck, held up a hand.

The other guard stepped out from behind the prisoners and gazed sullenly at the assembled police vehicles in front of them. 'Where's the van?' He turned to a mechanic who was working under the hood of a Toyota Prius hybrid. 'Mate,' he asked, nodding at his trio of prisoners, 'where's the transport for our friends here?'

The mechanic stood up and twiddled a spanner aimlessly. 'Huh?'

'The van for the Scrubs?'

'Oh yeah, it's outside.' The mechanic pointed with his spanner at the closed metal gates covering the entrance. 'They couldn't get it in. Some genius parked in front of the doors. We're waiting for them to get towed.'

The guards looked at each other.

Mills looked at the guards. His heart sank at the prospect of being sent back inside.

One of the other prisoners, the glue-sniffer, farted loudly and at length, eliciting a peal of hoarse laughter from the thief.

'I'll take them out one at a time,' Jeremy decided, after a while. 'You wait here with the others.'

'Okay,' the other guard nodded. 'My shift finishes at half-nine, so let's get on with it.'

Jeremy put a gentle hand on Mills's shoulder. 'Come on, sunshine,' he said, gesturing towards a side door, right next to the main gates. 'Over there.'

Less than a minute later, Henry Mills was out on the street and, fleetingly, back in the real world that he'd imagined he'd left behind for good. Feeling the sun on his face, he squinted as he got his bearings. A couple of people walking by, on their way to work, stepped around him without a second glance. A taxi roared past. Life outside was going on as normal.

Towering over the other cars parked on Chandos Place, the Dennis high-security prison van was about ten yards down the road. After aiming a half-hearted kick at the Skoda Yeti illegally parked in front of the police garage, Jeremy walked Mills towards the back of the prison van, nodding at the driver as he passed. Mills waited patiently on the pavement while the guard stepped up on to the footplate to open the back door.

The door would not budge.

'Christ!' Jumping back down from the footplate, Jeremy pushed past his prisoner and jogged back to the front of the van. 'It's locked,' he shouted at the driver. 'Open it up!'

Engine revving, a blue flower-delivery van turned into the street, heading towards them. Mills watched the driver talking animatedly into his mobile phone while steering with one hand. Isn't there a law against that? he wondered. Either way, the driver was going far too fast. As he accelerated down the street, a woman pedestrian scuttled for cover. Ignoring the screeching of brakes and the blaring horn, Henry Mills smiled. He looked up at the clear blue sky and felt himself floating away. Blinking away his tears, he heard a second van racing down the street towards him. He knew that this was his moment. 'I'm coming, Agatha,' he mumbled to himself, as he stepped into the middle of the road and closed his eyes.

FOURTEEN

September 1973

During the first few days on board the *White Lady*, William Pettigrew's captors operated a rigorous sleep-deprivation programme. He was kept awake with regular soakings from the water jets and random beatings. A head-count was taken every hour. In case anyone ever took a chance to doze off in their hammock, a sailor known as the 'Bird of Torture' would bang on the metal doors to further keep sleep away. They were fed once a day – water and a thin porridge. A few shovelled it in, most picked disinterestedly; there was always plenty left over for the seagulls.

Every so often, a group of sailors would appear and three or four people would be taken away for interrogation in the cabins which had been turned into torture chambers on the decks below. It was impossible to tune out the yelling and screaming that came up through the floor as the electric shocks were applied. The sessions could last twenty minutes or they could last ten hours. Afterwards, some of the victims came back, others didn't.

The first time he was tortured, Pettigrew shat himself almost before the cattle prod tickled his balls. His interrogators laughed and then made him eat it. They laughed even more when he immediately vomited the shit back up. They told him to eat it again. He tried, but this time he could not even manage to get it into his mouth. After some curses and some punches, they hosed him down.

More electric shocks, this time to the anus. He started shitting blood, bright crimson splashes on the floor rapidly darkening in the heat. That caused more hilarity. They hosed him down again. By now he welcomed the water jet. If nothing else, he could be clean.

The questioning was random and perfunctory. This was not sophisticated intelligence-gathering, and they were not interested in any answers. They had a lot of people to get through and could only waste so much time on each individual. No one cared about anything he had to say. No one recorded anything. No one took any notes. He was like a fly having its wings pulled off by a bunch of sadistic schoolboys.

It was all a charade. Emotionally, Pettigrew had closed down. He could feel the pain, but he didn't have any thoughts about it. There was nothing he could say that could make him useful to these people, nothing to hang on to that could fire a determination inside him to live. It wasn't a question of trying to survive. It was just a question of seeing it through.

Their only question was *what do you know?*

'I know nothing,' he would say, as calmly as possible.

'What do you know?'

'I know nothing.' That was true enough, even in the beginning. By the third or fourth time they asked him, he could barely remember his own name.

They would give him a few slaps, maybe another shock, and ask again.

'What do you know?'

Slap.

'I know . . . nothing.' Pettigrew couldn't even think straight enough to make something up. Names? By the time that they finally got round to him, who was left? Who could they not have possibly rounded up already?

'What do you know?'

Slap.

'Nothing.'

Pettigrew didn't want to make anything up. He knew that if he started giving them any kind of 'information' that it could only prolong things. By now he just wanted it all to be over as quickly as possible.

'What do you know?'

Slap.

'What do you know?'

He had nothing more to say. There were no more words. He was on a journey back to a time before language, before words; to a time when all you could do was howl.

After his second torture session, Pettigrew was told that he would immediately be shot because he was a *fucking Communist whore* – both a traitor to the Church and a traitor to the country.

They blindfolded him and pushed him up against a wall. Someone stepped in front of his face and said softly, 'It's over for you. The good priests are coming back now. The ones Allende stopped from teaching; the ones who were banned from hearing confessions; the ones who had to work as taxi drivers to make a living. I mean the priests who defended the Supreme Court and the Constitution of the Republic of Chile and opposed the creation of a Communist state. The ones who love the Church and don't want to see it destroyed by faggot perverts like you.'

Pettigrew said nothing. All he could think was, It's finally over.

'Understand this: the Marxist invasion of the Church is at an end. The theology of liberation is dead.'

He could sense the excitement in his beating breast. *Thank you, God.*

'You are dead.'

The voice stepped away and there was silence for five, ten, fifteen seconds. The safety-catch of a pistol was flicked off.

Someone cried, '*Fire!*'

A gull squawked overhead.

He stood there, shaking, refusing to still be alive. It should have been all over by now.

On the way back to the hammocks, someone clipped him round the ear, mistaking his sobs of frustration for sobs of relief.

His torturers soon became bored. After his fifth session, they left Pettigrew chained to a metal bedframe with a muslin hood over his head. At some point, he heard shouting. The sounds of people running around. General activity of men doing their jobs. Slowly, the ship's anchor came up.

A little later, he heard the door to the cabin open. Excited youthful voices gathered by the door. Then they brought in a woman and he heard them chain her to the bed next to his. Then they argued over who should go first.

Apart from a few shadows moving across the bottom corner of his field of vision, he couldn't see anything because of the hood over his head.

But he heard her screams.

Maybe he had died; died and gone to Hell. The sounds were bad, but the smell was worse. He lost count after the fifth time they raped her. Most were quick about it, but one man seemed to take an eternity. 'Hurry up, Julio,' one of his companions squealed. 'We'll find you another one later.'

'You can do *him*,' someone else said, kicking Pettigrew's bedframe so hard that it bounced off the floor. 'Just flip him over, you won't know the difference.' There was laughter and he felt spittle spray across his chest.

Another voice, closer this time, said to him: 'How would you like that, priest? You can be next. If you're still tight enough, that is.'

Finally they left. After the cabin door slammed shut, he listened to her sobs.

And then her whimpering.

And – finally – her silence.

Much later, he moved his head in the direction of the woman. Their beds were less than six inches apart. She was nearly close enough to touch. If he flexed the fingers on his left hand, he imagined that he could almost brush her right forearm. He tried to ignore the beating of his heart, the rasping of his breath and the buzzing in his ears, and instead concentrated on listening. There was nothing to be heard. Maybe it was his hearing – they had hit him on the ears many times. It was a torture technique called 'the telephone' and perhaps he had taken one call too many. Either way, the silence was a blessing. He hoped that it meant that his unknown companion was gone. That Death had finally shown her its soft heart. And he hoped that he would soon be shown the same mercy.

The hours passed with his body encased in a gentle rhythm of pain. At some point Pettigrew imagined that he was floating on the ceiling, looking down on the two beds: their bare frames, no mattresses, no blankets, no pillows; nothing else in the room but their naked, bloodied, bruised pulps.

He wanted to cry, but no tears came.

He wanted to scream, but no sound came.

He wanted to leave this place, but he could not move.

After a while, he felt a hand on his shoulder. He turned to see a messenger from the celestial court close by. Dressed only in a loincloth, he had the concerned expression of a man. With a warm, sincere gaze, he looked deep into Pettigrew's eyes as he hovered above him.

'I am Dismas, your guardian angel,' said the vision.

The priest smiled. He knew that Dismas was the Good Thief who had been crucified with Christ on Calvary, and then accompanied Him to Paradise. Dismas was the only human to be canonized by Jesus. He was also the patron saint of condemned criminals.

'Take me with you,' Pettigrew sobbed.

'I cannot.' Dismas stroked his ragged beard with one hand, and pointed at Pettigrew's body, lying on the bed below them with the other. 'You must go back to face the torment of your own creation.'

'B-but this is not my doing!' Pettigrew stammered. 'How can you say that it is?'

'My son,' Dismas smiled sadly, 'you betrayed the Church. You have to accept your fate.'

'No!' Now he felt an anger uncoiling within him that his torturers had never yet unleashed, igniting the life-force that he thought had been extinguished forever. 'I have followed in the footsteps of Jesus. I have served the poor. That is why I am here. That is why I did not run away when I had the chance! I knew I had to be with them, for that is the role of a priest. I have not betrayed the Church. The Church has betrayed *me*!'

'Such pride! Such arrogance!' Dismas took Pettigrew's head in his hands; the priest felt giddy. The room slowly flooded with a gentle white light. 'You have to go back in order to go forward. Only then can you respond to God's love and be welcomed into bliss. Do not worry. From now on, no evil shall befall you, nor shall affliction come near your tent, for to His angels God has given command about you. Upon their hands they will bear you up. They will guard you in all your ways.'

Pettigrew felt the tears running down his face. Looking down, he could see them fall on to his broken body, moistening his wounds. 'Can it be true?' he asked.

'Make your legacy one of penance.' Dismas smiled. 'Be sorry for your wicked life. Be the epitome of a repentant malefactor. God's willingness to forgive is timeless. With the love of God, it is never too late.'

'The love of God . . .' Pettigrew repeated, searching the vision's face for further comfort. But Dismas was already fading into the light. He watched him disappear and waited for his spirit to return to his body. The light engulfed him with calmness and love and, finally, finally, finally, he felt that he was truly on his way to Heaven.

* * *

When they came back, he was ready. He could hear distant voices – two people, maybe three. The handcuffs were unlocked. He rubbed his wrists and placed his arms across his chest, but made no effort to move from the bed. Instantly, he felt the now all-too familiar pressure of a rifle muzzle against his temple.

'Get up, you pig!'

Still hooded, the priest slowly swung his legs off the bed and stood unsteadily on the floor. Feeling dizzy and nauseous, he made to sit back down before a hand grabbed him by the back of the neck and jerked him forward.

'Out!'

Looking down, he could see a tiny patch of floor between his bruised feet. The floor was cool to the touch. It hurt to put too much weight on either foot, so he shuffled along as best he could, down a corridor and up some stairs. Suddenly on deck, he stopped to fill his lungs.

'Move!'

The deck was wet. It had been freshly scrubbed and there was just the slightest hint of disinfectant on the breeze. He felt a weak sun on his back. Someone behind him pulled the hood off with a flourish and he screwed up his eyes against the light. He looked at his hands, still with green paint under the fingernails, and let them touch his face for the last time.

Somewhere above his head a seagull cried. The sky was a gentle blue. Summer was on its way.

Due process was coming to an end.

This was to be the final scene of the Inquisitorial process, his auto-da-fé, the Act of Faith where he would be sentenced, and the sentence carried out. Pettigrew imagined himself with a smile on his face. This was where he would escape the trap of victimhood and retribution.

One of the sailors pointed to an open gate in the side-rail. He padded over and looked down. The drop looked to be about 60 feet. In front of him was nothing but the blue of the Pacific Ocean. To his left, he could see the coast. He guessed that they were maybe a mile or so out of Valparaíso. He thought of Cerro Los Placeres, of what he was leaving behind. What he had already left behind, his parents, his sister. What they would think of him? How would they mourn?

'Turn around.'

He did as he was told, facing his executioners with equanimity. There were four of them. Three were pointing guns at his chest. They looked scared witless, as if the exhausted, naked, delirious, broken man in front of them was poised to run amok.

Squinting, Pettigrew looked at them expectantly. The trio with guns were only boys – teenagers with faces that were round and smooth and questioning. Not so long ago, that had been him. But these boys were not like him. They were torturers, murderers, liars and thieves. They were missing something that should make them human. Still, he couldn't hate them. Despite everything, he felt a pang of empathy. How difficult must all this be for them, to be put in this position? Ten years from now, or twenty, thirty, would they remember this day? Would it be a defining moment in their lives? Would they ever suffer from depression? Nightmares? Insomnia? Would they ever atone for their sins?

Their fingers tightened on the triggers of the ancient-looking rifles. One of the boys turned to the fourth man, who looked older than the rest, maybe twenty-four or twenty-five. His voice quivered as he asked: 'Shall I shoot him?'

'What?' The older man tried to laugh but only a hoarse mumble came out, as if he was trying to clear his throat. He looked past the priest and into the wide blue yonder. 'And waste a bullet?'

The boy blushed with embarrassment and he lowered his gun. His companions followed suit, and the trio slouched away like kids who have just had their football confiscated by an annoyed neighbour. The older man sniffed theatrically and spat at his feet. He swayed back on his heels and then stepped forward, not looking at the priest; not looking away either. Six long steps brought him to within inches of Pettigrew's face. His eyes were bloodshot. He looked shattered.

A wave of euphoria swept over the priest. His time had come at last.

Here I am, good and gentle Jesus.

There was an almost imperceptible nod of recognition before the officer placed the fingertips of his left hand on Pettigrew's chest. The priest looked down at the man's hand and then back at his face. It was the face of a man who passed no judgement.

With great fervour, I pray and ask You to instil in me genuine convictions of faith, hope and love . . .

The sailor took another step forward, pushing gently, as if he was walking through a half-open door.

Pettigrew's jaw ached as a smile broke across his face. Agatha is going to kill me, he thought. In slow motion, he fell backwards into space. Arms outstretched, he finally embraced his fate.

. . . with true sorrow for my sins and a firm resolve to amend them.

FIFTEEN

Heading north, Carlyle and Joe walked up Endell Street, enjoying the warm sunshine. It had been a slow morning in the fight against crime in the capital, and the atmosphere in Charing Cross police station was soporific. Despite his best intentions, Carlyle had still not completed his report into the Mills case. Partly that was down to ennui; partly it was a determination – inherited from both his parents – to look every gift horse that came along in the mouth, very carefully indeed. With the last traces of wife-murderer Henry washed from the tarmac outside, the Mills case was now firmly closed. It had solved itself. This was, Carlyle knew as well as anyone, a good thing. Two unnatural deaths accounted for was a nice little gift for the statisticians and the performance tables. All he had to do was wrap it all up in some understated prose, hand it over to Carole Simpson and then everyone would be happy. If something else had come through the door, demanding his time and attention, maybe he would have done that. But, apart from Mills, all he had on his plate at the moment was a domestic, where the wife was battering the husband, and a spate of pickpocketings around Cambridge Circus. Not enough to keep a grown man occupied.

As much to avoid these other cases as anything else, Carlyle was reluctant to close the Mills case just yet. Joe was not impressed when Carlyle told him that he had decided they should take another look at the Millses' flat. However, the prospect of stopping off for a mid-morning snack on the way won him over.

As they reached the top of Endell Street, the usual traffic jam came into view. This was where High Holborn, St Giles High Street, Bloomsbury Street and Shaftesbury Avenue converged. Traffic that knew where it was going mixed with traffic lost in Covent Garden's tortuous one-way system. Gridlock was the norm here, and a familiar cacophony of horns and shouts greeted the two policemen as they approached. Carlyle did a quick calculation in his head; they would have to cross five roads and fourteen lanes of traffic to reach Ridgemount Mansions, which was barely a quarter of a mile away. Not for the first time, he cursed the city's ineffectual Mayor. Despite ostentatiously cycling to work once or twice a month, Christian Holyrod was criminally soft on the Congestion Charge that had been introduced by a predecessor in an attempt to get people out of their cars and on to public transport. Carlyle, a Central London resident, firmly believed that it should cost fifty pounds a day, or even a hundred, to drive your car into the centre of London. Hell, if you were serious about improving things, why not ban private cars altogether? Or only allow electric vehicles?

The current £10 charge was a complete joke, Carlyle thought. The traffic was as bad as ever. Meanwhile, all you ever heard was the endless moaning of lazy rich people who thought that it was their inalienable human right to clog the place up with their monster, gas-guzzling, road-hogging 4x4s, popularly known as 'Chelsea tractors'. These were the people who got Holyrod elected, so the charge wouldn't be raised to a sensible level any time soon.

It was only after they had slalomed through two lanes of stationary traffic that Carlyle realised that this particular jam was primarily the result of a number 55 bus which had been brought to a halt at a forty-five-degree angle across three lanes of traffic at the corner of Bloomsbury Street and St Giles High Street. Standing in the middle of Shaftesbury Avenue, it took him a little while longer to appreciate that the bus was also on the wrong route. The 55, a single-operator, red double-decker Plaxton President, which came in from Leyton in the east, normally went along Bloomsbury Way and New Oxford Street, before terminating at Oxford Circus. For some reason, it had left its route and was a block south of where it should be.

Bemused, Carlyle took a couple of steps forward and squinted at the vehicle, which was about twenty feet in front of him. The 55 wasn't indicating that it was out of service and he could see that a couple of passengers were still on board. Nor did the driver appear injured or incapacitated in any way. Rather, he was sitting in his cab like a lemon, watching the chaos unfold all around him, seemingly oblivious to a couple of tourists who were standing straight in front of the bus, videoing him.

The noise levels were rising as more and more drivers vented their displeasure. The temperature felt as if it had risen ten degrees in the last couple of minutes and the exhaust fumes were making Carlyle nauseous. He could taste the pollution collecting in the back of his throat. A familiar grinding sensation at the top of his spine, where it joined his skull, meant a monster headache was on the way. What he most wanted to do now was skip through the rest of the traffic and leave them all to it.

'We'd better find out what this is all about,' he shouted to Joe.

They made their way over to the bus and Carlyle rapped on the door at the front opposite the driver. The man was an unhealthy-looking off-white colour, in his twenties, with terrible skin and a pudding-bowl haircut. He gazed at them and then looked away. The passengers on the back seats sat gazing blankly out of the windows. Well used to the vagaries of London's public transport, they were apparently unconcerned at events.

Walking round to the front of the bus, Carlyle pressed his ID up against the window, in front of the driver's face. 'We're the police!' he shouted. 'Open the door!'

The driver blinked a couple of times, but said nothing. Instead, he sat with his hands on the steering wheel and didn't move. Maybe he's on drugs, Carlyle thought. His mood was deteriorating by the second. He could sense that a small crowd was gathering behind him and he needed to get the bus moved.

‘This guy is heading for the cells,’ Joe sighed.

The inspector banged his fist on the window. ‘Open the fucking door!’

Joe put a hand on his shoulder. ‘Hold on a second.’

Carlyle followed his sergeant back round to the side of the bus. He watched Joe reach down and open a small panel by the left-hand side of the exit doors. Inside was a green button about the size of a 10p piece, with the legend *EMERGENCY DOOR OPEN* above it in small script. Joe pressed the button and the doors whooshed open.

‘Why didn’t you do that in the first place?’ Carlyle snapped.

Joe just smiled and stepped back, moving slightly to allow his boss to get on.

‘Get rid of the gawkers,’ Carlyle barked, ‘and call for some uniforms.’ He jumped on the bus and slammed the palm of his hand into the Plexiglas partition that kept the driver safe from the travelling public. ‘What the fuck is going on?’ he asked. ‘Are you lost?’

The driver looked straight ahead, ignoring Carlyle and remaining mute.

‘Is this your bus?’

Finally, the man turned to look straight at Carlyle. Taking the right lapel of his jacket between his thumb and forefinger, he indicated his name badge to the policeman. ‘Yes,’ he said in a shaky voice, ‘it’s my bus. And this is a protest. What does it look like?’

‘It looks like piss-poor parking,’ said Carlyle, relaxing slightly. At least the silly sod seemed compos mentis. ‘What’s your name?’

‘Clive.’

‘And what exactly are you protesting about, Clive?’

‘The advertising.’

Carlyle was confused. ‘What advertising?’

‘The advertising on this side of the bus,’ said Clive huffily, as if that was obvious.

Carlyle frowned. Turning round, he stepped back off the bus

and stared up at the poster running horizontally between the upper and lower decks.

In disgusting pink letters, the text read: *THERE'S PROBABLY NO GOD. NOW STOP WORRYING AND ENJOY YOUR LIFE.*

Carlyle blinked, did a double-take and started laughing. He stepped back on the bus and said to the driver: 'What's wrong with that?'

'It offends my religious beliefs.' Clive actually looked hurt.

'And what are those, exactly?' Carlyle asked, failing to keep the *as-if-I-could-give-a-fuck* tone out of his voice.

'I am a member of the East London Tabernacle Missionary Baptist Church,' Clive said solemnly. 'Haven't missed a Sunday in almost six years.'

'Very impressive,' said Carlyle. He knew nothing much about religion and cared less. As far as he was concerned, people could believe what they liked, as long as they didn't make a song and dance about it and kept within the law. 'Now that we've got *that* sorted out, it's time to move the bus.'

'No.'

Fuck it, Carlyle thought, no more Mr Nice Guy. 'Move the bus or I will arrest you.'

Clive gave him a look as if he was a hurt puppy, but said nothing.

'You will go to jail. That means no more Missionary . . . whatnot Church for you for a long time.'

For the first time, a look of discomfort passed across Clive's face.

'They're all atheists in prison, you know,' Carlyle continued. 'They'll fuck you up the arse every night. God won't save you then.'

Clive's bottom lip quivered, but still he remained mute.

So much for psychology, Carlyle thought. Taking half a step forwards, he hit the Perspex so hard his hand hurt. 'Wait till I get you out of there, you little bastard. Move the fucking bus!'

'No,' replied a tiny voice.

'For fuck's sake, Clive!' Seething, Carlyle wheeled away and walked straight into a woman holding a small video camera. She stepped back towards the stairs leading to the upper deck, bringing the camera back up to her face, keeping it focused on Carlyle.

'What the fuck are *you* doing?' Carlyle growled. He wished that he had stayed at the station. The feeling that some kind of cosmic conspiracy was determined to fuck up his day was beginning to eat into his brain. With some effort, he resisted the urge to stick his hand over the lens. The woman took another step backwards towards a ratty-looking bloke, and he realised that they were the pair of 'tourists' he had seen outside the bus earlier.

Letting the camera drop to her side, the woman stopped filming. 'We're the Daughters of Dismas. We're recording this protest for our website.'

'The what?'

'The Daughters of Dismas,' the woman repeated slowly. 'It's the feminist wing of the Tabernacle Church.'

Carlyle gestured at the man behind her. 'What's he doing here then?'

'Stuart is an honorary member of the DoD. He's my boyfriend.'

'Lucky boy,' Carlyle leered, looking the woman up and down. Thin, pasty-faced, wearing a red T-shirt and green combat pants, she could have been anywhere from eighteen to thirty-eight. It struck him that she looked like a weedy heroine from one of those wretched Mike Leigh movies that Helen sometimes made him watch; boring people pissing about masquerading as 'social realism'.

The woman ignored his sarcastic tone. 'Dismas was the Penitent Thief, a friend of Jesus.'

'Good for him,' Carlyle said, not having the remotest clue what she was talking about. Dismas could have been a character on *Sesame Street* for all he knew. Or Fulham's new Hungarian left-back. He held out his right hand. 'Give me the camera.'

The woman immediately lifted the machine back to her face and resumed filming. 'We have a perfect right to be here. Are you arresting Clive?'

Carlyle glanced over at Joe, who was standing in the doorway trying not to laugh. Turning back to the woman, he said, 'Give me the camera,' as calmly as he could manage. 'Please.'

Hemmed in by her boyfriend, the woman kicked Carlyle in the shin.

Instinctively, Carlyle kicked her back.

'Ouch!' she squealed. 'That hurt!'

Without waiting for her to start screaming about 'police brutality', Carlyle grabbed the camera and quickly tossed it to Joe. 'You are under arrest,' he said, spinning her round and snapping on a pair of cuffs, 'for breach of the peace and assaulting a police officer.' He pointed at the boyfriend. 'That goes for you too, Stuart.'

'Boss,' said Joe from behind him, 'the uniforms are here.'

'Good. Tell 'em to take these two and the driver back to the station and we'll get them charged. And get someone out here to move this bloody bus.'

'Yes, boss.'

'What about my camera?' the woman whined.

'That's evidence, love,' said Joe, smiling. 'But don't worry – we'll look after it.'

SIXTEEN

Today I write not to gloat. Instead, I am writing to say goodbye.

Commander Carole Simpson dropped the letter on to her desk and sighed. Why her 'genius' fund manager husband had decided to write a 'fuck you' letter to the world in general and to his clients in particular, was beyond her. Simpson had never quite understood how her husband, Joshua Hunt, had transformed himself from the rather geeky Imperial College computer scientist that she had married into a financial guru with an estimated net worth – so she read in the papers – of almost £120 million. For a long time, she had taken comfort in the belief that the 4,000 square-foot house in Highgate, the expensive restaurants, the needy clients and the political networking had not turned Joshua into a completely different person, robbing her of what she had seen in him in the first place. Now, however, she wasn't so sure. Maybe the money had finally gone to his head.

Joshua Hunt's company, McGowan Capital, had run four of the best performing investment funds in London for each of the last six years. In the last two years, as the world's financial markets had imploded, he had made an incredible 723 per cent return, mostly from betting against bank stocks and sterling. However, he had taken a beating in the last quarter, calling the oil market wrong, and was finding it harder and harder to convince his clients that this was not the time that they should be pulling out their money.

Sitting at the kitchen table a couple of weeks earlier, he had told her that he was shutting down the firm. He wanted to retire. Retire to what? He didn't know. Still, that was fine by her – Joshua had never been the type of man who had allowed himself to be defined by his work. But now he had written this goodbye letter. That worried her. Glossing over recent losses, it smacked of hubris.

What I have learned about the investment business is that I hate it. I was in the game simply for the money. The low-hanging fruit – the idiots whose parents paid for public school and then the MBA – was there for the taking. These people were truly not worthy of everything they received as they rose effortlessly to the top of corporate and public life as if it was their right – which, of course, it was. All of this behaviour supporting the continuation of the Establishment, only ended up making it easier for me to find people stupid enough to take the other side of my trades. God bless you all.

There are many people for me to sincerely thank for my success. However, I do not want to sound like a credulous actor accepting a meaningless award. The money was reward enough. Furthermore, the people on the long, long list of those deserving thanks are almost certainly too stupid to appreciate who they are.

I will no longer manage money for other people. I have enough of my own. I am more than happy with my remuneration in exchange for ten prime years of my life. My message to the rest of you is: throw the BlackBerry away and enjoy life.

Goodbye and good luck.

Carole Simpson had no idea where all of this bile had come from. It seemed completely out of character. Deciding to walk away from the City with an obscene amount of money was one thing. Rubbing everyone else's noses in it was quite another. Particularly as Joshua still had his political ambitions. If anything, they seemed to be growing. She fretted that this farewell message would come back to haunt him. It was juvenile. Biting the hand that feeds you is never a good idea.

The letter had yet to be posted to investors or published on McGowan Capital's website, so maybe she could talk him out of it at tonight's reception. Drinks followed by dinner. Another evening lost to playing the dutiful wife, as if she didn't have a career of her own. The heavy card invite lay on her desk. Glancing at it, Simpson calculated that she would have to leave in about fifteen minutes. That would be more than enough time.

Picking up the telephone, she punched a button and waited for her PA in the room next door to answer. 'Send him in,' she said briskly, immediately dropping the receiver back on to its cradle, without waiting for a response.

The office door opened. Simpson watched Carlyle come in and stand in front of her desk. Another man who's causing me needless aggravation, she thought. Letting him wait there for a few seconds, she looked him up and down, on the off-chance that she might find some new insight into her under-achieving – if sporadically impressive – colleague. There was none to be found.

Scribbling some notes on a pad, she instructed him to sit down with a curt wave of the hand. 'How are you, Inspector?' she said finally.

'Fine.' Carlyle sat upright in his chair, as if he was back in the Headmaster's office at the Henry Compton secondary school, thirty years ago, waiting to take his punishment for some minor indiscretion. Unwilling to engage in any fake pleasantries, he kept his response to the one word, and let his gaze wander. Nothing here seemed different from his last visit. Aside from the basics, the office was empty, the desk spectacularly bare save for a photograph of a smug-looking middle-aged man gone to seed. Carlyle assumed that was Simpson's husband.

The inspector was always on his guard with his boss. They were very different animals and both knew it. Five or six years younger than Carlyle, the commander could still realistically anticipate moving further up the career ladder before her time was up. He had known Simpson for almost twelve years now, coming under her direction not long after his move to Charing Cross. She was, he had to admit, a hell of an operator – she only ever looked upwards – and had taken to her management role like a duck to water. She could be charming too – if you were a man of a certain age (i.e. between ten and fifteen years older than she was) and she wanted something from you.

Simpson rarely wanted anything from Inspector John Carlyle. The inspector knew that she was frustrated by what she saw as his refusal to play the game. Just as important, perhaps more so, was his inability to hide his feelings towards her. Simpson left Carlyle cold. He hated the feeling that he had been co-opted on to her mission for personal glory. Somehow, the collective good always seemed nicely aligned with the interests of the commander. Her approach to the job he found completely introverted, indeed almost demented. She was too busy climbing the greasy pole to worry about anything else.

The way he saw it, she was either extremely selfish or she had the self-awareness of a goldfish. Either way, Carlyle eyed her with a mixture of extreme distrust and antipathy. However, with much effort, he found that he could tolerate her well enough, as long as their paths did not cross too often. When they did, he felt as if his brain was overheating, and he was always too close to speaking his mind.

Simpson looked down at the notes she had scribbled on her pad. 'About this bus . . .'

'Yes?'

'There's been a complaint.' Simpson kept her voice firmly neutral.

'Oh?' He placed what he hoped was a butter-wouldn't-melt look on his face and concentrated on trying to keep it there.

'A woman called Sandra Groves says that you assaulted her,' Simpson continued. 'She says that there is video evidence.'

Sandra Groves? It suddenly dawned on Carlyle that she must be the religious loony from the bus; he had never checked the woman's name. He grinned sheepishly and adopted the tone of a casual observer with no axe to grind.

'Well, what happened was . . .'

For the next few minutes, he talked the commander through the events of the previous week, throwing in as much detail as he could recall, relevant or not, without addressing Ms Groves's accusation either directly or indirectly. He did this safe in the knowledge that Joe Szyszkowski's report backed him up 100 per cent. Moreover, Groves and her boyfriend not only had been charged, but already had records for previous public-order offences, as well as a couple of outstanding parking tickets. The only thing that could have caused him any problem, the video, had since been erased from the camera's memory stick. Just to be on the safe side, the camera itself had accidentally been run over – several times – by the back wheel of a police Range Rover in the garage of Charing Cross police station before being deposited in a rubbish bin on the Strand. Carlyle was confident that its remains were well on their way to some illegal landfill-dump in India by now. The complaint might lead to a formal investigation, but he knew that he was in the clear.

'And then . . .'

His monologue was interrupted by the sound of a mobile phone. Irritated, Simpson plucked at various pieces of paper before finding it buzzing on the desk. Checking the caller's identity, without preamble she said, 'Hold on one minute.' Standing up, she raised a forefinger to Carlyle, indicating that she would not be long, before quickly stepping out of the room.

As the door closed behind her, Carlyle's gaze fell on Simpson's desk. Leaning forward, he couldn't resist a quick peek. Over the years, he had become quite adept at reading things upside down from a short distance. Next to what were clearly the reports of the Groves case, which he could easily read when he got back to Charing Cross if he felt the need, was a fancy-looking invitation card. The black script was a bit small, but he could make it out without having to leave his seat:

Christian Holyrod, Mayor of London, and Claudio Orb, Ambassador of Chile to the Court of St James's, invite you to a reception at City Hall organised by the Anglo-Chilean Defence Technologies Association. The event will celebrate our two great countries' long history of co-operation and support, as well as England's long-standing association with Chilean naval hero Agustín Arturo Prat Chacón.

More Chileans. What were the odds of some connection? He was wondering who Agustín Arturo Prat Chacón was, when he heard the commander re-enter the room.

Simpson smiled thinly as she sat down behind her desk. 'So, where were we?' she asked, folding her arms and sitting back.

'Sandra Groves,' said Carlyle amiably. 'After *I* had been assaulted, we restrained her and her boyfriend . . .'

A minute or so into his continuing monologue, Simpson held up her hand. She had heard enough. Carlyle could argue for England, indeed the irritating little sod could argue for a World Select XI, and she knew that he would not be so stupid as to be caught out on something like this. She could never hope to get so lucky. 'All right, Inspector,' she said wearily, 'I get the drift. I'm sure, if it ever gets that far, that the Police Federation will make mincemeat out of this complaint. But next time, please try to show a tiny bit more restraint.'

'Restraint is my middle name,' Carlyle said genially.

'Yes, well . . .' Even Simpson had to repress a grin at his chutzpah. 'Well done on that Mills thing, by the way.'

'Thank you,' Carlyle said.

'Nice and neat,' she said, resisting the temptation to add '*for once*'.

'It looks that way,' Carlyle agreed, 'but there are still one or two loose ends.'

'Like what?' Simpson groaned. How could this irritating little man turn even the most straightforward domestic homicide of the year into a problem?

'Mrs Mills, the victim, had made some enemies.'

'Including her husband.'

'Maybe.'

'He's dead, isn't he?' Simpson huffed. 'You know as well as I do, that in domestic cases like these, killing yourself is usually a fairly clear admission of guilt. Take the win, Inspector, and move on.'

'I will.' Standing up, he decided not to push his luck any further.

'Good,' said Simpson stiffly, gathering up the papers on her desk. 'You know the way out.'

SEVENTEEN

A solitary young man sat at a table on the pavement outside Café La Marquise on the Edgware Road. Holding a small cube of sugar to the surface of his strong, syrupy Turkish coffee, he watched it turn brown before letting it drop it into the demitasse. Picking up his teaspoon, he began carefully stirring his coffee, eyeing the small band of anti-war protestors as he did so.

What a rabble, he thought. There were maybe seventy people taking part, at the very most, with almost as many police in attendance. All they were doing was holding up the traffic and preventing normal, law-abiding people from going about their business as they made their way slowly down the middle of the road, heading towards Hyde Park and a rally at Speakers' Corner. All the usual banners that he'd become familiar with recently were there: *Socialist Worker*, *Stop the War Coalition*, *Students for Justice*, etc., etc., carried by sallow, ill-looking people you would cross the road to avoid; all in all, nothing more than a bunch of pathetic, disorganised, ego-crazed losers.

He took a sip of his coffee and let the sweetness soften his mood. Towards the back of the crowd, he saw the banner he had been waiting for, and the three women underneath it, two of them holding the poles and one handing out leaflets while trying to start the occasional chant that invariably petered out almost as quickly as it began:

'*What do we want?*

'*Troops out!*

'*When do we want it?*

'*NOW!*'

The conversations at the tables had stopped as the other patrons watched the protestors go by. Those British and their passions! To foreigners living in London, they were an endless source of amusement. Catching the eye of a gawping waiter, he ordered another coffee as the semi-organised shouting started up again.

Get a life, he thought. As far as he could see, the three women leading the chants were virtually the whole organisation, yet they were trying to cause him so much trouble. He felt the familiar fury rising up inside him. It was ridiculous that he should have to waste his time on them; ridiculous but necessary – for his own sake and that of his comrades.

He fingered the leaflet that another protestor had dropped on his table as he had passed by. More slogans, more platitudes, more hopeless posturing:

'*Justice for the victims of the Ishaqi massacre!*'

Like the victims care any more, he thought.

'*STOP THE WAR!*'

I was there; you weren't.

'*END THE MERCENARY KILLINGS!*'

The anger blossomed in his chest. *You don't know what you're talking about.*

Leaning down, he grabbed an anti-war flyer from the pavement, carefully folding it in half and then folding it in half again, before dropping it into his jacket pocket. The waiter arrived with his fresh coffee. Downing it in one, he pulled out his wallet and fished out a five-pound note, which he placed under his saucer. Sitting back in his chair, he let the demonstration go past, accompanied by the hooting of angry motorists and some pointing and laughter from a group of Arab customers enjoying their shisha pipes at the table beside him.

Pulling a cigarette from the packet of Royal Crown Blue sitting on the table, he lit it with a match and stuck it between his lips, inhaling deeply. Dropping the match in the ashtray, he rose from the table, before starting slowly along the road, heading in the same direction as the protestors.

By the time he reached the park, the speeches were in full swing. Standing under a nearby tree, he smoked another cigarette, keeping a careful eye on the women as he tried to tune out the ritual denunciations of America, Britain and every other tool of imperialism that they could lay their hands on.

Mercifully, the speeches ended before his packet of smokes was empty. He watched the women pack up their banner and say their goodbyes, before heading off in different directions. After a moment's thought, he decided to follow the older one. Once he knew where she lived, it would be time to begin.

EIGHTEEN

Carlyle stood on the walkway that spiralled up the inside of the triangulated glass façade of City Hall, looking down into the foyer of the Greater London Assembly, while listening to the clink of glasses and the hum of polite conversation from below. He had been scanning the room for several minutes now, without being able to find any sign of Simpson or her husband. He had, however, seen the Mayor, Christian Holyrod, shoulder-to-shoulder with the man he assumed was the Chilean Ambassador, as they worked the room together.

The upper terrace had been closed off to the public for tonight's event, so Carlyle found himself alone. As the Mayor stepped up on to a small raised platform to make some introductory remarks, Carlyle turned his back on the throng to take in the views over the river towards the Tower of London. For the next few minutes, he let his mind wander. An occasional phrase drifted up from the floor below but the words were no more than the usual trite nothings that accompanied events like this. He ignored them, as he watched the boats go by on the Thames, and reflected on his previous dealings with the Mayor.

Christian Holyrod was a *Boy's Own* story made flesh. That alone would have been enough for Carlyle to be deeply suspicious of the man, even before they crossed swords on what turned out to be one of the more unpleasant cases he had recently had to deal with.

Before turning his hand to politics, Major Holyrod had

commanded the 2nd Battalion of the Duke of Wellington's Regiment (motto: *Virtutis Fortuna Comes* – Fortune Favours the Brave), one of the first British battle groups to go into action in Helmand Province in south-west Afghanistan, as part of Britain's latest unsuccessful foray into the world's most inhospitable country. His subsequent journey from unsung hero to big-time politician began when an American documentary crew arrived to film the story of Operation Clockwork Orange, a mission to capture a terrorist commander who had been hiding out in a mud compound in the middle of nowhere. The mission was a fiasco. Holyrod's boys were ambushed and a swift retreat followed, leaving the target happily ensconced in his mountain lair, but the firefights and general chaos that followed made for great television. Shaky hand-held pictures of the major shouting 'Contact, contact, contact!' while squeezing off rounds from his SA80-A2 assault rifle and trying to drag a wounded squaddie back to his truck were as entertaining as anything that Hollywood could come up with. They made all the main news bulletins back home in Britain even before the show had aired in the US. For almost two days, it was the number one most-viewed video on YouTube, with more than 45 million hits around the world.

Holyrod became an instant celebrity. Within a fortnight, he was offered his own radio talk show, signed up to do a newspaper column, acquired an agent and had received more than a hundred offers of marriage.

Initially, the Ministry of Defence was more than happy to let a stream of journalists beat a path to his door, given their desperation for any kind of 'good news' out of a story that had been a complete disaster from day one. For his part, Holyrod quite enjoyed the attention, using this platform to argue that the MoD had seriously underestimated the task in hand, i.e. fighting the enemy. The tone of his interviews became more and more downbeat as he contemplated 'the big picture'. After telling a very nice girl from the *Sunday Express* that 'the whole thing's gone to rats', he was hauled back to London 'for discussions'. His return to the front line was then cut short when he was caught on camera berating the Foreign Secretary, who was in the middle of a four-hour tour of the troops, about the lack of support from politicians back home for 'his boys'.

Of course, the media had lapped it all up. Opinion polls suggested that Holyrod's approval ratings were in the high eighties. No politician could live with him. The major's window of opportunity had arrived. Now he had to decide what to do with it. It was at this point that the leader of the Opposition, Edgar Carlton MP, persuaded his old Cambridge University pal (and brother-in-law, for Christian had married Edgar's sister, Sophia, some eight years earlier) to run for election as Mayor of London.

So it came to pass that Holyrod resigned from the Army, swapping his fatigues for a selection of very sharp Richard James suits. After six months campaigning under the party slogan *Change that keeps changing* he won a landslide victory, thus providing a template for Edgar Carlton's first national government, which duly followed less than two years later.

It was during Edgar's victorious General Election campaign that Carlyle had first come across both men. It was a nasty case, involving the deaths of several of their friends. With their stellar careers to protect, Carlton and Holyrod did not want the reason for the killings to be made public. All too predictably, the Metropolitan Police was no match for their united front. Although the case itself was nominally solved, the truth – or rather, the underlying facts of the case – never saw the light of day.

Having seen off this particular threat, the two men seemed to have cemented their political relationship. But the alliance was beginning to show signs of wear and tear. In Westminster village, Christian Holyrod was quickly identified as Edgar Carlton's obvious successor and, therefore, his de facto rival.

Turning all this over in his head, Carlyle felt the familiar stab of anger and frustration that came when he thought about cases with too many loose ends. He remained deeply unhappy about what had happened, and still fretted over whether he could have dealt with it better. Above all, he still felt irritated at his inability to close the case properly, lay all the facts on the table and let all the principals take responsibility for their actions. As the investigation had reached its conclusion, Carlyle had attempted to pressure Holyrod into at least acknowledging what had taken place. But the Mayor was not going to be browbeaten by a lowly policeman, and he stood his ground.

A lowly policeman.

That was what rankled as much as anything. Being treated like the hired help. A gamma male who had stumbled into an alpha world.

One of the little people.

Well, now their paths had crossed again. Maybe belatedly there would be a chance to settle the score.

Frowning, the inspector leaned over the railing and looked down at the small crowd. Holyrod was speaking from notes written on pieces of card: '*Britain and Chile are two countries sharing a belief in fairness, democracy and freedom . . .*' He paused, waiting for the smattering of polite applause which duly followed.

Carlyle yawned and glanced at his watch.

This evening, however, Holyrod chose to keep his remarks mercifully brief. After barely two minutes, he signed off with a reference to 'our long-standing political, social and military links with Chile', and invited his guests back to London to attend a conference called TEMPO, which was taking place in September. Acknowledging the further applause, he handed the microphone over to the Ambassador.

Being a diplomat rather than a politician, Claudio Orb's remarks were even shorter and blander that those of Christian Holyrod. As the Ambassador stepped away from the microphone, to exactly the same applause as his host, Carlyle began making his way down towards the throng.

The free bar must have been closed before the speeches had started, because the place had pretty much cleared in the forty seconds or so that it took the inspector to descend the stairs. Passing the guests heading out, he made straight for the Mayor, who was still in discussion with the Ambassador and another man by the front of the stage.

Fixing a big smile on his face, Carlyle stepped up to Holyrod with his hand outstretched. 'Mr Mayor,' he said warmly, gratified to see that the former soldier had put on quite a few pounds. The extra weight didn't suit him, for it looked as if he had gone in age from thirty-five to fifty-five in about twelve months. 'How very nice to see you again.'

Holyrod broke off from his discussion and looked up. Recognising the policeman, he fought to keep a look of displeasure off his face. 'Inspector . . .' He shook Carlyle's hand firmly, trying to step away from his guests at the same time. But Carlyle had deliberately boxed him in and he had no alternative but to remain at Orb's side.

'. . . Carlyle,' he prompted. 'Inspector John Carlyle, from Charing Cross police station.'

Holyrod scanned some interesting spot in the middle distance. 'Yes, yes, of course.'

'Nice speech,' said Carlyle, looking at the Ambassador.

'Thank you,' Holyrod replied, even more concerned now lest he become Carlyle's quarry.

Still grinning like an idiot, Carlyle returned his gaze to the Mayor. 'I thought perhaps you could introduce us?'

'Ah, yes,' said Holyrod, looking unhappier by the second. 'Mr Ambassador,' he said stiffly, 'this is Inspector John Carlyle of the Metropolitan Police.'

'Pleased to meet you, Inspector.' Claudio Orb extended a hand and flashed the smile of a man who had nothing to fear from London's finest. He was a trim, dapper man in an elegant three-piece navy suit, white shirt and bright red tie. About 5 feet 8 inches, with a shock of white hair and bright blue eyes, he looked to be well into his seventies. I hope I age that well, Carlyle thought, knowing that it was extremely unlikely. He glanced at the much younger man standing next to Orb. At most in his late thirties, the guy looked fit and tanned. He had the most well-tended beard that Carlyle had ever seen. He made no attempt to introduce himself, so Carlyle, writing him off as some flunky, quickly returned his full attention to the Ambassador. 'I was wondering if I could have a few minutes of your time, sir,' he asked in his most deferential tone, ignoring the baleful glare coming from Holyrod.

'Of course!' Orb's eyes twinkled with delight. Carlyle wondered if the Ambassador had had a few; maybe he was even a little drunk. 'It would be my pleasure to help the police with their enquiries.' He nodded to the others. 'Excuse us, gentlemen.' He took Carlyle's elbow and began marching him back up the walkway, in the direction from which he had arrived. 'Why don't we step outside for a minute. I could do with some air.'

Out on the vast empty terrace, Carlyle felt the cool breeze from the river on his face and realised how stuffy it had been inside.

'What a pleasant evening,' Orb said, holding on to the rail and inhaling deeply. 'It's nice to enjoy some fresh air, is it not?'

'Or as near to fresh as it gets in London,' Carlyle replied.

'Hah!' The older man grinned. 'You should try Santiago sometime.' He looked the policeman up and down. 'Have you ever been to Chile, Inspector?'

'No.'

'Ah, you should. It's well worth a visit. I know I'm biased, but it's a great country.'

'Maybe one day.' Carlyle shrugged.

'So . . . what can I do for you?' the Ambassador continued cheerily. 'Ask and you shall receive, as they say. I'm already in your debt for saving me from your Mayor, if only for a short time.'

Carlyle laughed. 'So he's not to your taste either?'

'No, no.' Orb wagged an admonishing finger, 'it's not that. I'm a diplomat, so taste doesn't come into it. And, in many ways, Mr Holyrod is a very admirable man. Apart from anything else, he was a fine soldier.'

'But?' Carlyle, relaxed about being distracted from what was, at best, a fishing exercise, was curious about the man's opinion of the Mayor.

'But he's playing games with us a little bit.'

'How so?'

'The last time I looked,' the Ambassador said gently, 'I was Ambassador to the Court of St James's, not to the Court of St Christian Holyrod. The Mayor wants to use people like us as he tries to develop his own mini-foreign policy on the side, while expanding his own business interests at the same time. He wants to be the next Prime Minister and needs to fill in gaps in his CV. That's why he's touting TEMPO.'

'What is that?' Carlyle asked.

'TEMPO is a big arms fair, held in London every other year,' Orb explained. 'Chile has a successful military technology industry, so it is an important event for us. But we do not seek publicity.'

'No?'

'It should be a discreet place to do business. If Mayor Holyrod goes and turns the event into a political platform, well, that is not good for anyone.'

'No,' Carlyle agreed. He had never stopped to consider the problems faced by international arms dealers before, but he could see the Ambassador's point.

'Then there's the whole question of conflict of interest,' the Ambassador continued. 'I thought that you British were always quite . . . proper when it came to that kind of thing.'

'What conflict of interest?' Carlyle asked, trying not to sound too interested.

'Christian Holyrod is a non-executive director of the company called Pierrepoint Aerospace.'

Carlyle shrugged, none the wiser.

'"Aerospace",' Orb continued, 'is a widely-used euphemism for "arms manufacturer" these days, Inspector. Sophisticated arms, true, but they still kill – when they work, that is. Holyrod is busy trying to drum up business for his company – and, no doubt commission for himself – at the same time as he's supposed to be running this city.'

Carlyle made a face. 'I thought that you had to give up outside interests like that when you took office?'

'Apparently not,' Orb sniffed.

'And you think that's wrong?'

'It's not my country.' Orb held up a cautionary hand. 'And it's not my business. It would be wrong for me to express a view. Anyway, I have seen a lot worse activities in my time.'

Carlyle smiled. 'I'm sure you have.'

'I am just an amused observer.'

Watching a pleasure craft head upriver, Carlyle pondered what the Ambassador had said. 'Are we talking about corruption here?' he asked finally.

A gust of wind from the river blew across the terrace, and Orb shivered. 'That is such a vague term,' he said. 'Look at it this way, there is no danger of him going to jail. All I'm saying is that I've been around a long time and there are certain ways of doing business. No one likes it when confronted with someone who is becoming too pushy.'

'Isn't that just the modern world in microcosm?' Carlyle said.

'You are absolutely right,' Orb laughed. 'Anyway,' he took his hands from the rail and spread his arms wide, 'you didn't come here to listen to me being *un*diplomatic, Inspector. I am sure that you will ignore my indiscretion.'

Carlyle nodded. 'Of course.'

'The end of my career is looming,' Orb said solemnly. 'I don't have to worry so much about my every utterance, but even so . . .'

'I have no interest in causing you any embarrassment, sir,' Carlyle said. 'After all, that is not what I was seeking out your opinion on.'

'Good,' the Ambassador nodded. 'Thank you. So . . . what is it that you want to talk about?'

'Well,' Carlyle looked at his shoes, which needed a polish, 'I am conducting an investigation, which maybe has a Chilean angle, and I thought that you might be able to help me out with some advice.'

The Ambassador listened intently as Carlyle explained the Mills case, as well as the story of William Pettigrew and the belated attempt to bring his killers to justice. After the inspector had finished, he pondered for a while.

'It sounds as if you have already done a good job, Inspector,' Orb said eventually. 'What help do you need from me?'

'I was wondering whether there could be any credibility in Henry Mills's claims about his wife having had enemies in Chile.'

'We all have enemies.'

'Enemies who might want her dead,' Carlyle clarified.

Orb knitted his eyebrows, making him look older. 'But I thought that the matter had been closed. You have charged the husband?'

'Yes,' he said, omitting to mention that the suspect was no longer on this earth.

Orb looked at him carefully. 'Don't you believe that he did it?'

Carlyle wasn't going to share his personal concerns about the investigation with a man he had only just met. 'I am just tying up some loose ends,' he said, as casually as possible. 'This is a very serious matter and I would not want a cynical defence lawyer to suggest that we had been less than thorough.'

'Of course. Of course.' Hand on chin, Orb struck a thoughtful pose. 'I don't know the particular individuals, obviously, but it is true that the particular chapter in our history to which you refer has not yet been fully closed. Plenty of people disappeared at that time, not just priests. Many of them have still not been found.' He looked at Carlyle. 'Can you imagine the anguish that must cause their families?'

Carlyle said nothing. That kind of pain, he didn't want to imagine.

'If, as you say,' Orb continued, 'there is a case like this coming to court back home, old wounds may well have been reopened. How could it be otherwise? We Chileans are only human, after all. It was a very difficult time.'

'I understand.'

'Look at the passions the Civil War in Spain still arouses, for example. That occurred a lot earlier than our . . . situation. But so long as there are generations still alive who were touched directly, it will always remain a very emotive subject.'

'Emotive enough for people to kill?' Carlyle asked.

'That is a very difficult question to answer.' The Ambassador ran a hand through his hair. 'Theoretically, yes. But, in my experience, theory and practice can often be far removed from each other. It is indeed possible, but that is a long way from saying people would take the law into their own hands in such a way – especially so far from home. Times are different now, but back then . . .' Orb's voice trailed off as he scanned the river, maybe looking for a distraction. Finding none, he turned back to Carlyle. 'Well, back then I would not have been so happy about helping a policeman with his enquiries.'

'People could kill and get away with it?' Carlyle asked.

'Yes, they could. People like you.'

Carlyle smiled to show that he hadn't taken offence. 'I'm sure that you are right, but what about people like *you*?'

'People like me?' Orb frowned. 'Oh, people like me never have to get our hands dirty.'

'So you got through it all unscathed?'

'Of course. It was a terrible time, but life goes on. You go to work, you have dinner parties at home, you take your children to the zoo; the world doesn't stop turning because some people are being murdered in a football stadium a few blocks down the road. Even if you know about it, even if you can hear the shots, what can you do? Nothing. So you get on with your life. Hard to imagine now, but that was the case.'

'It's not that hard to imagine,' Carlyle remarked.

'What?' Orb raised an eyebrow. 'Here in England? One of the most civilised countries in the world? And you, a man who has never known war or serious civil unrest?'

'I know,' Carlyle said. 'I am very lucky. But at least I know how lucky I am. I also know how quickly it can all fall apart. The veneer of civilised society is thin. Under the right circumstances – the *wrong* circumstances – what happened in Chile, what happened to William Pettigrew, can happen to anyone.'

'Indeed,' the Ambassador nodded.

The light was going. It was time for Carlyle to ask for what he really wanted. 'Do you have a list of the people who were invited here tonight?'

'Of course. My office was responsible for the invitations.'

'Can I have a copy?'

'Absolutely,' the Ambassador said. 'I will have it sent to you in the morning.'

'Thank you.' A thought suddenly struck Carlyle as he handed over a business card with his email address and fax number on it. 'What were you doing back then?'

'Me?' A look of surprise spread across Orb's face. 'In seventy-three?'

'Yes.'

The old man raised his gaze to the darkening sky. 'Back in 1973, I was what you might call a rising star in the Christian Democratic Party. I taught Economics at the Universidad Católica de Chile in Santiago. My specialism was agrarian reform.' He sighed. 'It's a long time ago now.'

The man did not seem embarrassed about discussing his past, so Carlyle kept going. 'Did you support Pinochet?' he asked.

Orb shrugged. 'It was not a question of being for or against him, Inspector. It happened. I made sure my family came through relatively unscathed.'

'You're a survivor.'

'I've had a long career,' Orb said to that. 'Now I work for a Socialist president, who is also a woman. You never know how things will turn out, so it is better not to nail your colours too firmly to the mast.' He touched Carlyle gently on the arm. 'I'm sure you already know that well.'

'Yes,' said Carlyle, who had spent his whole life pointlessly nailing colours to masts, usually on ships that were already sinking. 'I suppose that's right.'

'Now, if you'd excuse me,' Orb held out his hand, 'I must be going. I'm hosting a dinner with your multi-tasking Mayor.' He grinned. 'I will give him your best wishes, since I get the impression that you are a big supporter of his.'

NINETEEN

'Take a look – this is really funny,' said Dominic Silver.

Carlyle grunted non-committingly as he sucked down on a latte that was way too cold for his liking. He always asked for it 'extra hot' and the Brazilian/Indian/Ukrainian/whatever boy/girl behind the counter would nod happily and then serve him up something that was barely lukewarm. It drove him mad. Often he would take it back and complain; get them to make it again. One time he caused such a fuss that the manager followed him out into the street and threatened him with a good kicking. It was a great example of traditional British customer service at its finest. Carlyle would have happily arrested him on the spot if he hadn't been late for a court appearance,

This morning, however, he refused to get angst-ridden about his coffee. Rather, he just wanted to get as much caffeine as possible into his system as quickly as possible, cold or not, to try and compensate for the fact that he wasn't still tucked up in bed. Twenty yards away, Alice was squealing in delight as a couple of young boys chased her round a tree. When they caught her, she squealed even more. Carlyle felt a smile spreading across his face as he watched her. Whatever grumpiness he felt about standing here in the middle of Regent's Park at ten o'clock on a Sunday morning was offset more than a hundredfold by his pleasure in witnessing his daughter's uncomplicated delight in a simple game of tag on a fresh summer morning, when the world seemed full of promise. Not for the first time, he wondered how much she was missing out on, being an only child. Not that there was much they could do about that now.

The two boys, Tom and Oliver Silver, were a year older and younger respectively than Alice. They were the youngest of five children belonging to Dominic Silver and Eva Hollander. The fact that Dominic and Eva had managed to produce five kids only added to Carlyle's worry about Alice not having any siblings. Helen, practical as always, suggested that they should just be grateful for those ready-made playmates.

His wife had arranged this particular play-date with Eva earlier in the week, but Carlyle had only been told about it the night before – so that he couldn't come up with an excuse for not going along. He wondered if the same had happened to Dominic. People in Dominic's line of work weren't known for their early morning starts, but Dominic was a big family man, so Carlyle expected that he was similarly philosophical about being here. The women were both probably still enjoying a lie-in, but each man recognised that you just had to accept being outmanoeuvred by your other half more often than not.

Happy to let the kids run off as much energy as possible, the two men took up residence on a bench and contemplated the view in comfortable silence, looking west across the playing-fields towards the London Central Mosque. They knew each other well enough not to worry about small talk. In fact, their relationship went all the way back to their Metropolitan Police training at Hendon College in the early 1980s.

Dominic was a genuine, 100 per cent cockney. He came from East London and was a West Ham fan. Carlyle came from West London and supported Fulham. Straight out of college, they had worked the bitter Miners' Strike together. They had spent much of the time speeding their tits off on the picket line together, courtesy of Dominic's ready supply of amphetamines. They had both been outsiders, piss-takers, awkward-question-askers. They were chippy bastards – but solid chippy bastards always willing to do more than their share of the dirty work, and more than happy to do extra overtime. There was enough common ground for them to build a solid friendship during the fourteen-hour shifts far from home.

Once the strike was over, Dom didn't take to the relatively sedate life of a policeman back on the beat. There was an entrepreneurial spirit gnawing away inside him, and in the end he had just too much get-up-and-go for the Force to satisfy him. Within a year of the strike ending, he left the Metropolitan Police and went into business for himself. Once, in the early days, he had asked Carlyle to join him. But then, as now, Carlyle couldn't see himself working for a drug dealer. Even if he was rather ambivalent about what Dominic did for a living, he certainly didn't want to get involved.

Over the following years, their paths had crossed many times since, sometimes by accident, sometimes by one seeking the other out. That was not so surprising: they had a lot of mutual interests, given what Dominic Silver did for a living. Almost three decades later, while Carlyle was merely an undistinguished career cop, Dominic Silver had become something of a legend among certain sections of the Metropolitan police force. The son of a policeman, the nephew of a policeman, he was the archetypal good boy turned bad, but with an honesty and a style that gleaned a little goodwill from even the most hard-nosed copper. Even now there was still a part of Dom that remained 'one of us' in the eyes of many police officers of a certain age.

However, there was also a large part of Dominic Silver that had left his life in uniform a very long way behind indeed. Now at his professional peak, Silver was maybe in the third or fourth tier of drug dealers across the whole of London. This was not a bad place to be, reasonably comfortable, avoiding the problems facing those higher up the ladder as well as those below him. His operation was turning over maybe low millions each year, with clients including a swathe of minor celebrities and some of the newer entries in *Who's Who*. He even had a couple of corporate clients who still bought on account, despite the recession.

Dominic had built up his business slowly, one step at a time, always avoiding conflicts and solving problems without resorting to violence, wherever possible. As the years turned into decades, his reputation grew. In a business where to survive three years was rare, to have survived three decades was a major miracle. He had never been arrested, never mind convicted, of any offence. He was not some nut job who'd let success and so-called 'easy' money go to his head. Nor did he dabble in all the nasty related shit that was associated with his business, notably prostitution, modern-day slavery and people-trafficking.

In short, he was not your average criminal.

At the heart of this success was a very pragmatic attitude to money. Dominic never spelled it out, but Carlyle was vaguely aware that he handed over a very high proportion of his take to his key suppliers, in exchange for protection. 'I'm kind of freelance, kind of not,' he once told Carlyle, 'kind of independent, kind of not. Basically, they outsource this part of their operation to me. It's like anything else – if I'm quicker, cheaper and less hassle, I get the job.'

Pragmatic and self-aware himself, Carlyle recognised that they had a lot in common. Indeed, there were many things about Dominic Silver that the inspector genuinely liked. Over the years, Dominic had shed his cheeky-chappy demeanour and become more serious. He had obtained a degree in Business and Management from Queen Mary College, and with his greying shoulder-length hair and rimless spectacles, he looked like a writer or an academic or maybe the keyboard player in some soft rock outfit like Genesis. For someone with a net worth that was probably heading towards fifty million, Dom enjoyed a very down-to-earth lifestyle. He wasn't bling and kept an extremely low profile. He didn't do drugs. He didn't smoke, and only took the occasional drink. He went to the gym regularly and kept himself in shape – although he was almost six feet tall, he couldn't weigh much more than seventy kilos.

In short, their relationship was both stable and cordial. It wasn't complicated, but it wasn't very *clear* either. Neither of them would necessarily have wanted to create it if it didn't already exist, but they could both see its advantages as well as its drawbacks. Of course, Carlyle could never go after him, even if he wanted to: he would be compromised by the favours that Dominic had done for him in the past. But he was confident that he was not alone in that regard; for years, the rumour was that Silver had some fairly serious protection even further up the food chain, both inside the Met and outside. He also had a close-knit inner circle of advisers which Carlyle would join on an ad hoc basis, as part of the unspoken quid pro quo for Dominic's help whenever he needed it.

Carlyle felt very ambivalent about their relationship. If someone chose to use it against him, he knew what it could do to his career and to his family. That did cause him concern, but the reality was that it was too late to do anything about it now.

Carlyle watched Dominic fiddle with his phone. Finally finding the clip he wanted, he hit the play button. 'There's a lot of crap at the beginning, but the party piece is worth waiting for.'

'Mm.' Dominic offered him the phone. 'Go on, take a look.'

Taking the handset, Carlyle watched Alice race off through the middle of someone's football game, followed by Tom and Oliver. He turned and eyed the video jerking across the mobile's tiny screen, without focusing on it. In his book, phones were meant for voice calls. Since when did everyone suddenly need to make their own videos? He glanced back at the kids to make sure that they were not straying too far. 'What's that?' he asked.

'It's a guy called Jerome Sullivan.'

'Who's he?'

'He is – *was* – in the same business as me. Not really a competitor, but I'd met him a couple of times.'

'What happened to him?' Carlyle asked, wary now that they had moved on to business.

'He shot himself in the head,' said Dominic, amused.

'What?' Carlyle scrutinised the handset. 'He filmed himself committing suicide? I didn't think that people in your line of work tended to suffer from depression.'

'Not exactly,' Dominic grinned. 'He was showing off to a mate and didn't realise there was a round still in the breech.'

Carlyle watched Jerome put the gun to his head. 'Darwinism in action.'

'That isn't what killed him, though,' said Dominic cheerily. 'The bullet kind of bounced off his skull and missed his brain.'

'Which, presumably,' Carlyle mused, 'was tiny.'

'Yeah.' Dominic laughed. 'What actually killed him was the hundred-foot fall off the top of his building.'

'What an outstanding effort,' Carlyle said, then: 'How did you come by the video?'

'Lots of people have it now,' said Dominic. 'Jerome's acquaintances were unusually co-operative with the police. No one wanted to be accused of killing him.'

'That's understandable.' When the video clip ended, Carlyle idly hit the play button and watched the final moments of Jerome Sullivan unfold again from the beginning. If you didn't know what had happened, you wouldn't have been able to say if the video was real or fake.

'They'll be wanting something to drink,' Dominic said suddenly, nodding at the kids, who were running back towards them.

'Yes,' Carlyle agreed. But that thought was quickly pushed aside as something else popped into his mind. He halted the Sullivan video once again and went back to the start. Letting it run for about five or six seconds, he paused at the point where one of the other men on the roof stuck his hands in the air in mock surrender. Squinting, he brought the phone closer to his face, until it was only about four inches from his nose. The quality of the image was poor, but, if you knew who you were looking at, you could make out the man's face.

'Dominic,' he asked, 'what's Michael Hagger doing in this video?'

TWENTY

Suffer the little children, thought Carlyle, and forbid them not, to come unto me: for of such is the kingdom of heaven.

A-fucking-men to that.

Helen was been incandescent at having another Sunday interrupted. She had booked a yoga workshop for that afternoon and Carlyle had been supposed to take Alice to the zoo. But he had insisted, trying to explain to her that he was *obliged* to deal with this one. He had promised Amelia Jacobs that he would speak to Michael Hagger, to stop things getting out of control. But he hadn't. And they had.

Jake had been picked up from nursery by his father almost a fortnight ago. Neither of them had been seen since. Except for Michael Hagger's appearance in the video clip, which Carlyle now had stored on his phone. That afternoon he had spent some time in Kentish Town, trying to track Hagger down. Zero success. Now he had to go and face the music.

Sam Laidlaw lived less than five minutes' walk away from Carlyle's flat. Walking through Covent Garden, Carlyle counted nine A4-sized MISSING posters in shop windows or tied to lamp posts. The flyer had a blurred digital image of a frowning Jake Hagger, above a text that offered a £2,000 reward for information about the boy's whereabouts. Carlyle had no idea who had put up the money, but he was fairly sure that it would never be claimed. Already, the posters had a grubby and forlorn look about them. Jake was a fairly nondescript kid, whose most memorable characteristic was that his mother was a hooker and his father an all-round, general purpose scumbag. He was most definitely not the kind of pretty, middle-class kid with articulate, professional parents who could drum up a large supply of media interest and public sympathy. His time in the media spotlight had been brief and perfunctory. Within a few hours, he was usurped in the news agenda by a mentally ill man who had climbed into the lion enclosure at London Zoo.

To the extent that it was doing anything at all, the police investigation was busy chasing dead ends. In any child disappearance case, 99 per cent of members of the public who came up with 'information' were simply time-wasters – psychics, visionaries, dreamers, nutters or 'well-wishers' who simply wanted to wallow in other people's misery. Even these wretches had shown only a minimal interest in the disappearance of Jake Hagger. As far as the inspector was aware, there had been no decent leads at all. Sidestepping the tourists, and keeping out of the sun, Carlyle knew that those posters wouldn't last another week.

Two minutes after arriving at Phoenix House, he found himself back on the same orange leather sofa that he had sat on during his last visit. This time it was dirtier, with even more stains and a new collection of cigarette burns on one arm. Sam Laidlaw sat in an armchair opposite him, staring doggedly at the carpet. Carlyle looked for improved signs of life but Laidlaw still looked like a zombie. Aside from the odd sniffle, she made no sound.

Amelia Jacobs was considerably more presentable. Dressed in black jeans and a grey, long-sleeved T-shirt, she paced the floor between them. Carlyle said nothing while Amelia gave him a hard stare, looking him up and down as if he was some John who couldn't get it up. Finally she asked: 'Did you ever talk to Michael?'

'I did try.' Carlyle leaned forward and gave her some proper eye contact. 'I couldn't find him.' Not that I tried very hard, he thought. 'Did you know a guy called Jerome Sullivan?'

Laidlaw made no sign of even hearing his question.

Jacobs frowned. 'No. Why? Has he got something to do with this?'

'I don't know,' Carlyle replied, 'but I know Michael has been hanging out with him recently.'

'He must be a right scumbag then,' Amelia snapped. 'Have you spoken to him yet?'

'He's dead,' Carlyle said casually.

'Great! So what are you going to do about it *now*?' Amelia's question was a reasonable one. If nothing else, he admired her determination. She seemed to be the only person who really cared about the kid. Even if Jake came back, he would go straight into the care of Camden Children's Social Services. His mother had blown her last chance. It would be a miracle – or, rather, a scandal – if she ever got her kid back. Amelia knew all this already, but she would still not give up.

Carlyle shrugged. 'It's not my case.'

'The other guy,' Amelia snorted, 'doesn't give a toss.'

'Cutler?'

'Yeah. A copper in search of a freebie, if I ever saw one.'

'I spoke to him about the case the other evening.'

She looked doubtful. 'And?'

'And they are on top of everything,' said Carlyle, parrying the query as best he could.

'Right.' Amelia looked as if she wanted to give him a slap. He couldn't blame her.

'I'm sure that they,' Carlyle corrected himself, 'that *we* will find him.' The reality was that he wasn't sure at all.

Amelia Jacobs balled her fists, her face locked into a brittle stare. 'Someone has got to show some interest in this little boy.'

Giving up on the eye contact, Carlyle stared at his shoes.

'Otherwise, it's like the poor little sod never even existed.'

'Yes.'

'That bastard can't have just vanished.'

'No.'

'It's been weeks now . . .' Her voice trailed off.

Carlyle stared harder at the floor. 'I know.' He did know. He could shut his eyes and paint a very clear picture in his head. But that didn't mean he could do anything about it.

Waking the next morning, Carlyle watched Helen pad out of the bedroom to make a cup of green tea. Declining her offer of coffee, he got up, stretched and headed into the bathroom. After getting dressed, he decided on one last effort at conciliation. The TV was still playing, but Alice's fifteen minutes were up and it was time for school. He wandered into the kitchen, where Helen stood gazing aimlessly out of the window at the London skyline, sipping her tea.

'Why don't I take Alice to school this morning?' Carlyle suggested.

Helen turned to face him. 'No need.' She reached for the kettle and poured more hot water in her mug.

He looked at her carefully. This had to be a test. He needed to show more willing. 'I don't mind,' he continued carefully. 'It'll give you a bit of extra time before work.'

Helen sipped her tea demurely. 'Actually, I spoke to Alice about it yesterday, while you were out making your enquiries.' A small smirk crossed her mouth. 'She's going on her own.'

'What?' A sense of panic flashed through Carlyle's brain. How could his daughter be travelling across London on her own at her age? There were so many dangers; all those nutters and perverts, watching and waiting for an opportunity to prey on the innocent. Not to mention all the crazy white-van men itching to knock down any careless pedestrians. What the hell was Helen thinking about?

His wife watched these emotions flash across his face and fought to stop her grin getting wider. 'Don't worry, she'll be fine.'

'Fine?'

'Yes. Alice, as if you hadn't noticed, is a very sensible child. Anyway, she has to do it.'

Carlyle frowned. 'She does?'

'Yes. The term is almost finished. After the summer she'll have to go on her own.'

'Says who?'

'Says the school. We got a letter about it, remember?'

Carlyle grunted. He remembered various letters, but none in particular.

'The school,' Helen dropped her mug in the sink, 'insists that all kids Alice's age have to be able to go to school on their own. The Headmaster says it's part of the process of becoming more independent as they grow up.'

'Becoming more independent?' Carlyle sniffed, not liking the sound of that one little bit.

'Exactly.' Helen put a hand on his arm. 'You can't remain a paranoid parent forever.'

Oh can't I? Carlyle wondered. Just watch me.

Helen squeezed his arm gently. 'She's got to start sometime.'

'I know, I know.' Carlyle pressed his thumbs to his temples. He could feel a headache coming on. He really needed something to eat. Breakfast, however, would not solve his problem. Far worse than the dangers of the big, bad city (most of which, he knew, were just down to media hype and invention) was the realisation that the golden years were coming to an end. His daughter was leaving him behind.

Almost on cue, there was a call from the hall. 'I'm off!'

Helen skipped out of the kitchen and gave Alice a hug. Carlyle sheepishly followed. He smiled at his daughter and tried to ignore the spasm of discomfort in his guts. 'Go carefully.'

'Yes, Dad!'

He looked her up and down. She looked younger in her uniform than she did in jeans and a T-shirt. He bit down on his fear once more. 'Will you get the bus?'

Alice pulled on her jacket. 'I've got plenty of time, so I might walk. I could pick up Sarah on the way.'

Carlyle looked at Helen.

'One of her classmates,' his wife explained. 'She lives in Hatton Garden.'

Carlyle turned back to his daughter. 'But you've got your Oyster card with you?' he asked.

She sighed theatrically. '*Yes.*'

'And your mobile?'

Another sigh, even more dramatic this time. 'Yes. And I'll text Mum when I get there.'

Carlyle glanced again at Helen, who nodded in confirmation.

'And you'll text me?' he asked his wife.

'Yes, on your work mobile. That way, you might just manage to pick up my message.' Helen had never been overly impressed by her husband's insistence on having two phones. In addition to his work-issue handset, Carlyle always carried his own cheap, pay-as-you-go mobile. Currently, it was a Sony Ericsson J132, which had cost him just a fiver at the Carphone Warehouse on Long Acre. He had bought it a couple of weeks earlier and would change it again in a couple of months. Meanwhile, very few people had the number to his personal phone, or even knew that he had one. Carlyle saw this as an attempt to keep at least some of his communications private in an increasingly trackable world. It was so private, in fact, that he had been known to go for days, even weeks, without remembering to check it.

'Okay.' He grabbed his daughter and gave her a tight hug, before she squirmed away. 'Have a great day at school.'

'I will.' Alice kissed her mum on the cheek and bounced through the front door. 'See you later.' Ignoring the lift, she disappeared round the corner towards the stairs.

Carlyle listened to her footsteps on the stairs until they faded to nothing. He turned and noticed Helen's eyes welling up. 'I know,' he said, putting his arm around her and pulling her close. 'I know, fucking hell.'

TWENTY-ONE

Sitting in the front seat of the BMW, Rosanna Snowdon cursed the late-night traffic. She was hoping that the congestion would ease, so she could manage to make it home before she had to throw up. The bottle of supermarket Rioja after taping the latest edition of *London Crime* – on top of the two double vodkas she had taken to relax before recording her show – had not been a good idea. She had vowed to go easy on the booze, but that plan had gone out the window after her boss's boss had started hitting on her for the umpteenth time. Alcohol was a key part of her coping strategy when it came to fighting off the unwanted attentions of fat, menopausal television executives, something of which Rosanna had plenty of previous experience.

There was a long BBC tradition of management 'mentoring' the talent. It was something that she had always robustly resisted, even if sometimes her would-be suitors put up quite a struggle. Ian Dale, the Managing Editor of Factual Programming (London), had been chasing his 'little star' for almost a year now. If Rosanna was not really in a position to tell him to get lost, she did nothing to give him any encouragement either. Now he had offered to drive her home. That should have been a major red flag, but she was pissed and tired and couldn't be bothered to wait for a taxi, which could take ages at this time of night. It was already almost midnight and she had to be back in the studio by 8 a.m. tomorrow morning. Anyway, pissed or not, she was confident that she could handle Dale. If all else failed, she had her ace card, his wife Erica's mobile number, prudently acquired from Dale's secretary when it became apparent that he was going to be an ongoing nuisance. The number was programmed into her own phone. If he got out of order, she could just call up Mrs Dale, hand her husband the phone and invite him to explain himself.

Finally the Beemer made it through the last set of traffic-lights and turned into Gladstone Terrace. In front of her mansion block, Dale pulled into a bay marked *Motorcycles Only* and put the car into neutral. Spandau Ballet's 'Gold' started playing on the radio. Rosanna didn't know if she would make it inside in time; if not she could make use of the bushes either side of the front door. It wouldn't be the first time, she thought ruefully.

'That's great, Ian, thank you.' Before the car even stopped, she was trying to release the seat belt and make good her escape. However, in her intoxicated state, it was proving a difficult task.

Seeing her difficulty, Dale smiled lecherously. 'Here, let me help.'

Putting one hand on her knee, he reached over for the buckle with the other, copping a quick feel of her left breast on the way.

'Ian!' It came out as a squeak rather than a shout. With a click, the belt released itself and he was all over her. She could smell his sweat and could hear his panting. She tried to sound forceful: 'Get off!'

Grunting, he kept on pawing her, trying to force his tongue into her mouth. He was stuck half on top of her now, too heavy for her to try and lever him off. Her sense of nausea was overwhelming. A hand went between her legs. Energised, she pulled her thumb out of her right fist and slowly, deliberately, jabbed it into his left eye.

Immediately, both hands went to his face, and he slumped back into the driver's seat. 'Hell! My eye! You've blinded me.'

It took Rosanna a second to realise that she was no longer wearing the seat belt. But then, even as she reached for the door release, she felt a terrible pain in her stomach. Turning back to face Ian Dale, she was able to catch the look of horror in his good eye as she started to puke. For what seemed like an eternity, a prodigious stream of projectile vomit bounced off his shirt and pooled in his lap. Finally the retching finished. Rosanna took a moment to ensure that there was nothing more to come before taking some deep breaths through her mouth. Pulling a tissue from her pocket, she wiped her mouth daintily, before rolling it up into a ball and tossing it in the pile of sick. 'Phew!' She grinned, wiping a tear from her eye. 'I feel a lot better for that.'

Ian Dale still had one eye clamped shut. The other was bulging in shock. It looked as if he was going to cry. The inside of the car was a complete mess and the smell was truly appalling. Rosanna opened the passenger door and swung her legs on to the pavement. 'This is your wife's car, isn't it?' She asked, turning back to take one last look at the mess. 'It looks as if you will have some explaining to do when you get home.'

'Can I at least come in and clean up?' Dale whimpered.

'Are you kidding?' Rosanna asked, edging out of her seat. 'After you just tried to rape me?'

'What?' This time he did let out a sob. 'It wasn't rape.'

'No, but it jolly well would have been,' Rosanna said. She felt sober now and, even better, in control. 'We'll call it quits, then, but if you are still here by the time I get upstairs I'll call the police. And then I will call Erica.'

'But . . .' Dale's protests died in his throat.

'I'm sure that Mrs Dale would be very impressed by the sexual urges you are still able to display at your age.'

At the mention of his wife, Dale finally put the car into gear and released the handbrake.

'Well done, Ian,' Rosanna said, stepping out of the car. 'That's a good boy. Now, remember, you are getting off very lightly indeed. Have a good evening and see you tomorrow.' Slamming the door firmly shut, she threw her shoulders back and walked as steadily as she could manage towards the front door.

The windows of the rusty old Peugeot 307 were wound all the way down, but the smell inside the car was still disgusting. It was as if someone had vomited and then curled up in a nest of fast-food wrappers and died under one of the front seats. Even with his latex gloves on, the man was reluctant to touch anything. He had already decided that when he got back to his apartment he would shower – twice.

Trying to suck in cold air from outside, he stuck his head out of the driver's window and fired up another cigarette, careful to drop the stub from the previous one into his jacket pocket. As the smoke percolated into his lungs, he at least felt a little better. He had been waiting outside the dilapidated student pub in North London now for more than two hours. Every time a knot of punters emerged, he let his hand hover over the ignition, ready to spring into action. But, so far, his target had not emerged.

Every minute that ticked by on the car's electronic clock increased his annoyance level another notch. He was missing a poker game for this, and he loved his poker, even if it was an expensive habit. Grinding his teeth, he thought about how ridiculous it was that he was having to sit here, waiting. In any proper country, he would be able to have someone walk right into the Cow Pub, put a couple of .45s in the girl's head, toss the gun on the floor and walk out. No questions, no problems, no comeback and there would be change out of $100 US. But this was not a proper country, he knew that well enough. The weather was vile, smoking was almost a criminal offence, and shooting people in public was considered 'bad form'.

The thought made him laugh. Bad form was what he did best.

He glanced at his watch: eleven fifty. Yawning, he started picking his nose.

When she finally appeared, he was just flicking a ball of snot at a passing mongrel.

'How nice to see you,' he muttered.

Finally, after all this time, he had caught a break. The woman was on her own, singing along quietly to a tune playing on her iPod. Swaying to the music. Probably drunk.

Perfect.

He started the engine and watched as she stepped between a couple of parked cars, twenty yards or so further up the two-lane road. Peering out from behind a small Ford, she saw that there was no traffic in either direction. Stepping out, she got halfway across before realising that the pavement on the far side had been closed off for repairs. Turning away from him, she continued walking down the road itself, heading towards the traffic-lights at the next junction.

Putting the car into gear, he carefully manoeuvred it out into the roadway. She was thirty yards in front of him now, as he moved his foot on to the accelerator. By the time she realised what was happening, he was almost upon her. Half-turning, there was barely time for the incredulity to register on her face. There was a satisfying thud and she was flipped up over the car bonnet, and sent bouncing down the road.

Did she recognise him as she flew past? It was unlikely but he hoped so. He wanted her to know *why* – why this was happening to her; why she had got herself killed. That should be the last thought crawling through her brain before she expired.

Looking back, he saw the street was still empty – no witnesses, no reaction, plenty of time for him to go back and make sure the job was done properly. But the satisfied grin had not reached his face when his thoughts were interrupted by the scream of a horn. He was sailing through the junction before he realised it, through a red light, almost sideswiping a black cab as it roared past him.

'Mother of God!' he cursed, bringing the Peugeot to a halt.

The taxi stopped in a squeal of rubber off to his left. He could see the driver get out and head towards him with fury in his eyes. The cabbie hadn't seen the girl yet, but there was no question of going back now. No matter: a look in the rear-view mirror showed her still lying prostrate on the tarmac. He'd hit her at speed. She wasn't getting up again. He was confident that the job was done. Stomping on the accelerator for a second time, he left the taxi driver's curses flailing on the wind, and headed off into the night.

TWENTY-TWO

Rosanna closed the front door and stood in the entry hall of Reith Mansions, listening for the sound of Ian Dale's BMW pulling away from the kerb. Peeking through the letter box, to make sure that her unwelcome suitor had finally gone, she let out a drunken squeak of triumph. 'Good riddance, you odious little man,' she cackled. 'Let's see how you talk your way out of *that* one when you get home.' Taking her mobile from her jacket pocket, she pulled up Erica Dale's number on the screen. For a few moments, her finger hovered over the call button, before she thought better of it. 'You've had enough excitement for one day, girl,' she mumbled to herself. 'Time for some sleep.'

Recalling vaguely that the building's lift was out of order, Rosanna slowly staggered up two flights of stairs. Swaying slightly in front of the door to her flat, she began rummaging through her bag in search of her keys. When they were not immediately forthcoming, she tipped the bag upside down, emptying the contents on to the carpet in the corridor. What a pile of crap, she thought. I really must sort it out. Falling to her knees, she began sifting through the debris.

'Hurrah!' Grabbing the keys, she slowly struggled back to her feet. Reaching for the lock, it took her another moment to realise that she was not alone. She made a face as her pickled brain tried to process this information.

'What are *you* doing here?' she asked, not looking up. 'It's late and I've got work in the morning. Plus, I don't feel well.' She tried to insert the key in the lock and missed. When she tried again, it fell back to the floor. 'Shit!' She bent down and felt woozy.

Then she felt a firm hand on her collar, pulling her backwards. 'Hey!' Rosanna tried to stand upright, but her legs buckled. Her stomach surged and she thought she was going to be sick again. She half-fell away from the door, tottering back towards the stairs. One of her shoes came off and she felt the ground disappear from beneath her. The same hand reached out towards her, but she couldn't grab hold of it as she started bouncing backwards down the stairs.

TWENTY-THREE

It was hot and Carlyle was bothered. Standing on the cobbles of Covent Garden piazza, inside the flaccid police tape, he wiped some sweat from his brow and looked at the tourists staring back at him. Didn't they have anything better to do than gawp at some poor bloke who had keeled over while playing the bongos for their entertainment? Over the last hour, people had come and gone, but nevertheless the crowd had been growing steadily. Now it was easily more than a hundred strong, which was probably a much bigger audience than poor Dennis Felix had ever enjoyed while he was alive. Carlyle was almost tempted to pass the dead man's hat round and ask for contributions towards the funeral expenses. If nothing else, that would have cleared away the crowd.

Standing next to him, sweating profusely, was Sergeant Dave Prentice. On a rare and unwelcome foray from his usual position behind the front desk at the station, he was reciting the basic facts that had so far been gleaned about the unfortunate musician: 'Mid-thirties apparently. From Estonia apparently. Lives somewhere in East London.'

'Apparently,' Carlyle said, without thinking.

Prentice shot him a dirty look. 'He's been playing at this pitch three or four times a week for over a year.'

'Well done,' said Carlyle, trying to retrieve the situation. 'That was quick.'

'Speak to *her*.' Prentice pointed at a woman standing nearby. 'She knows him.'

Carlyle caught the woman's eye and beckoned her over. Young and gaunt, she was about 5 feet 4 inches, with dark rings round her eyes that matched her black hair. You need a good feed and some prolonged exposure to sunlight, he thought. She was dressed in baggy green trousers and a cropped pink vest, allowing her to display a selection of rings protruding from her belly button. With too much jewellery and not enough make-up, she looked primed to run away and join the circus. Maybe she already had.

'I'm Inspector Carlyle and I work with Sergeant Prentice here.'

The girl stepped directly in front of Carlyle, but said nothing. Despite the heat, she was shivering and he could see that she had been crying.

'What's your name?' he asked.

The girl eyed him suspiciously. Then she glanced at the body lying on a trolley, hidden under a blanket, waiting to be taken away by the crew that had edged their ambulance to one corner of the square.

'It's not a trick question,' Carlyle snapped, his meagre reserves of empathy already exhausted.

'Kylie.'

How unlucky, thought Carlyle, to be named after a midget Australian pop star. He focused his gaze on a spot an inch above her head. 'Okay, Kylie, what can you tell me about Mr Felix?'

'He was from Tallinn, in Estonia.' She scratched her neck. 'That's like, Russia, I think. Somewhere round there anyway.'

'What else?'

Kylie thought it over at length. 'I've known him for about six months,' she said finally.

'How?'

'How what?' She gave him a look like an inquisitive puppy.

Carlyle took a deep breath and counted to ten. Calm yourself, he thought. Don't let little things wind you up. You have to try and keep things under control.

'How did you know him?' *Were you fucking him? Did he try*

and dump you? Could you have cared enough to try and kill him? How did he die?

'I work over there.' She pointed to a fast-food trailer that had been parked by the entrance to the Jubilee Hall gym.

Carlyle realised that he hadn't been to the gym for almost a week. He felt sluggish. I need a workout, he thought.

'Dennis would often stop by for a smoothie and a chat. And I would listen to him play. He was good. Did an amazing version of "Wonderwall".'

Shame I missed that one, Carlyle thought. 'So what happened this morning?'

'I dunno,' she shrugged. 'I saw him arrive and set up. He started drumming and then I had to get a customer a cappuccino. When I looked again, Felix was kind of slumped over to one side. No one seemed to be paying him any attention.' Her eyes lost focus. 'Maybe they thought it was part of his act.'

'Why would they do that?'

She ignored his question. 'I knew something was wrong, so I went over to see if I could help. I gave him a shake and then checked for a pulse . . . but there was nothing.' She paused and a tear appeared at the corner of her right eye.

Give it a rest, Carlyle thought uncharitably. All you did was sell the poor sod the odd juice.

'Did he do drugs?'

She looked at him blankly in a way that Carlyle read as: *Yes, of course he did, you idiot!* 'No.'

'Are you sure?'

She shook her head. 'I never saw Felix touch anything illegal.'

I'd need some serious drugs if I had to play the bloody bongo drums all day, Carlyle mused. 'Okay, was he ill?'

'No, no, he was very healthy.'

'What else did he do?' Carlyle asked. 'Apart from play for the tourists here?'

'He loved his music. He often worked with kids doing drumming workshops.'

'Here?'

'No, in Hackney. He also had his own band. They're called Toompea. They play alternative folk rock.'

'Uhuh.' Carlyle was switching off; this dead guy was getting less interesting by the second.

Kylie looked at him expectantly, obviously waiting for another question, but his mind had gone blank.

'John?' He was saved by Susan Phillips, who had appeared from somewhere.

He held up a hand to signal to the pathologist that he would come over in a minute. 'Thank you for that,' he said to the girl. 'Give Sergeant Prentice here your details, and we will be in touch.'

'What happened to him?' Kylie asked.

'That's what we need to find out. If you can think of anything else that might be relevant, let us know straight away.' Turning away from the girl before she could start crying again, he stepped over to the pathologist and smiled. 'Nice to see you, Susan.'

'You, too, John. You've got an interesting one here.'

Based ten minutes up the road, at Holborn police station, Susan Phillips had been a staff pathologist with the Met for more than fifteen years. Slim and blonde, with a healthy glow and a cheery smile, she brought a smidgen of much-needed glamour to The Job. More to the point, she was quick, no-nonsense and dependable – just what Carlyle liked in a colleague. They had worked together many times before and he was always pleased to see her at a crime scene.

'What can you tell me?' Carlyle asked.

'Not a lot,' Phillips grinned, pushing a pair of oversized sunglasses back up her nose.

'Foul play?' he asked casually.

'No signs of it that I can see, first off.'

'Heart attack, then? The girl says he just kind of keeled over.'

'Maybe,' she shrugged. 'He's still young, but it can happen. I'm sorry, but I can't speculate at this stage. It's not immediately apparent what killed him. We're going to take him away now. I'll get him on to the slab and let you know what I find out.'

'Okay,' Carlyle nodded. 'Thanks for coming.'

'No problem,' Phillips said. 'Let's speak later.'

The body was carefully loaded into the ambulance by a couple of paramedics. Carlyle watched as it slowly edged its way into the traffic on Bow Street before heading away from the piazza.

'What shall we do with the bongos?' Prentice asked.

Carlyle looked at the pair of forlorn-looking drums standing on the cobbles alongside Felix's other bits and pieces. 'Take them back to the station with the rest of the guy's stuff. They're evidence.'

'Okay,' said Prentice, happy to be getting back to his desk.

As Prentice trudged off, Carlyle glanced back across the police tape. With the show over, the crowd had largely dispersed, heading off in search of other diversions. It was hard work being a tourist, Carlyle thought.

Finally, there were only a handful of people still standing by the tape. One man caught Carlyle's eye and grinned. 'Well, fuck me!' the inspector mumbled under his breath. Instinctively, he felt for his handcuffs, cursing when he remembered that – not for the first time – he had left them at the station or at home or God knows where. He looked around for some support, moral or otherwise. In the distance, he could see Prentice already on the far side of the piazza, heading back to the station with a bongo drum under each arm. Everyone else had left.

Taking a deep breath, Carlyle stepped towards the tape.

'Inspector.' Michael Hagger doffed an imaginary cap and let the grin spread even wider across his face.

Just short of six feet, Hagger was taller and heavier than Carlyle, not to mention at least fifteen years younger. They both knew that the policeman could not take him down, one on one.

More to the point, there was no sign of the child.

'Michael, nice to see you.'

'I hear you've been looking for me.'

'Quite a few people have.'

'Well, here I am.'

'Yeah, but people are also looking for the boy. Where's Jake?'

Hagger did a little half-step dance on the cobbles. 'The kid's okay.'

'That's good.'

Hagger sniggered. 'You know that if you lay a finger on me now, well . . . that might change.'

'Yes,' said Carlyle, holding his hands up in supplication. 'I do.'

Hagger put on an expression of mock hurt. 'It's a shame that a father isn't allowed to have some quality time with his son these days.'

Carlyle bit his tongue.

'It's not like his mother – that useless bitch – is doing much of a job anyway.'

At least that's something we can agree on, Carlyle reflected.

Hagger gave him a sly look. 'I'm guessing that when you do get Jake back, Social Services will take over, anyway.'

When. Carlyle liked the sound of that. On the other hand, Hagger talked shit most of the time; gibberish the rest. 'Where is he, Michael?'

Hagger raised a fist, but only for emphasis. 'He's safe. And he's well. I only need him for a few more days, and then you'll get him back. In the meantime, tell your people to back off.'

My people? Carlyle wondered what he meant. Maybe Inspector Cutler was outperforming any expectations. 'Okay.'

'If Jake gets hurt,' Hagger continued, sounding more agitated, 'it will be your fault.'

'No one wants Jake to get hurt,' Carlyle said, as soothingly as he could manage.

'Well, tell your chum Silver to behave himself, then.'

Silver? Carlyle frowned. 'What's he got to do with all this?'

Thrusting his hands into his trouser pockets, Hagger turned on his heel and began walking briskly away. 'Just bloody tell him,' he shouted over his shoulder.

Carlyle watched him go, while replaying in his head what had just been said. As Hagger disappeared round a corner, he reached into his jacket pocket, pulled out his private and untraceable (he hoped) mobile, and called Dominic Silver's number. Almost immediately, it went to voicemail. Gripping the handset tighter in frustration, he spat out a message: *Dominic, it's me. Call me back asap. I am waiting for your call, so I will definitely pick up.*

For a few moments, he stared at his phone, willing it to ring, while wondering whether he had time to pop up to Il Buffone for lunch. But the phone didn't ring and he decided, regretfully, that he didn't have time for a proper lunch. Plan B was a cheese sandwich and an orange juice, which he bought from a cheerful girl working in Kylie's trailer to take back to the station.

Five minutes later, aware of the rumbling in his stomach, Carlyle stepped out of the lift and headed towards his desk. As he approached, he wasn't best pleased to find someone sitting in his chair.

'John Carlyle?'

'Yes.'

The tall Asian-looking bloke lifted his spotless Nike trainers off Carlyle's desk and planted them on the floor. 'I'm Inspector Nick Chan.' He nodded at another man hovering nearby. 'That is Sergeant Greg Brown.'

Both men wore a smug look that said *We know something you don't*.

Chan and Brown? After a few seconds' thought, Carlyle came to the conclusion that he didn't know anything about this duo. That made it doubly certain that now was a good time for caution.

'What can I do for you gentlemen?' Carlyle asked. He couldn't wait any longer for some food, so he flopped into a nearby chair and began unwrapping his sandwich.

Chan took that as his cue to stand up. 'Let's go into one of the conference rooms.'

'Fine.' Carlyle took a large bite out of his sandwich and chewed it vigorously, getting back to his feet and following his two colleagues towards the row of empty rooms situated at the rear of that floor.

* * *

Conference room number seven was filled by a long rectangular table, surrounded by a dozen chairs. Carlyle quickly took a seat at the far end of the table, by the window. Someone had left a copy of the *Mirror* on the table. The newspaper was folded in half and Carlyle could only see part of the front-page headline: *TELEVISION PRESENTER* . . . Resisting the temptation to open it out, he polished off the last of his sandwich and took a long swig of juice.

Behind him, Brown entered the room, followed by Chan, who closed the door and then removed his jacket, dropping it over the back of a chair. Both policemen remained standing. 'Do you know Sandra Groves?' Chan asked.

Carlyle downed the last of the juice and screwed the cap back on the empty bottle. 'Yes.'

'She claims you assaulted her.'

'So I hear.' Knowing now what this was about, Carlyle relaxed a little.

'And did you?'

'No.' Carlyle smiled at Brown, who stared grimly back at him. 'Have you guys not seen the reports?'

'She's in hospital,' said Brown.

'As far as I'm aware,' Carlyle said, as casually as he could manage, 'she was fine when she left this station.'

Brown folded his arms and leaned against the wall. 'She's in intensive care.'

Carlyle squeezed the juice bottle tightly, saying nothing. The room was hot and stuffy, but now was not the time to get up and try to open a window. In the breast pocket of his jacket, his phone started vibrating. That would be Dominic, but now was not the time to answer it. In fact, now was not the time to do anything but sit very still and listen.

'Someone tried to run her over last night,' Brown continued.

'So?'

'So,' Chan replied, trying and failing to keep a grin from his face, 'she says that it was you.'

TWENTY-FOUR

After a further twenty minutes, Chan and Brown departed. Carlyle had explained that firstly, he didn't know how to drive, and secondly his wife could provide him with an alibi for the time when Sandra Groves was suffering a vehicular assault. The pair didn't seem particularly concerned by what he had to say one way or another and, after mumbling the usual stuff about being back after making further enquiries, they left him sitting alone in the conference room, wondering what to do next.

The first thing he did was check his voicemail. As expected, it was Dominic Silver: *John, it's me. I thought you were definitely going to pick up? Anyway, don't call me back. I'm busy this afternoon. I'll try you again tonight.*

It took Carlyle a moment to remember what he had called Dominic about in the first place, even though it was barely an hour ago. When he remembered, it didn't seem so much of a priority any more. Standing up, he dropped his empty juice bottle into a bin in one corner of the room. Then he unfolded the newspaper and laid it out on the table. Reading the full headline, he grimaced:

TELEVISION PRESENTER FOUND DEAD AT HER FLAT

With a sick feeling in his stomach, he read on:

Leading London television presenter Rosanna Snowdon was found dead at her flat in Fulham early this morning. She had fallen down some stairs and it is believed she suffered a broken neck, as well as arm and head injuries. The police have declined to comment, but at this stage, sources suggest that foul play has not been ruled out.

Under a picture of Reith Mansions, the block where Rosanna had lived, the rest of the article consisted of filler about her career-history and her personal life. Thinking back to their meeting, Carlyle reread the article. If she fell down the stairs, maybe it was an accident. But if the police hadn't ruled out something more sinister then they must have some serious doubts.

There was no reference in the paper to the stalker that Rosanna had been worried about. Carlyle tried and failed to recall the guy's name. Perhaps he was involved? Refolding the paper, he dropped it back on the table.

Should he have taken her concerns more seriously?

Could he have stopped this?

As usual, there were lots of questions and no answers.

'John,' he whispered to himself as he left the room, 'this is really not looking like it's going to be a great day.'

Under the circumstances, Carlyle decided that it would be sensible to make himself scarce, for a while at least. That meant switching off his work mobile and getting out of the station for the rest of the afternoon. Deciding to head for the one place where he knew that he wouldn't be disturbed, he took the keys to the Mills flat from his desk and headed for the street. Once outside, he walked slowly up through Covent Garden to Ridgemount Mansions, taking care to avoid any more arguments with bus drivers, protestors or anyone else on his way there.

Stepping inside, however, he realised that coming back to the flat had been a bad idea. The place had not been aired for a fortnight. The heat was oppressive and the atmosphere was rank.

Closing the front door behind him, Carlyle stepped quickly down the hallway, heading for the kitchen. Glancing round the room, he saw that nothing had been touched since the original investigation. A chair lay overturned beside the kitchen table and Agatha Mills's dried blood was still caked on the floor. Carlyle wondered how long the place would stay like this. It could take months, if not years due to legal reasons for the flat to get sold and have someone else move in. It struck him that this place would be great for Helen and Alice and himself, but it was way out of their league – probably about a million quid out of their league. He wondered who actually owned it now – whether the Millses had left it to anyone in their wills, or whether it would just revert to the Government, to help pay down the National Debt. God knows, the public finances needed all the help they could get.

Moving over to the kitchen window, he flicked open the latch and stepped out on to the same fire escape where he had found Sylvester Bassett, the pathologist, having a smoke on the morning after Agatha Mills's death. Sitting on the small landing just below the windowsill, Carlyle let his head rest against the metal handrail of the fire escape and closed his eyes. In the cool silence of the stairwell, he spent a minute or so running through the day's events in his head. Reaching no particular conclusions, he dug into his inside jacket pocket and pulled out a list of the Chilean guests who had attended the Mayor's reception at City Hall, a week earlier.

The list had arrived, as promised, from the Ambassador's office the day after the actual event. A couple of days after that, Carlyle had stuck it in his jacket pocket and basically forgotten about it. Now, for want of anything better to do, he began scanning the rows of names and organisations, none of which meant anything to him. After a short while, his eyes glazed over. Putting the list back in his pocket, he just sat there, staring into the darkened windows of the empty flats opposite.

After a while, his thoughts turned to Rosanna Snowdon. She

had asked for his help: had he let her down? He really had no idea. Had he got her killed? Surely not. The bastard who killed her was the bastard who killed her. He had long ago realised that he was not the kind of guy who tried on other people's guilt for size.

He was spared any extended reflection by the phone vibrating in the breast pocket of his jacket. He frowned, convinced that he had switched it off, before realising that the one ringing was his private phone. Muttering to himself, he checked the incoming number – Dominic Silver.

'Hello?' he barked.

'So you do actually know how to answer your phone,' Dominic chuckled.

'I thought you were supposed to be busy,' Carlyle said, remembering the man's last message.

'I was . . . I am, but you sounded harassed.'

'I am.'

'That's what I thought,' said Dominic, exuding unreasonable reasonableness. 'So how can I help?'

Carlyle took a moment to remember the problem in question. 'Michael Hagger.'

'Yes,' Dominic said breezily, 'what about him?'

'He came to see me.'

'Did he indeed?' Dominic's tone remained determinedly cheery, but Carlyle could now detect an underlying wariness. 'Did he bring the boy?'

'No, but he said that Jake was okay.'

'That's something, I suppose.'

'Hagger also said that he would be returning him soon.'

Dominic said nothing to that.

'And he *also* said,' Carlyle continued, 'that I was to tell *you* to back off.'

Dominic laughed. 'And what did you say?'

'What could I say?' Carlyle shot back, with more than a hint of exasperation in his voice. 'I didn't have a bloody clue what he was talking about.'

'Where is he now?'

'How should I know?' Carlyle snapped.

'You let him go?'

'Dominic, what was I supposed to do? We don't know where the kid is or even why he's being held,' Carlyle pointed out, glossing over the fact that Hagger could have easily decked him if he had been silly enough to try and arrest him.

'Ever the pragmatist,' Silver joked. 'Let's hope that no one finds out how you let London's Most Wanted walk away from you.'

'Hardly,' Carlyle muttered.

There was a pause on the other end of the line. 'No, but you can see how it could look.'

Carlyle felt a stab of anger. 'Are you threatening me?'

'No, no,' Dominic said quickly. 'Of course not.'

Carlyle grunted.

'Don't be silly,' Dominic continued. 'All I'm suggesting is, don't go round telling anyone.'

'As if.'

'Good.'

'So,' Carlyle asked, 'what *is* going on here?' There was a pause and the inspector could almost hear the hum of his mate's brain as he edited the information that he was about to share.

Finally, Dominic spoke. 'As you know, Hagger sometimes worked for Jerome Sullivan.'

'Who?'

'You know – the bloke on that video I showed you; the genius who shot himself and fell off the roof of his own building. The clip on the mobile phone where you spotted Hagger in the background?'

'Yes, yes,' said Carlyle, not liking where this was going.

'Well, it seems that Hagger and Jerome's other idiot mate, Eric Christian, have been trying to keep the show on the road since the demise of their glorious leader. But they're clearly not up to it. One of my . . . associates has asked me to sort it out.'

'*Asked* you?'

'Instructed me.'

Carlyle sighed. Normally, he didn't like knowing too much about the mechanics of Dominic Silver's profession, but here he needed to know what he was getting wrapped up in. 'I didn't think you did that sort of thing,' he remarked.

'I don't,' Dominic said. 'All I'm trying to do is facilitate a satisfactory resolution for the mess.'

'Including Jake?'

'Including Jake.'

Carlyle shifted uneasily on his perch. 'Will it involve more people falling off buildings?'

'Let's hope not,' was the best Dominic could manage.

'So where does the kid fit into all of this?' Carlyle asked.

'Hagger put him up as collateral for a debt owed by Jerome.'

'Collateral?' Carlyle snorted. 'How much can the boy be worth?'

There was another pause. 'Quite a bit, if you know the wrong sort of people.'

Carlyle felt his stomach turn. 'How much?'

'I don't know.'

'Who holds the debt?'

'Not sure.'

'Speculate.'

'No, I won't. Not at this stage.'

'How long have we got?'

'I don't know.'

'What happens if Hagger doesn't come up with the money?'

'The kid gets auctioned off,' said Dominic matter-of-factly, as if it was obvious.

'C'mon,' Carlyle whined, 'don't give me this bollocks.'

'I'm not giving you any bollocks,' Dominic retorted. 'I'm just telling you how it is. Don't shoot the fucking messenger. I'm only trying to help you here.'

'Jesus,' Carlyle said wearily. 'What are you doing, getting involved in this type of shit?'

'I'm trying to sort it out,' Dominic said testily.

Carlyle coughed up a wad of phlegm and spat it out over the side of the fire escape and into the alley below. His mouth was dry and he felt terrible. What type of degenerate scumbag would sell their own kid? Never mind Dominic: how did *he* manage to get involved in these type of situations?

'John, I've got to go . . .'

'Okay.' Carlyle pulled himself together. 'All I want is the boy. Whatever you need to do to get him back, I will do my best to make sure that any official fallout gets dealt with.'

'I appreciate that,' Dominic said.

'Just fucking get him back,' Carlyle growled. 'Unhurt and unmolested.'

'Don't worry, I'll make sure nothing happens to Jake, even if I have to pay for him out of my own pocket.'

'You'd better.'

'What sort of a man do you think I am?'

You really don't expect me to answer that, do you? Carlyle thought. 'Where is he now?'

'I can't tell you.'

'Can't or won't?'

'Can't, because I have no idea. Look, just sit tight – this thing will get resolved soon.'

'Do I have a choice?' Carlyle said resentfully.

'Don't worry, I'll be in touch. I'll make sure you get the tip-off, rather than that idiot Cutler.'

With that gentle reminder to Carlyle that he wasn't the only policeman in town, the line went dead. The inspector put the phone back in his pocket and scratched his ear. Stepping back to the window, he tried to lift it open again, but it was stuck. Cursing, he gave the frame a push with both hands, but with no success. Peering inside, he could see that the latch must have re-engaged itself after he had stepped outside. His initial thought was to break the glass, then he realised he could just walk on down the fire escape and out on to the street. He thought about that for the moment. Even if the window had been locked when they found Agatha Mills – and he would have to check that with Bassett – someone could still have left the flat and exited the building this same way. Maybe they could have got in this way too. With the possibilities bouncing round in his brain, Carlyle carefully made his way down to the alley below.

Reaching the bottom of the fire escape, Carlyle opened a metal gate and stepped out into a short passageway filled with waste bins and bags of rubbish, which led out on to Great Russell Street. Noting the familiar stench of rotting food and urine, he lengthened his stride and held his breath. He was about ten feet from the street itself when a large black sack in front of him started moving. Assuming that it was disturbed by a rat, Carlyle kept moving. However, his further progress was impeded when the mound of rubbish stood up in front of him, yawned and let out an enormous belch. Unable to hold his breath any longer, Carlyle was forced to inhale an eye-watering mix of curry, eggs and Special Brew. Taking a step backwards, he watched the tramp shake himself fully awake. The guy was dressed for winter, with at least three layers of clothing under a heavy black woollen overcoat. He wore a pair of grey slacks that looked as if they had not been cleaned during this century, and some fairly expensive-looking but heavily worn tan shoes. A blue Chelsea beanie hat rounded off the ensemble nicely.

Belatedly realising that he was not home alone, the man looked Carlyle up and down. He spent a few moments trying to work out what to make of the policeman, his eyes widening all the while, as if he had never seen another human being before. Finally, his mouth opened. A couple of seconds later, some words crawled out.

'Got any money?'

It look Carlyle another moment to realise who he had standing in front of him, larger than life and ten times as smelly. 'Dog?' he said, puzzled. 'I thought you were dead.'

Walter Poonoosamy thought about that for a moment, as he looked around the alley. 'Maybe I am,' he sniffed.

Stepping away from the pile of rubbish from which he had emerged, Dog continued to block Carlyle's exit from the alley. If anything, the smell was getting worse, and the inspector was keen to be getting on his way. 'Well,' he mumbled, with as much fake bonhomie as he could manage, 'it's good to see you are still with us. I'm sure we'll be seeing you at the station some time soon.'

The tramp grunted and looked down at the mess from which he had emerged. Tentatively, he began poking at one of the bags with his foot, in case there was some tasty morsel that he had missed. Taking this as his cue to leave, Carlyle eased his way past, heading for the bustle and the glare of the street beyond.

'Excuse us, please?'

No sooner had the inspector emerged on to the street, than a couple of Chinese tourists thrust a street map in his face and asked him very politely – and in the kind of perfect English that no one in England had used for as long as he could remember – for directions to the British Museum. Resisting the temptation to send them in totally the wrong direction, he pointed at the massive building just across the road and forced himself to smile. With a cheery 'Thank you', the pair stepped off the pavement and almost walked straight into the path of an oversized tour bus. Once they had finally made it safely across the road, Carlyle watched them negotiate the pavement artists and the hot-dog sellers and safely reach the museum gates. Turning away, he decided to head for home.

He had barely gone twenty yards, however, when an idea popped into his head. Turning round, he retraced his steps back towards the alley. When he arrived, the tramp was still there, sitting serenely on a mound of rubbish sacks, as if surveying his kingdom. In his hand was an anonymous-looking bottle from which he carefully sipped a brownish liquid.

The tramp gave no indication of noticing the policeman's return. Trying once again to ignore the smell, Carlyle stepped towards him. 'Dog,' he asked, when he thought he might finally have gained the tramp's attention, 'do you come here often?'

Walter didn't even look up, but took his lips far enough from the bottle to mumble, 'Sometimes.'

'At night?'

Nodding, Dog stuck his lips back on the bottle and sucked out the remaining dregs.

'Were you here a couple of weeks ago?' Carlyle persisted.

Dog scratched himself behind his left ear, like a man trying to come to terms with the concept of time. Finding it too much though, he gave Carlyle a look of infinite weariness. 'Dunno.'

'The last few times you were here,' Carlyle persisted, 'did you see anyone else?'

Dog did another excellent impersonation of a man thinking for a long time. 'No,' he said finally.

Damn! Carlyle thought. 'No one?'

Another pause.

'Just the man with the beard.'

'The man with the beard?'

Dog tossed the bottle over his shoulder and stood up. He looked at Carlyle. 'You don't have to repeat everything I say,' he grumbled. Reaching into an inside pocket of his overcoat, he pulled out what looked like a slice of beef. Tilting his head back, he dropped the morsel into his mouth. Resisting the urge to gag, Carlyle waited for the man to chew his food, swallow and then let out a satisfied burp. He willed himself to show some patience. After all, he had caught Dog on one of his more lucid days – maybe coming back from the dead had helped sharpen up his thought processes – and knew that he should now be prepared to wait it out.

Finally, Dog wiped his hand on his belly. 'Came down the stairs back there, just like you. I asked him for some money. He said somethin' foreign.'

'In Spanish?' Carlyle asked.

'Mebbe.'

'What did he look like?'

'Had a beard,' said Dog, his eyes returning to the piles of

rubbish; his mind doubtless wondering where he was most likely to find something else to drink.

'Okay,' said Carlyle, realising that the wino's mind was beginning to wander and that he wasn't going to get anything else from him right now. 'Thanks.' He fished a ten-pound note out of his trouser pocket and offered it to Dog. 'Here, get yourself some Diamond White or something.'

Mention of the demon drink instantly got Dog's attention, but he eyed the money suspiciously. 'Will it work?'

'I suppose so,' said Carlyle, 'if you drink enough of it.'

'No,' said Dog, still not accepting the banknote. 'The money, will it work? They wouldn't take the other one.'

'Who wouldn't?' said Carlyle, instinctively asking the wrong question.

'The bloke in the newsagent's,' Dog said, as if that was obvious. 'He said my money was no good.'

'What money?'

Dog started rooting around in his pockets. 'The money the man with the beard gave me.'

Carlyle watched as Dog pulled out various crumpled pieces of paper from different pockets, looking at each one carefully, before slowly returning it to its original hiding place.

The fourth or fifth scrap that Dog extracted looked a bit like an old one-pound note. He waved it at Carlyle. 'This.'

'I tell you what,' Carlyle said, still holding out the tenner. 'I'll swap with you. My one here will work.'

'It better had,' said Dog, pulling himself to his feet and exchanging the notes. After carefully considering both sides of the ten-pound note, he reached a decision and quickly shuffled out of the alley, in search of suitable refreshment.

When the wino had gone, Carlyle stood there examining the piece of paper Dog had given him. It was a worn, thousand-peso note in a colour he could only describe as aquamarine, with the legend *Banco Central de Chile* printed on both sides. On one side was a picture of a statue, on the other a Victorian-looking military gentleman, with a battleship behind him. After much squinting, Carlyle made out the man's name: *Agustín Arturo Prat Chacón.*

Smiling, Carlyle thrust the note into his trouser pocket. He had no idea how much a thousand pesos was worth, but he knew this was evidence that could prove priceless for his investigation.

TENTY-FIVE

The Mayor took a cautious sip of his Auchentoshan 3 Wood, a malt whisky described by the advertising men as 'best enjoyed on its own when in a ponderous and contemplative mood'. More to the point, it was 43 per cent alcohol. Christian Holyrod was not a man given to excessive contemplation but at the moment he definitely needed a drink – several drinks, in fact. Taking a second sip, he looked carefully at the man standing in front of him. 'I don't know what you are up to,' he said quietly, 'and I don't want to know either. Just remember rule number one . . .'

The Mayor's companion smiled weakly and half-pretended to be interested in what the harried politician was telling him. 'And what is rule number one?' he asked dutifully.

The Mayor leaned closer. 'It's simple: *don't get caught.*'

'Come, come now, Mr Mayor. What makes you think I am up to anything illicit?'

Holyrod, now enjoying the first flush of Auchentoshan-inspired warmth, said nothing.

'We are both military men,' his companion continued, 'officer class.'

Not so you'd notice, Holyrod thought sourly. There are officers and there are *officers.*

'We both know the importance of discretion,' the other man went on, 'and honour.'

We'll see, the Mayor thought.

The man gazed into his glass of mineral water. 'Do not worry,' he said. 'Everything will go as planned. We will support the TEMPO conference as arranged. And, even more importantly for your friends at Pierrepoint Aerospace, the contract will be signed before the opening gala dinner.'

Holyrod took another swig of Scotch. He had eaten nothing all day and the whisky was going straight to his head, leaving him feeling tired and irritable. 'That is good to hear. What you have to remember is that the deal should have been signed by now. If it isn't done by the time the conference starts, Pierrepoint will look to sue LAHC.'

The other man stiffened. 'We both know that will not be necessary.'

'I hope you are right,' the Mayor said. 'The last thing we need is another example of an equipment-procurement project suffering from horrendous delays and going way over budget.'

'Ah, yes.' A broad smile broke out on the man's face. 'The Green Report – the one that your government tried to suppress.'

'Without success,' Holyrod said bitterly.

'I've only seen what's in the papers, but your Ministry of Defence does not come out of it looking too good. No one likes the idea of money being wasted while front-line soldiers go without the equipment they need.'

'Well,' Holyrod sighed, 'managing money was never their strong point. But, having been on both sides of the fence, I can see the difficulties the civil servants in Whitehall face.'

'I'm sure you can, but that's a compelling reason for you to come to us.'

'Assuming you can deliver what we need,' Holyrod interjected.

'We can. On time and on budget.'

'Good.'

'And you, in turn, will be able to supply the MoD with the equipment they need, almost on time and almost on budget.'

Holyrod chose to ignore the last barb. 'I have told the Pierrepoint Board that I think that any form of legal action would be totally counter-productive, even as a last resort. Apart from anything else, it would incur the risk of considerable publicity. But I am just one voice among many. And, as things stand, they are not inclined to take my point of view.'

'Ah, yes, the travails of the non-executive director. To be honest, I am surprised that you are able to combine such a job with your political office.'

Was that a threat? Holyrod wondered. Bloody foreigners, he should never have gotten into bed with them. Ah, well, there it was. Draining his glass, he signalled to a nearby waiter for another whisky. He knew that he really shouldn't, but what the hell. 'It's all above board. I made it very clear before I ran for Mayor that I was in the process of building up a portfolio of business interests and that I would not – that I *could* not – give them up if I was elected.'

The other man nodded. 'Indeed.'

'The voters like the idea that I can earn a living in the real world.'

The man looked bemused.

'In the private sector,' the Mayor explained.

'Ah, yes.'

The empty glass was whisked from Holyrod's hand and replaced by another large tumbler of Auchentoshan 3 Wood. He weighed the glass in his hand: it felt satisfyingly heavy. A couple more of these and I won't need to bother about dinner, he thought. I might even get a good night's sleep for once. 'No one can doubt my commitment to public service,' he continued, 'but that does not put bread on the table.'

'No, absolutely not.'

Holyrod started on his fresh drink. 'I spent more than a decade in the service of Queen and country, stuck in many of those same hell-holes of which you have personal experience . . .'

'Yes.'

'. . . and I am still completely committed to public service, but not at the expense of keeping my family in penury.'

'Of course not.' His companion gave the Mayor a comforting

pat on the shoulder. Presumably the £500,000 you are due to collect for closing our deal will help in that regard, he thought.

'After all,' Holyrod explained, 'I don't have the kind of family wealth behind me that you have.'

'That is a very fair point.' The other man stared into his glass of mineral water. 'I am very fortunate.'

A deeper wave of warmth from the Scotch eased through the Mayor's body and he realised that it was time to move the conversation on. 'What does the Ambassador think of all this?'

'Orb?' The man made a face. 'He is a bystander, nothing more than a passive observer. He has spent his whole life watching other people act, while making sure that he does nothing to get in the way. It is amazing that anyone can spend so long doing so little. At least that means he is nothing to worry about.'

'And the policeman?'

The man placed his glass on the tray of a passing waiter and pulled out a packet of cigarettes. 'Who?'

The Mayor thought about mentioning that this was a no-smoking building, but thought better of it. He hoped there weren't any smoke-detectors nearby. 'Carlyle,' he said, 'Inspector John Carlyle. That policeman who spoke with the Ambassador at the reception.'

The man lit his cigarette and inhaled deeply. 'Surely you don't have to worry about a mere policeman?' He looked around for somewhere to deposit the ash from his cigarette. Finding nothing suitable, he flicked it on to the floor.

Aghast, Holyrod looked around, hoping that no one had seen. A waitress caught his eye and started heading towards them, but he glared at her and she hurriedly turned away. 'I have come across him before,' he said, 'and he is a professional nuisance.'

'Okay.' The man shrugged. 'I hear you, Mr Mayor. I can take care of him.'

'No, no, no,' Holyrod said hastily. 'You can't do that.'

The man looked at him with an air of faint amusement.

'Let me assure you,' the Mayor continued, 'you shouldn't try to interfere with the workings of our police here. That would be very . . . unprofessional. It would jeopardise everything.'

An irritated look swept across the man's face. 'As you wish.'

'These kinds of problems can be dealt with in other ways.'

The man made a small bow. 'As you wish,' he repeated, in an almost mocking tone.

The Mayor felt a ripple of unease spread through his stomach. Maybe he should go easy on the Scotch. 'My country, my rules.'

'Of course.'

Holyrod emptied his glass. 'Things are still at a delicate stage. We need to stay under the radar.'

'You have my word.'

TWENTY-SIX

Squat and brooding on the south bank of the Thames, St Thomas's Hospital offered fine views of the Palace of Westminster. From the third floor, Carlyle looked out over the river towards the Parliament building. Darkness had fallen and lights shone brightly from almost every window. Doubtless the place was full of Members of Parliament fiddling their expenses, shagging their interns and preparing for their extended summer holidays, he thought. No wonder the country was run so poorly – the only apparent qualifications needed for the job of MP were ego and avarice.

For her part, Sandra Groves would not be contemplating this view for a while. Lying in a bed by the window in a room she shared with two other patients, she was drugged up to the eyeballs and fast asleep. Moved out of intensive care a few hours earlier, she was still in a very weak state. In addition to a smashed leg and a broken hip, she had suffered a couple of cracked ribs and a fractured wrist. Although she was out of immediate danger, the doctors were still worried about the concussion she had suffered, as well as the internal bleeding.

Standing in the corridor outside, Carlyle gazed at the sleeping woman. She certainly looked a mess, with tubes coming out of her nose and her left arm, as well as bandages on her head.

Sitting by her bedside, in front of an array of machines, Carlyle recognised Stuart Joyce, the boyfriend who had been involved in the confrontation on the number 55 bus. Holding the girl's hand, Joyce had his back to Carlyle as the inspector now entered the room. A couple of the other patients, hoping that he had perhaps come to visit them, tried to catch the inspector's eye as he stepped inside, but he studiously ignored them.

When he reached the end of the bed, the boy finally looked up. Carlyle was surprised to see him flinch.

'You!' Joyce hissed, eyeing the panic button by the bed. He half-rose out of his seat. 'What are *you* doing here?'

Carlyle, aware of the Ward Sister hovering nearby, ready to throw him out at the first sign of any trouble, held up a hand. 'A couple of quick things before we go any further,' he said, quietly but firmly, staring the boy down. 'First – I didn't run your girlfriend over.'

The boy looked at him suspiciously but returned to his seat.

'On the one hand,' Carlyle explained, 'I don't drive. On the other hand, I have a perfectly good alibi, which the officers investigating the case have checked out.' He knew this was true because of the ear-bashing he'd received from his wife, complaining about the disruption his 'colleagues' had caused to her working day. Helen had been very disgruntled indeed at having to help the police with their enquiries. Carlyle had been left in no doubt that he would need to provide a full explanation of exactly what the hell was going on, once he got home.

'So,' he continued, as soothingly as he could manage, 'you have nothing to worry about from me.'

Still the boy said nothing. Behind him, a machine bleeped. Carlyle gave the machine a professional stare. As he was the wrong kind of professional, he didn't know if the bleeping was anything important or not. If it was, a crack team of medical professionals would presumably come roaring in and take some action. The machine bleeped for a final time and then fell silent. The woman in the bed hadn't stopped breathing, so Carlyle assumed that things were okay. He returned his attention to the boyfriend. However, with his train of thought interrupted, he struggled to recall the second thing he wanted to say. For a moment, his mind went blank, then he pulled it back. 'Point number two,' he said, eyeing Joyce carefully, 'I'm here to help, if I can. I'm certainly not here to cause you any more trouble.'

'Like on the bus?' the boy whined.

Carlyle felt a twinge of embarrassment. 'What happened on the bus has been and gone. This,' he nodded at Sandra Groves, 'is much more serious.'

The boy shrugged. 'I told the other policemen all that I know.'

'Which is basically nothing.' Carlyle had read the preliminary report. Groves had been knocked down on Moreland Street, near City University, by a stolen Peugeot which had later been abandoned up past King's Cross station. A taxi had almost collided with the Peugeot, but the cabbie had not witnessed Groves being run down, nor had he been able to provide any kind of meaningful description of the Peugeot's driver. There were no other witnesses. The only available CCTV showed the car accelerating towards Groves, suggesting that it wasn't an accident but, again, it didn't get a clear view of the driver. The Peugeot had been taken to a nearby police depot and given the once-over by a team of technicians. They recovered traces of the injured woman's blood on the grille. Inside the car were various sets of fingerprints – none of which had shown a match on the national database.

This boy, apparently home alone at the time of the incident, had no alibi, but Carlyle couldn't see him doing it – he seemed too much of a wimp. Anyway, domestics rarely involved stolen cars; it was so much easier just to smack the offending partner over the head with a frying pan.

'What I'm wondering,' Carlyle continued, 'is why someone would want to do this to her.'

'Why would you care?'

'I didn't say I cared.' Carlyle smiled nastily, just to keep the boy on his toes. If the little do-gooder wanted to believe in the fascist bullyboy stereotype, that was fine by Carlyle. 'It's just that . . . well, it's just that it's come on to my radar.' Thinking about it on his way over to the hospital, that was the best explanation he had been able to come up with.

'What about the other policemen?' Joyce asked.

'This is still their case,' Carlyle replied. 'But I have another case currently under investigation and I'm wondering if there might be a connection.'

'So what do you want from me?' Joyce asked, clearly not convinced that he should be having this conversation.

'Tell me about what you guys were involved in.'

'We weren't involved in anything,' Joyce said defensively.

'You're political,' Carlyle said evenly. 'You were campaigning for – what?' His mind went blank. 'That advertising business on the side of the bus.'

'Religious beliefs.'

What about the beliefs of atheists? Carlyle thought, but he bit his tongue. 'That's right, I remember. It's kind of political, I suppose.'

'That's not a crime.'

'I didn't say that it was.' Carlyle fought to keep his irritation in check. 'Tell me about the things that are important to you guys. Tell about the campaigns you've supported.'

The boy looked at the woman in the bed. Then, realising he didn't have much else to do, he launched into a monologue he had clearly delivered many times before: 'We draw our inspiration from the Bible and from the social teachings of the Church . . .'

Which church? Carlyle wondered. That's the thing about churches; they all think they're 'the' church. His irritation level rose another notch, but again he said nothing.

'We want to help people who are poor, marginalised or oppressed,' the boy continued, 'and to fight injustice and poverty. There needs to be a global community that respects the rights and dignity of everyone. Discrimination must be ended.'

Good luck, sunshine, Carlyle thought. He wondered what all this had to do with filming the antics of Clive the nutty bus driver and making the traffic congestion on St Giles High Street even worse than normal.

'The bounty of creation should be shared by all. To do that we need social justice, underpinned by the Christian faith and the values of the Gospel.'

Carlyle failed to stifle a yawn.

'Am I boring you?' the boy asked sharply.

Of course you bloody are, Carlyle thought. 'No, no,' he mumbled, yawning again. 'Sorry, it's just that it has been a very long day.'

The boy looked at him doubtfully.

The next yawn the inspector managed to stifle – third time lucky. 'The Church – the campaign against unfairness – do you do any work in Latin America?'

'Of course. We campaign wherever there is injustice and poverty.'

'Anything specifically in Chile?'

The boy eyed him. 'Why?'

Just answer the fucking question. 'Humour me.'

'Maybe,' Joyce said. 'I'd have to check.'

'That organisation Sandra mentioned – the Daughters of Something or other – is that what you use to achieve all this?'

'Daughters of Dismas is one of the organisations that gets involved in the campaign, yes,' Joyce replied. 'But, obviously, it's for women only, so I can't really get involved that much.'

'How many members does it have?'

'Quite a few.'

I bet, Carlyle thought. 'What does that mean? Dozens? Hundreds? Thousands?'

'I wouldn't know exactly.'

Probably less than ten, Carlyle thought dismissively. He ploughed on. 'What type of people are members?'

'There are all sorts, from young activists like Sandra, through to old-timers – women who remember Greenham Common, things like that.'

Old-timers, thought Carlyle. Helen would love that. His wife had been to Greenham, the Women's Peace camp in Berkshire, several times in the early 1980s, protesting against American cruise missiles being based there. Carlyle hadn't thought about that for a long time. It was from before they had got together; before he'd even joined the police force – which was just as well or they might have met under very different circumstances. CND – the Campaign for Nuclear Disarmament – had been a big deal back then, in the days when the Russians were the number one enemy and no one had heard of Muslim fundamentalism. Now, it was all you heard. Carlyle wondered if CND was still going.

For all their time, effort and commitment, had those protestors ever achieved anything of note? Not as far as he could recall. The situation now was as bad as ever. The country was skint and yet the politicians were still spending billions on fantastically expensive weapons systems. Were they still pointed at the Russians? Who knew?

He wondered if he dared ask Helen about it. Looking back, she was as ambivalent as most middle-aged people were about their youthful idealism. Holding hands and singing songs – it all seemed so naïve now; just one of those things you did when you didn't really understand the way the world worked. Still, the idea of people fighting the same battles almost thirty years on filled him with sadness. He looked at the boy directly. 'Have you ever heard of a woman called Agatha Mills?'

Joyce shook his head. 'I don't think so, no.'

Carlyle considered him, unsure if he was telling the truth. Sandra Groves let out a low moan, then shifted in the bed and started snoring lightly. Joyce looked at her, until he was happy that she was still sleeping soundly. 'I usually only tagged along with Sandra when she was on her own,' he told Carlyle, 'like that day on the bus. When she was with her "sisters", she didn't like me being there. The Daughters of Dismas is supposed to be a women-only organisation.'

'Ah, yes,' Carlyle mumbled to himself. 'The sisterhood in action.'

Joyce gave him a funny look. 'What?'

'Nothing,' he said hurriedly. 'Where would I find a membership list?'

'You wouldn't,' said Joyce. 'We are law-abiding people. We don't need to be harassed by the police.'

Harassment? Carlyle thought wearily. You don't know you're born, you middle-class muppet. 'All right,' he said, 'if I wanted to find out if my Mrs Mills had been involved in Sandra's group, how might I do that?'

Joyce told him: 'If we checked and she was a member, she'd need to agree to let us share the information.'

'She won't be able to do that.'

'Why not?'

'She's dead.'

Joyce looked confused. 'Dead?'

'She was murdered,' sad Carlyle, without going into any of the details.

'Um.' Joyce looked a bit sick.

'So,' Carlyle continued, 'I am wondering if there is any connection between Agatha Mills and Sandra here. Maybe the person who killed Agatha was the same person who tried to run Sandra over. If there *is* a connection, that is very important for our investigation. It will help us track him down.'

He didn't add *before he tries again*, not wanting to wind the boy up any more.

Joyce sat and thought about it. As the colour began returning to his cheeks, he pulled a mobile out of the back pocket of his jeans and started a text message. 'I'll see what I can find out,' he said, concentrating on his texting.

'Thanks,' said Carlyle limply. His stomach growled and he suddenly realised how hungry he felt. He remembered seeing a coffee shop on the ground floor as he came in. With luck, it would still be open. He waited for Joyce to send his message. 'I'm going to buy a coffee and something to eat. Can I get you anything?'

The boy grunted. Carlyle took that as a yes – or maybe a no? – and wandered off.

He reached the ground floor to find the café shuttered. Inevitably, his stomach complained loudly. Carlyle issued a curse under his breath which got him a censorious look from an old woman shuffling by with the help of a walking frame. For a moment, he stood there unable to decide what to do next. Finally, he strode through the main doors and headed down Westminster Bridge Road, in search of some sustenance.

A greasy spoon that catered for cab drivers and other servants of the twilight economy allowed the inspector to refuel with a fried-egg roll, a jam doughnut and a double espresso. Half an hour later, he strolled back into the hospital carrying a small latte for Joyce. After another couple of minutes waiting for the lift, he reached the third floor. Walking into Groves's room, he saw Joyce slumped face-down over the bed. Stepping closer, he could see a small hole where the boy had been shot in the back of the head. The stench indicated that he'd voided his bowels, and a pool of urine had collected at his feet.

'Jesus Christ Almighty,' the inspector groaned, 'what a fucking mess.' With his legs turning to jelly, he had to force himself to step closer to the bed. Careful not to disturb anything, he made himself look at the pulverized face of Sandra Groves lying on a pillow stained black with blood. Shot several times in the face, she was, to all intents and purposes, no longer recognisable, no longer obviously human. Carlyle's gaze followed the blood splatter, his eyes stopping on a clump of hair and skin that had stuck to the wall above the bed. He felt sick to his stomach.

'I'm sorry,' he mumbled, for his own benefit rather than anything else. Taking a couple of deep breaths, he swallowed the bile in his throat and waited for the risk of his meal regurgitating to subside. Quickly, he took in the rest of the scene. The machines that Groves was still hooked up to stood silently by her bed, their screens blank. The killer had been careful to switch them off, to stop the alarm going off when her vital organs stopped functioning. On the bed, by Joyce's head, lay a small semi-automatic pistol. Carlyle took out his mobile phone and called the front desk at Charing Cross. This business wouldn't fall to them, but if he didn't get things started on the right foot, Carlyle knew that he could be in for an even longer night than the one he was already facing.

Sensing movement behind him, he swivelled round to confront the Ward Sister. 'What in the name of . . . ?' She tried to look beyond him, at the mess in the corner, so he shuffled a couple of steps sideways in a half-hearted attempt to block her view.

They were distracted from this stand-off by some movement from the bed nearest the door. A head emerged from under the covers, followed by a bony finger which pointed at the inspector. 'It was him! It was him!' the patient yelled through her a drug-induced haze. '*He* did it!'

The Sister looked at Carlyle cautiously, unsure of whether she should stand her ground or run for help. Bouncing on the balls of her feet, she looked ready to bolt, but his accuser's glassy, unfocused eyes gave her pause. The woman was so out of it, it was amazing she even realised that a shooting had occurred. Holding up a hand, Carlyle issued precise instructions over the phone, speaking loudly enough for the Ward Sister to understand that he had the situation under control.

Ending the call, he held the Sister's gaze. She was a chunky, no-nonsense-looking blonde, maybe ten years younger than he was. Not a bad-looking woman but, you could clearly see, well on the way to being crushed by the daily grind. Excitement like this she could do without. 'The police . . .' Carlyle started. 'More police will be here in a couple of minutes, along with a team of technicians and a pathologist – the usual crew.'

'Yes,' the Sister replied, her voice shaking just a little.

'Make sure that they are shown straight here.'

The woman nodded.

'In the meantime,' Carlyle told her, 'I don't want anyone passing up and down that corridor outside.'

'I understand,' the Sister said, more composed now. She half-turned and then stopped. 'What about the others?' She gestured at the other beds occupying the room. The woman who had pointed the finger at Carlyle had retreated back under her sheets; the other patient was snoring away happily, as she had been when he had first arrived. Either she was the world's soundest sleeper, Carlyle reckoned, or she was on some truly excellent medication.

He made a snap judgement. 'Leave them where they are for the moment. We'll need to talk to them. But I'll make sure you can get them moved as soon as possible.'

'Okay.' She turned and swiftly left the room.

After she had gone, Carlyle stepped away from the murder scene and took the lid off Joyce's coffee. He sipped it carefully. It was at best lukewarm now, but it was strong and it tasted good. He certainly wasn't going to throw it away. 'Waste not, want not,' he said to no one in particular. 'After all, this is going to be a long night.'

In the end, Carlyle spent almost four hours hanging around the hospital corridor before he was able to go home. It had taken a couple of hours for his new pals, Nick Chan and Greg Brown, to show up, and another hour before they were ready to talk to him. As far as Carlyle was concerned, that was fine. On this occasion, he would have to be professional courtesy and co-operation personified. For a start, he knew that he had a bit of explaining to do. Chan and Brown could really drop him in it if they wanted to. He could appeal to their goodwill but Carlyle knew that was not a good idea. Otherwise, all he could do was share his thoughts on a possible connection with the Agatha Mills killing and see if that might spark their imaginations.

'Sounds like a load of rubbish to me,' Brown snorted, after he had talked them through it.

Carlyle looked to Chan.

Chan shook his head. '"Rubbish" is the polite way of putting it.'

Recognising the reasonableness of their reaction, Carlyle gave a shrug. 'The late Mr Joyce here sent a text to someone before I went off to the café, to check if Mills was part of the same group as his girlfriend. Did he get a reply?'

'Let me see.' Brown wandered off.

Chan watched him go and turned to Carlyle. 'The gun is an Israeli semi-automatic, the Jericho 941, about fifteen years old. Not very common in this country.'

'Not very common at all,' Carlyle agreed.

Brown reappeared. 'No texts for Mr Joyce this evening, but we can try and track down the recipient of the message he sent.'

'Good.' Chan turned away from his colleague to face Carlyle. 'Inspector,' he said, 'you can go home now. We'll be in touch.'

'Fine,' said Carlyle as he headed towards the main lifts. 'You know where to find me.'

TWENTY-SEVEN

Carefully balancing a fragile but expensive-looking cup and saucer on his knee, Carlyle sat quietly waiting for Claudio Orb to take a sip of his own tea. High on the wall to Carlyle's left was a large photograph of a Chanel-clad woman who presumably was the current Chilean President. From behind the Ambassador, light flooded in through the French windows opening on to a small balcony which looked over the busy square just outside.

He had arrived almost on a whim. When Henry Mills had walked out in front of that van, his case had apparently solved itself. It could be easily put to bed, and no one would give it another thought. Sandra Groves was Chan's problem. Carlyle could put his feet up for a while and wait for the next pile of shit to come along. Being a restless soul, however, he knew that he wouldn't be able to leave it alone. The sense that there was more to this than met the eye was lodged in his brain. It was a feeling that he'd experienced many times before. He hated the idea of being taken for a ride – whether it was due to professional pride or personal vanity – and he wasn't minded to let things drop just yet.

Turning up at the Embassy, he had been cheered that his arrival had been greeted with neither surprise nor dismay. After passing through the most rudimentary of security checks, he had been sent up, on his own, to the Ambassador's office, where a very pretty, very young-looking secretary told him that Orb would see him in a couple of minutes. Barely ninety seconds later, he was sitting in front of the Ambassador's desk, while his host weighed up the relative merits of Fortnum's Smoky Earl Grey or their Piccadilly Blend. Having decided on the latter, Orb surprised Carlyle by getting up and scooting out of his office to go and make the tea himself. By the time he came back, Carlyle's opinion of Chile and Chileans couldn't have been higher.

After a tentative sip, Orb returned his cup to its saucer in the middle of his otherwise uncluttered desk, and looked up at Carlyle. 'It's a pleasure to see you again, Inspector,' he smiled. 'Tell me, how is your investigation going?'

Carlyle made a vague gesture with one hand, while keeping a firm grasp of his saucer with the other. 'These things always need to run their course.'

'Indeed they do.' Orb clasped his hands together over the desk as if in prayer. 'And what, if I may ask, happened to the husband?'

Having had enough of the balancing act, Carlyle reached down and placed his cup and saucer on the carpet beside his chair. 'He walked in front of a van,' he said, sitting back up.

'An accident?'

'Suicide.'

'Oh?' Orb looked nonplussed. 'But he was your main suspect?'

'Yes.'

'So is that it?' Orb asked. 'Is the case now closed?'

Carlyle shifted in his seat. 'Maybe.'

'Maybe?' Orb repeated. 'Don't be coy, Inspector, you must be here for more than a cup of tea, very nice though it is.'

Carlyle grinned. 'Maybe.'

'So . . .' The Ambassador's smile faded slightly, indicating that, although his welcome was genuine, neither his time nor his patience were infinite. 'How can I help you?'

'That gentleman I saw you standing with at City Hall . . . at the reception when we were first introduced?'

Orb reflected on it for a moment. 'You mean the Mayor, Mr Holyrod?'

'No. The other man. About your height, in his thirties, had a beard – good-looking guy, with a nice tan.'

'Ah, yes,' Orb said. 'Matias Gori.'

'Who is he?'

'He works here at the Embassy, as one of our military attachés. Does he have anything to do with this?'

Carlyle ignored the question. 'I've always wondered,' he mused. 'What does a military attaché actually do?'

'I know what you mean.' Orb picked up his cup and again sipped his tea, content to wait a little longer for the policeman to get to the point. 'I'm only the Ambassador, Inspector, so much of it is a mystery to me too. I think most people would probably assume that "military attaché" is just a polite way of saying someone is a spy. But it is usually more mundane than that.'

'Not everyone can be James Bond, I suppose.'

'No, especially nowadays. You can find out about most things you want to know about on the Internet, assuming that you can be bothered to spend some time searching. It's an amazing invention – my grandchildren simply have no concept of how we could have ever lived without it.'

'No,' Carlyle agreed. 'So where does that leave a military attaché these days? Are spies now basically redundant?'

'More or less,' Orb said, 'as far as I can see. Certainly for a small country like Chile they are not particularly important. Our military attachés do a bit of marketing for our defence companies, and a bit of research to keep the folks back home up to speed on the latest developments in important markets like Britain.'

'Has Gori been here long?'

Orb drained his cup and shrugged. 'I don't really know. He was already here when I arrived.' He did the sums in his head. 'So . . . I suppose that means he's been here for at least three years.'

'Where was he before he came to London?'

'We all move around, Inspector,' Orb told him. 'Gori has had various postings in the US, Spain, Iraq—'

'Iraq?'

'Of course. We were strong supporters of the war on terror.'

Carlyle sat up in his chair. 'Can I talk to him?'

'About your case?'

'Yes.'

'Well, technically, he would be within his rights to decline to speak to the Metropolitan Police – diplomatic immunity and all that.' Seeing that Carlyle was about to speak again, Orb held up his hand. 'However, when I said the other day that I'm always happy to help the police with their enquiries, I meant it. If Señor Gori is happy to speak with you, then I would be happy to sanction such a conversation.'

'Thank you.'

Orb made a gesture indicating that it was nothing. 'But you understand that it has to be his decision.'

'Yes.'

'Very good.' Orb reached across his desk and pressed a button on the phone. 'Claudia?'

'*Si, embajador?*' the secretary replied instantly.

Orb looked at Carlyle. 'In English, please.'

'Yes?'

'Could you ask Matias Gori to come in here for a minute, please?'

'I'm very sorry, sir. I don't think Mr Gori is here at present.'

Orb raised his eyebrows and a look of irritation clouded his face. 'Do you know where he is?'

'I will double-check with his assistant,' the secretary replied, 'but I'm fairly sure that he had a flight to Madrid this morning. He was going back to Santiago.'

Orb sighed. 'I see. Please check for me and let me know if that's the case. And find out when he is due back in London.'

'Of course.'

Orb ended the call. 'I'm sorry, Inspector,' he said, pushing his chair away from the desk and getting to his feet. 'It looks as if you are out of luck today.'

Carlyle rose up and took a half-step towards the desk, hand outstretched. 'Not a problem. Thank you for your help.'

'My pleasure,' smiled Orb, shaking his hand.

Carlyle stood his ground, however, happy to push things a little further. 'Maybe I could see Mr Gori when he gets back to London?'

'Will the case still be open then?'

'Perhaps, perhaps not. In the meantime, if he could call me from Santiago, that would be a help.'

'I will see what I can do,' Orb said, shuffling round the table and guiding Carlyle towards the door. 'Now, sadly, I have a rather dull meeting to attend, so Claudia will show you out.'

'Thank you again for your time.'

'It's nothing.' Orb patted him on the shoulder. 'Let me know how you get on. I find this kind of thing fascinating.'

Back out on the street, watching the traffic snake erratically round Portman Square, Carlyle realised that the Embassy was little more than ten minutes' walk from the Paddington offices of Avalon, the international medical aid charity where his wife worked as a senior administrative manager. Deciding to seize the moment, he headed up the Edgware Road and presented himself in front of a comatose-looking receptionist with a ring through her nose that made her look even uglier than she already was.

After an extended discussion with Helen's PA about whether Ms Kennedy would want to see her husband, nose-ring girl informed Carlyle that he should take a seat and his wife would be down in a minute. Almost twenty minutes later, she finally appeared, looking hassled and not particularly pleased to see him.

'What are you doing here?' she asked suspiciously.

'I was on business nearby,' Carlyle said, raising himself out of the tatty faux-leather sofa. He set his jaw tight, determined to retain a cheery demeanour despite the grumpiness of his better half. 'I thought we could grab some lunch.'

'You could have called,' she replied, hoisting an oversized sack-type bag bearing a logo he didn't recognise on to her shoulder, before turning on her heel and heading for the revolving door leading to the street.

'I guess that's a "yes" then,' Carlyle muttered sotto voce, as he followed at a safe distance.

Once he had caught her up, they settled for a Mexican restaurant a brisk five-minute walk away, halfway between Paddington railway station and Hyde Park. The place was busy, but they had been here before and knew the service would be good. Confident that she could be in and out in forty-five minutes, Helen relaxed slightly. Once they had ordered a selection of quesadillas and enchiladas, she even managed a smile. 'This is a nice surprise,' she said, albeit belatedly, 'particularly as you were home so late last night.'

At least she didn't say *again*, Carlyle thought as he nibbled on a tortilla chip. Concentrating on trying to stay in the happy zone, he didn't really want to talk about his work, but he knew that wasn't an option. Helen was not one of those women who could let her husband go off to work every day and not give a moment's further thought to what he did or how he did it. She always kept track of what he was up to: his cases and, even more keenly, the endless cycle of the Met's internal politics. In this regard, Carlyle knew that he was a very lucky chap. Now, more than ever, Helen was his main sounding-board and adviser. She was discreet, decisive and insightful, and he trusted her judgement completely.

She looked at him expectantly, so Carlyle leaned across the table, keeping his voice low. He didn't want the people at the next table – a couple of girls currently discussing different mobile-phone tariffs – tuning into their conversation. 'It was quite a night . . .' He smiled wanly, before going on to explain how Sandra Groves and Stuart Joyce had been executed while he was down the road munching an egg roll.

He gave her the two-minute version, avoiding too many details that might put her off her lunch when it came. Even so, by the time he'd finished, Helen managed to look pale and angry at the same time. 'Thank Christ you weren't there!' she hissed.

But I was there, Carlyle thought. 'What do you mean?'

She picked a knife off the table and waved it in his general direction. 'I mean, Inspector bloody Carlyle, that if you hadn't gone off to get yourself something to eat, they'd have shot you as well.'

They were just then interrupted by the arrival of the waitress with their food, which saved him from having to admit that he hadn't thought of that.

For a short while they ate in silence. After a couple of mouthfuls of enchilada, Helen seemed to have successfully overcome her shock at Carlyle's near brush with death. 'So why *did* that poor girl get shot?' she asked.

'Dunno,' said Carlyle. 'It's not my case.'

Helen daintily wiped the corners of her mouth with a napkin. 'If it's not your case,' she said finally, 'then why were you at the hospital?'

'Well . . .' Once again, Carlyle gave her the short version: a quick explanation about the Daughters of Dismas, and his idea about a possible connection between Agatha Mills and Sandra Groves. 'The boyfriend said that they had some old-timers in their group; the kind of people who had been campaigning against all this sort of stuff for decades.' He smiled meekly. 'The kind of people who used to go to Greenham Common.'

'There was nothing wrong with going to Greenham,' Helen said tartly. 'I did it myself, after all.'

Carlyle sat back in his chair and held up a hand. 'I know, I know.'

'And if I'd come across you on the front line, I wouldn't have fancied your chances.'

Me neither, Carlyle thought.

'I'm glad I had the spirit to do that,' Helen continued. 'I hope Alice has it about her too.'

'Yes,' Carlyle agreed readily.

Helen watched him carefully, waiting to see if he could resist poking fun at her youthful idealism back in the day. When she was satisfied that he had, for once, managed to resist the temptation to tease her, she said: 'What was the name of that group of women again?'

'Daughters of Dismas.'

'Never heard of it.'

'No reason why you should have.' Carlyle shrugged. 'Dismas was some old-time religious guy in the Bible. He hung out with Jesus – something like that. They're just a bunch of religious loonies.'

'But I know someone who will.' Helen reached down under the table and pulled her bag on to her lap. After rummaging around for a few seconds, she found her mobile and started searching through the contacts list. The girls at the next table had moved on from talking about technology to discussing sex and were casually comparing STDs. Carlyle tried not to listen, watching Helen hit the call button as he began contemplating a plate of *churros y chocolate*.

'Clara, it's Helen. Hi! How are the boys? Good, yes, we're all fine.' She looked over at Carlyle and grinned. 'Yes, he's still a policeman. I know, I'm giving up hope of him ever getting a proper job.'

Carlyle made a face and she stuck her tongue out at him.

'Look, Clara, sorry to interrupt lunch, but I just wanted to check something quickly. Have you ever heard of an organisation called Daughters of Dismas – *Dismas*. They're a kind of international church campaign against poverty. What I need to know is whether a woman called . . .'

'Agatha Mills,' Carlyle chipped in.

'Whether a woman called Agatha Mills is a member. I think it's quite urgent, that's why I've rung. That's very kind of you. Yes, on the mobile. Speak soon – bye!'

Clara? Carlyle couldn't place her, but that was no great surprise. He only paid the vaguest attention to Helen's network of friends, acquaintances, colleagues and contacts, which was far bigger than his own. 'Who was that?' he asked.

'No one who would ever be prepared to talk to you,' Helen said sweetly, scanning the menu. 'Professionally speaking, of course.'

'That doesn't narrow it down much,' Carlyle grinned. 'Fancy a pudding?'

'Just a green tea for me,' she replied, 'but if you've got your eye on the chocolate doughnuts, don't let me stop you.'

The waitress cleared the table. With some effort, Carlyle restricted himself to a double espresso. The drinks arrived within a few minutes and he was on his first sip when Helen's mobile started vibrating on the table. She pressed it to her ear. 'Clara? My goodness, that was quick. Yes, all right . . . interesting. Look, thanks a million for coming back to me so quickly. If I need anything else on this, can I give you a call? Lovely. Thanks again. Speak soon. Bye!'

She ended the call and dropped the phone back into her bag.

'Well?' he asked.

'Well, well, Inspector,' she grinned, taking a sip of her tea. 'You might be on to something after all. Not only was Agatha Mills a member of Daughters of Dismas, she even worked for them for a couple of years.'

'Here, in London?'

'In Chile.'

Fuck, Carlyle thought, that *is* interesting.

Taking another mouthful of tea, Helen hauled her bag on to her shoulder and stood up. 'I've got to get back to work,' she said, reaching over the table to plant a kiss on his forehead. 'Try and get home early tonight.'

'I will.'

'Good,' she said, edging between the tables. 'Thank you for lunch. You can pay, as I think I've earned it.'

Having duly paid the bill, Carlyle took the tube back to Tottenham Court Road and walked down towards Charing

Cross police station. Turning into William IV Street, he was surprised to see the road cordoned off, with a small crowd milling by the police tape. Stepping past the gawkers and ducking under the tape, he flashed his warrant card at a young-looking WPC that he didn't recognise.

'What's going on?' Carlyle asked.

'I'm not sure, sir,' said the flustered officer, 'but everyone was ordered out of the building about an hour ago.' She nodded in the direction of the Ship and Shovel on the corner. 'Most of them have gone down the pub.'

That figures, Carlyle thought. Feeling a hand on his shoulder, he turned around.

'Hello, boss.' Joe Szyszkowski returned the hand to his jacket pocket and rocked gently on his heels.

'What's going on?' Carlyle repeated.

'It's Dennis Felix.'

'Who?'

'The bongo player in the piazza.' Joe pulled him away from the WPC, so they were now standing in the middle of the empty road. 'Apparently,' he said in a stage whisper, 'he'd contracted anthrax.'

Carlyle scratched his head. 'Jesus!'

'Quite. They reckon that he must have caught it from the animal skins he used on his bongo drums.'

'Unlucky,' said Carlyle, trying to dredge up some information from the recesses of his brain about what anthrax was and how exactly you caught it. As far as he could recall, you inhaled spores, but what that might have to do with animal skins, he had no idea. Bloody hell! He suddenly wondered – could he have caught it too? As far as he could recall, he hadn't actually touched the drums, but had got reasonably close to take a look. As casually as he could manage, he rubbed his throat and gave a little cough. Maybe he *was* feeling a bit under the weather today?

'They've sent in a couple of guys wearing biohazard suits,' Joe continued, oblivious to his boss's personal medical concerns, 'to collect the bongos from the evidence locker. The station was evacuated about half an hour ago.'

'Jesus.' Carlyle rubbed his throat more vigorously this time.

'It's caused quite a stir.'

'I can imagine,' Carlyle replied, worried about the little tickle he could now detect in his throat whenever he swallowed.

'And Dave Prentice has been sent off to the hospital for a check-up.'

Prentice? What about me? Telling himself not to be such a big girl's blouse, Carlyle considered how he had been the one who had told Prentice to bring the damn bongos back to the station. He couldn't have known that they were a bloody health hazard, but if Prentice got sick or, God forbid, died, Carlyle could easily see how it could end up being his fault. He felt his pulse quicken slightly. 'It can't be that serious, can it?'

'Nah,' Joe replied, looking slightly less than completely convinced. 'You know what these things are like – panic, scare people shitless, then walk away. It's the usual drill.'

Let's hope so, Carlyle thought.

'Anyway,' said Joe, 'I think I'm going to call it a day. The missus is cooking a curry tonight. See you tomorrow.'

'Okay, see you tomorrow.' Carlyle watched Joe set off down the road and wondered what he himself should do next. He had reached no particular conclusion, when Joe stopped, turned and walked halfway back towards him.

'I almost forgot,' the sergeant shouted. 'You had a call from a Fiona Singleton.'

Carlyle made a face indicating that the name hadn't registered.

'She's a sergeant at Fulham,' Joe explained.

Singleton, Carlyle now remembered, was the officer who had listened to Rosanna Snowdon's complaint about her stalker, a loser called . . . Carlyle tried to recall the guy's name from their meeting at Patisserie Valerie, but it was another detail that escaped him. Maybe anthrax made your memory go funny. 'Did she say what it was about?'

'No.' Joe shook his head.

At least she's discreet, Carlyle thought. He held up a hand to Joe. 'Okay, I'll give her a call. Thanks. See you tomorrow.'

'Sure, no problem.' Joe turned and headed off again. This time he kept going. Carlyle watched him disappear round the corner, then took his official work mobile out of his jacket pocket, found the number he wanted and listened to it ring. He was almost resigned to leaving a voicemail, when a real live person finally responded at the other end.

'Hello?'

'Susan?'

'Ah, John,' the woman laughed. 'Let me guess, you are standing on Agar Street, wondering what the hell is going on?'

'Actually,' he told her, 'I'm just round the corner wondering what the hell is going on.'

'Not a bad guess, huh?'

'Susan Phillips – so much more than just your everyday pathologist.'

'I'll take that as a compliment.'

'It most definitely is a compliment. What the hell *is* going on? My sergeant tells me it's an anthrax scare. Should I be running to find the nearest hospital or the nearest priest?'

'Neither really,' Phillips sighed, all laughter draining from her voice now. 'What's happening down there is a complete overreaction. Poor Mr Felix did indeed die as a result of inhaling anthrax, almost certainly transferred from the skins on his drums.'

'How did he manage that?'

'He was a guy who liked to travel and I'm guessing that he got the skins in Africa. It's fairly common for animals to ingest or inhale the spores while grazing. Diseased animals can spread anthrax to humans. Maybe he ate the flesh or, more likely, inhaled some spores while putting the skins on the drums himself.'

'Poor sod,' said Carlyle, with feeling.

'He was very, very unlucky,' Phillips agreed. 'It's not unheard of, but the risk to anyone else has got to be negligible.'

'So what's with the boys in the Noddy suits?' Carlyle asked.

'Good question,' Phillips replied. 'Someone should have come along and quietly removed the evidence. Then I could have run some further tests and we could have kept an eye on anyone we thought might have had even a tiny chance of catching anything. Going into the station like that was way over the top.'

'Whose decision was it?'

There was a pause on the other end of the line. 'Who do you think?'

'Simpson?'

Phillips lowered her voice a notch. 'Commander Carole Simpson, everyone's favourite bureaucrat.'

'But how did this problem reach all the way up to her?'

'You know how these things work, John,' Phillips said. 'No one would make a decision, so it was kicked up the chain of command until it got to someone who couldn't pass the buck any further and had to do something.'

'Safety-first Simpson.'

'This isn't safety first,' Phillips scoffed, 'this is blind panic. She's probably petrified of being sued by anyone who's stepped inside Charing Cross in the last twenty-four hours.'

'Quite,' Carlyle agreed. 'Maybe I should sue her myself.'

Phillips laughed. 'Maybe you should. I'm sure your Federation rep would be only too happy to help.'

'No question about it.'

There were voices in the background. Phillips told someone, 'Don't worry, I'm coming,' and there was a pause while she listened to a reply. 'John,' she said, coming back on the line, 'I need to get on now. But don't worry. Trust me, there's no risk. Doubtless there'll be lots of messing about for the next few hours, but everything should be back to normal by tomorrow morning. If I were you, I'd just take the rest of the afternoon off.'

'Good idea!' Carlyle was pleased that his fears had been

allayed. 'Thanks for the tip. Good to speak to you, Susan. See you soon.'

'You too, John. Take care.'

The line went dead and Carlyle stood for a moment glancing up and down the street. Nothing much had changed: still the same WPC on one side of the tape and a small group of onlookers on the other. Then he saw a camera crew making its way towards them from the direction of St Martin's Lane. 'That's my cue to leave,' he said to himself and set off in the opposite direction, heading towards the piazza where Dennis Felix had drummed his last.

Reaching King Street, he checked the clock on his mobile. He just about had time for a quick workout at Jubilee Hall gym and still get home in time to meet Alice when she got back from school. That was the kind of metrosexual multi-tasking that would impress Helen more than his making it over to Paddington for lunch. At least, he hoped so. Bringing the handset to his ear, he let a smile cross his lips as he prepared to give her the good news.

TWENTY-EIGHT

The weather had turned cold. It was grey and damp. Three hours earlier, when Carlyle had left the flat, clear blue skies offered the hint of a pleasant summer day. Now it seemed a facsimile of February in June. Cursing himself for ignoring the weather forecast and leaving his raincoat at home, he cast his gaze to the heavens and hoped that the surrounding trees would offer him some protection from the imminent rain.

Despite his discomfort, this was the right kind of weather for a funeral. Carlyle had long ago decided that getting buried on a beautiful summer's day would just be the final insult – the universe taking the piss. Dark, dank and introspective – that was how he wanted the proceedings when his own time came.

Waiting for the deluge, he forced himself to lighten up. With luck, his time would be a while in coming yet. For Agatha and Henry Mills, however, their time had already come. In their respective wills, the pair had stipulated that they be buried together in the Pettigrew family mausoleum at Lavender Hill Cemetery in North London. Carlyle had picked up a leaflet at the main gate. Pulling it from his pocket, he found his present location on the small map.

The Pettigrew family had a vestibule mausoleum on a plot near the centre of the cemetery. It looked like a small granite house (or a very big children's playhouse). Walking around it, Carlyle could still hear music coming from the non-conformist chapel by the main gate. The idea struck him that this was the kind of place that he himself would want to be buried in – above ground, with some fresh air, a little sunlight and a good view.

Walking around the plot for a second time, Carlyle now realised that the door to the mausoleum had been unlocked in anticipation of the two new arrivals. Glancing around to make sure he wasn't being watched, he gave it a gentle push and, ducking his head, stepped inside. Illuminated by the light from a small round window at the back was a narrow aisle, long enough for each casket to be slid sideways into one of the three crypts on each side. One side was already full, the other empty. Each crypt had a small wooden plaque listing a name, and the deceased's dates of birth and death. Crouching down even further, Carlyle read the names of Tomas and Sylvie Pettigrew, Agatha's parents, who had been buried there in the 1970s, along with one Walter Henry, who died on 4 August 1956 – presumably one of her grandparents. On the empty side, he read the freshly added names of Agatha *née* Pettigrew and Henry Mills. At the back, in faded script, was a plaque below the space that had been reserved for William Pettigrew, the missing priest. No date of death had been added.

Since there was no remaining family, there was no one to suggest that the circumstances of her departure from this life might have caused Agatha to change her mind about being buried beside her husband and suspected killer. Carlyle was pleased about that; he was more convinced than ever that Henry Mills had not killed his wife. That theory of course, was not playing well back at the station. Simpson was pressing him for his final report, so that the case could be formally declared closed and another tick placed in the 'win' box. The report, however, had yet to be completed. Simpson's patience was wearing thin and the inspector knew that he would not be able to stall her for much longer.

Indeed, Simpson would be horrified to know that he was here rather than devoting his energies to the latest case she had dropped on his desk – a series of robberies targeting wealthy members of the audience at the Royal Opera House. Carlyle, like Simpson and everyone else, knew that it had to be an inside job, but interviewing dozens of highly strung staff, with only Joe Szyszkowski and a couple of Community Support officers to help him, was going to take him weeks. Anyway, Carlyle thought, if the victims could afford £350 for a ticket and another £200 or so for dinner in the Amphitheatre restaurant afterwards, it was hard to be too sympathetic to their plight.

The inspector stepped back outside. As expected, the rain had started coming down quite heavily, and he ran for the cover of a large pine tree that stood about twenty yards from the mausoleum. From there, he watched a large, sleek, midnight-blue Volvo hearse containing both coffins heading slowly towards him. It was followed by what he thought was a surprisingly large number of mourners, who were making their way up the gentle slope on foot. A minute or so later, the hearse stopped in front of the mausoleum. As if on cue, the rain eased off to almost nothing. Four undertakers jumped out smartly and readied themselves, before waiting for the group of mourners – maybe thirty strong – to take their places, before opening the back of the Volvo and removing the first coffin.

At that moment, without warning, Justin Timberlake blared out across the cemetery. Eyes turned and mouths muttered; this might have been a non-conformist ceremony but a blast of 'LoveStoned' was clearly taking things a bit too far. Mortified at the disturbance he was causing, the inspector tried to pull the phone out of his pocket and shut it up. 'Bloody Alice!' he muttered as he jogged behind the tree, hoping that out of sight would be out of mind. It wasn't the first time his daughter had changed the ringtone on his phone without him knowing it; he would kill the little so-and-so when he got home. In his panic, he hit the 'receive', rather than the 'end' button. His relief at Justin's departure from the scene was offset by the unpleasant realisation that someone was still on the line.

Feeling completely put upon by the technology, Carlyle moved further away from the disapproving mourners, in the hope that his continuing breach of funeral etiquette would be less intrusive. He lifted the handset to his ear. 'Hello?' he half-whispered.

'Inspector Carlyle? This is Fiona Singleton from Fulham.' The words came out quickly, as if she was trying to get them out before he could stop her.

Shit, Carlyle thought.

'I've been trying to get hold of you for a few days now,' Singleton continued. 'I left you a couple of messages at Agar Street . . .'

'Ah, yes,' Carlyle said keeping his voice low and his eyes on the coffins, which were now being carried inside the mausoleum. 'Apologies for that. We've been having a few problems at Charing Cross.'

'Yes,' said Singleton sympathetically, 'the anthrax thing. It must have caused quite a scare.'

'Not really,' Carlyle replied. Singleton's tone caused him to relax a bit; at least she wasn't giving him a hard time for not returning her call. 'It was probably all a rather OTT, to be honest.' Phillips was right; it had all been a twenty-four-hour wonder. No one had been discovered with any symptoms and even Dave Prentice had been given a clean bill of health. The station had returned to normal the next day.

'Anyway,' said Singleton, 'you know why I'm ringing?'

'Yes,' Carlyle said, looking back down the slope. The rain had stopped, for the moment at least. Agatha and Henry Mills had been laid to rest and the mourners were already beginning to drift away. If he was going to get anything useful from this trip, he had to get going. 'Look,' he said hastily, 'I'm at a funeral right now. Can I call you back in an hour or so?'

'I suppose,' Singleton sighed, resigning herself to being fobbed off yet again.

'Okay, thanks.' Carlyle ended the call and walked back round the tree towards the mausoleum. The funeral directors were standing patiently by their hearse, waiting for the last of the mourners to begin making their way back to the front gate. They watched Carlyle amble by, saying nothing.

The inspector stopped a couple of yards beyond their Volvo, watching the scattered groups of people heading down the road. What was he looking for here? Someone who looked as if she might be a member of Daughters of Dismas? Someone who looked Chilean? Someone who might know Sandra Groves? Distracted by the phone call from Singleton, his mind seemed unable to focus on the matter in hand. Thoughts of Rosanna Snowdon began monopolising his brain. It struck him that there had been nothing more of substance in the newspapers about her death. He was surprised that the stalker hadn't been arrested yet. Not for the first time, he wondered if he should feel guilty about his failure to help Rosanna at the time, but once again concluded that there wasn't much he could have done anyway. As his minded wandered, he also wondered what he was going to say to Fiona Singleton, and what he was going to have for lunch – but not necessarily in that order.

Trying to snap out of his funk, Carlyle set his gaze on a pair of women – perhaps a mother and daughter – walking thirty yards further down the road. He had just resolved to talk to them when he became aware of someone arriving by his shoulder. He turned to face a tanned, handsome man wearing an expensive-looking raincoat, which he wore over a classic black suit, with a white shirt and a black tie. The overall effect was of someone who had just stepped out of an Armani advert. The man was holding out his hand, so Carlyle shook it.

'Matias Gori.'

You've shaved off the beard, Carlyle thought. 'Inspector John Carlyle.'

'Yes,' Gori smiled, 'I know.'

That's enough of a preamble, you smug git, Carlyle thought. 'What are you doing here?' he asked abruptly.

Gori lowered his eyes, but retained the smile. 'The Ambassador told me you wanted to speak to me. He also wished the

Embassy to pay our respects to the Mills family.' He gestured to a large wreath propped up against the entrance to the mausoleum. Attached to the front of it was a message in Spanish – *con más sentido pésame* – which Carlyle didn't understand, but he got the drift. Carlyle recalled the funeral notice – *No flowers. Please send any donations to the Catholic Aid Foundation* – but said nothing. His gaze fell to the military attaché's beautifully polished shoes.

'How did you know that I would be here?'

'I didn't,' Gori shrugged. 'But here you are, so I can kill two birds with the one stone, as the saying goes.'

Carlyle let Gori place a gentle hand on his back and steer him down the access road. The rain was still holding off but he knew it would soon start pouring again. After a few moments, the Volvo rolled up behind them and they stepped off the tarmac and on to the grass to let it pass. As they waited, Gori opened his raincoat and pulled out a packet of Marlboros from an inside pocket. He offered one to Carlyle.

'No, thanks.' The inspector shook his head.

Gori took a cigarette and stuck it between his teeth. As he fumbled in another pocket for his lighter, Carlyle noticed a pin, like a small golden dagger, attached to his jacket lapel. Gori lit his cigarette and inhaled deeply, holding in the smoke for a few seconds before exhaling it past Carlyle's head. Noticing Carlyle staring at the dagger emblem, he casually but quickly closed up his raincoat, before stepping back on to the tarmac.

Carlyle waited patiently while Gori took another drag on his cigarette.

'So why are *you* here?' the military attaché asked finally.

'Simply to pay my respects,' Carlyle said evenly.

Gori gave him a quizzical look. 'Do you attend the funerals of all your victims?'

'They're not *my* victims.' Carlyle smiled politely, to show that he wasn't put out at being questioned. 'And, no, I don't always go to the funerals, not at all.'

'But in this case, yes.'

'Well, Agatha Mills was a remarkable woman.'

Gori removed the cigarette from his mouth and looked at it carefully. 'So they tell me.'

Carlyle waited for Gori to expand on this comment. When it was clear that nothing else would be forthcoming, he changed tack: 'I thought that you were supposed to be in Santiago.'

Gori contemplated his surroundings, 7,000 miles from home, and sighed. 'I was, but it was just a flying visit, only three days.'

'That's a long way to go for such a short time.'

'I know,' Gori shrugged. 'It's a shame, but that's part of the job.'

'So, what is the job?' Carlyle asked. 'What is it that you do?'

Gori laughed. 'The Ambassador told me that you two had discussed that.' He stopped and wagged a friendly finger. 'Don't worry, Inspector, there's nothing illegal or controversial involved, apart from maybe the odd unpaid parking ticket. And all embassies have those.'

'Indeed.'

'It's all very dull really.'

Never trust a man who can't – or won't – explain what he does for a living, Carlyle reflected. 'Did you know Agatha Mills?' he asked.

'No.' Gori bit his lower lip. 'Why?'

'You know about her connection to Chile?' the inspector asked.

'As I understand it, she had a Chilean father.'

'And a brother who was a priest there.'

Gori said nothing but there was a clear flicker of interest in his eyes as he waited to see if the annoying policeman would show his hand.

'He died during the coup in 1973.' Carlyle gestured towards the mausoleum. 'His name was William Pettigrew. There's a place waiting for him in there. They're still looking for the body. Or they were.'

Gori's eyes narrowed slightly. 'Thanks to your conversations with the Ambassador, we know about the family's long-standing links to our country.'

'What do you think about all that?' Carlyle probed.

'About what?' Gori resumed his leisurely pace back towards the front gate.

'About what happened to her brother?'

'Her brother!' Gori snorted. 'Isn't that the whole point, Inspector? No one knows what happened to him.'

'But there will be a trial?' Carlyle replied almost casually.

'Perhaps.' Gori did a little quickstep dance on the tarmac, gesticulating with his hands in front of his face. 'But, after all this time, how can anyone hope to get to the truth?'

'So you think it's a waste of time?'

Realising that he was giving too much away, Gori quickly got his body language back under control. 'It's nothing to do with me, Inspector. The legal process will take its course.'

'But you must have a view?'

Gori sighed theatrically. 'For what it's worth, I think that one should always look forwards, rather than back.'

How very convenient, Carlyle thought. 'Were you involved in what happened back then?'

'In 1973?' Gori frowned. 'I was barely two years old.'

'But your family?' Carlyle persisted.

'Not really.'

Not really? It was a yes or no question, Carlyle thought angrily.

'No more so than anyone else,' Gori added. 'Anyway, as I said, we are the kind of people who look to the future, Inspector. We do not wallow in the vagaries of the barely remembered past.'

They reached the front gate. It was starting to rain again, and Carlyle faced a long walk down Cedar Road in search of a bus stop. Gori pulled something out of his pocket and aimed it at the gleaming grey Mercedes sports car parked on a double yellow line across the road. The car beeped noisily as the doors unlocked. 'I would offer you a lift, Inspector,' he said, glancing at the leaden skies, 'but I'm going the opposite way.'

'Don't worry,' replied Carlyle through gritted teeth as he felt a fat raindrop land directly on the crown of his head. He forced what he hoped was something approaching a nonchalant grin onto his face. 'One last thing, though?'

'Yes?' said Gori, stepping quickly over towards his car.

'Do you know a woman called Sandra Groves?'

In one fluid movement, Gori pulled open the car door and slid inside. He looked past Carlyle as if wishing for the heavens to open up completely. An increasingly rapid procession of raindrops bounced off the windshield and he licked his lips. 'No,' he said finally. 'Should I?'

'No,' said Carlyle, getting ready to beat a hasty retreat to the gatehouse. 'Thank you for your time. And give the Ambassador my regards.'

But Gori had already slammed the car door shut and put the car into gear. As Carlyle watched the Mercedes pull away, the rain became heavier. Within seconds, he was soaked to the skin. Giving up the search for shelter, he began slowly walking down the road.

TWENTY-NINE

Sitting in her office on the twelfth floor of the ugly 1960s office block that was invariably described as 'Britain's most intimidating police station', Commander Carole Simpson held her head in her hands as she fought back the urge to burst into tears. Things were not going according to plan. Without doubt, this was turning into the worst day of her life.

In the basement below, one of her assistants was giving a small group of select journalists a guided tour of the station's special cells for terrorist suspects, which had just been refurbished at a cost of half a million pounds. With brown paper lining the walls – to ensure that suspects would not come into contact with anything that they could later claim contaminated them – and facilities for watching films and listening to music, this project had been Simpson's baby. She had managed it well, and today was supposed to see her reward for getting the work finished on time and (more or less) on budget, as well as her putting up with all the moaning from anti-Terror officers that these new arrangements were too luxurious for some of Britain's most wanted criminals.

Never shy when it came to personal publicity, Simpson had been looking forward for several weeks to another all-too-fleeting moment in the media spotlight. The Commander had come to understand that she had to work hard for her 'share of voice' in the media, and no opportunity to promote the personal Simpson brand could be passed up. Building a profile was essential if she was to keep climbing up the Met hierarchy. All through her career, she had seen journalists as allies.

Not any more.

Now she was shark chum.

That morning, just before 6 a.m., she had been rudely awakened by a couple of burly, unshaven men hammering on the front door of her Highgate home. Always a light sleeper, Simpson jumped out of bed, cursing her husband, who was happily snoring away. Pulling back the curtains, she opened the window and stuck her head out.

'Bugger off,' she shouted, 'or I'll call the police.'

'We *are* the police, madam,' one of the men had smirked up at her; his tone all the more galling given that he had to know exactly who she was.

She hadn't realised it at the time, but the officers had a camera crew and a couple of newspaper journalists in tow. The first copy was already being filed, the first pictures transmitted down the wires, as Simpson went downstairs and sheepishly opened the front door. She was in the process of being done up like a kipper.

Forty-five minutes later, she was again standing on the doorstep, nursing a mug of black coffee, as she watched her husband, now in handcuffs, being bundled into the back of a black Range Rover by one of the officers. The other was busy loading cardboard boxes full of documents into the car boot. Earlier she had watched in disbelief as Joshua was informed of his rights and told he was being arrested on suspicion of conspiracy to defraud.

'Get me the lawyer,' was the only thing he had said to her, before they led him out of the house.

Now, more than six hours later, the enormity of the mess she was in was becoming painfully clear. The front page of the evening paper's website had a picture of Carole and Joshua posing on their wedding day – where on earth had they got *that* from? – under a headline that screamed ***TOP COP'S HUSBAND***

ARRESTED FOR £650M PONZI SCAM. Joshua was dubbed '*the British Bernie Madoff*', after the disgraced American financier who had been given 150 years in prison for masterminding a £30 billion fraud that had wiped out thousands of investors.

Simpson finished reading the story and winced. The way the piece read, she herself had to be either a knowing accomplice or a complete fool for not noticing what was going on right under her nose. She placed her palms flat on the desk and tried some deep breathing. Next to her right hand lay a single sheet of A4 with a statement typed on it, running to just a couple of paragraphs. It hadn't yet been picked up on by the denizens of the worldwide web, but the Met had at least managed to put out a press release stating that the commander herself was in no way suspected of any wrongdoing and that she would continue to perform her duties.

Simpson thought about that for a moment. How had they managed to come to such a definitive conclusion about her so quickly? Simpson didn't want to think about it. Both she and Joshua must have been under long-term surveillance in the run-up to his arrest. The buggers would have gone through everything – bank statements, phone records, emails – with a fine-tooth comb.

With a trembling hand, she picked up the statement and read it again. As messages of support went, it was as much as she could hope for right now. In the longer term, she knew that her career was over. So far today there had been precisely zero messages of support from any of the higher-ups. The only call had come from Human Resources, offering her some 'compassionate leave'. Simpson snorted at the thought. What kind of mug did they take her for? Once they got her out the door it would be hard, maybe even impossible, to get back in. The leave would drift into (very) early retirement or, worse, a posting to some hopeless Community Liaison job in some shitty part of the capital.

Drumming her fingers on the desk, the Commander tried to force herself to think. The family lawyer, a former Government prosecutor called John Lucas who charged an astonishing £800 an hour, was currently meeting with Joshua at Kentish Town police station (at least they hadn't brought him here, to Paddington!). Once that was over, Simpson would need to speak to Lucas in order to get a full debriefing. In the meantime she could only wait.

At no time did it cross her mind that Joshua might be innocent. Now it was all about the process. In her head Simpson could hear the gears of the system grinding into action. For the first time in her life, she was on the wrong side of the law. She felt chilled and helpless.

Slowly, the shock gave way to frustration and anger at her husband. As she had feared, Joshua had been laid low by a toxic mixture of his greed and his hubris. It was that letter, she thought, that bloody letter: *Farewell, you suckers!* Full of arrogance and spite, it had been good for a couple of amusing diary stories in the *Financial Times*, but ultimately served only to annoy some very important investors, the kind of people who could bring you down. Carole felt the tears begin to well up again. If Joshua really thought he could close his business down and get out without anyone realising that there was a huge black hole, he must have been crazy. Then again, he must have been crazy to create the black hole in the first place.

When the phone rang, it made her jump. She let it ring until it stopped. A few seconds later, her secretary, a temp who had started only the day before, nervously stuck her head round the door.

'Commander? It's the Mayor on the phone,' the girl said, ploughing on in the face of her boss's apparent catatonia. 'He says he wants a word. It sounds quite important.'

Without waiting for a reply, the girl disappeared. A couple of seconds later, the phone started ringing again. Simpson slowly picked up the receiver. 'Hello?'

'Carole?'

Simpson forced herself to sit up straight in her chair. 'Yes?'

'It's Christian Holyrod.'

She tried to think back to the last time they'd met. It was less than a fortnight ago at City Hall, at a reception followed by a fundraising dinner. Joshua had spent a ridiculous amount of money for their table. Holyrod had been very amiable to them that night, talking about his plans to move into national politics. He had even hinted – hinted heavily once he got stuck into the Scotch – about his plans for a long-awaited assault on Downing Street. He outlined his 'medium-term campaign strategy' for replacing Edgar Carlton as Prime Minister, but it was clearly becoming more short-term all the time. The party had been in government for a while now, and support was waning. Holyrod was not the only one with his eyes on the top job. Diehards like Joshua – rich supporters who could bankroll a leadership bid – were more courted than ever as rival factions prepared for battle.

All that seemed a very long time ago now. 'Yes, Mr Mayor?' she sniffed. 'What can I do for you?'

'Look, Carole, I'm very sorry to hear about this . . . thing with Joshua.' Holyrod sounded embarrassed and distracted; there were voices in the background, as if he was at a lunch. 'I'm sure that it is just a misunderstanding – a malicious complaint.'

'Let's hope so.'

'I'm sure it is,' Holyrod said soothingly. 'You know what it's like these days. Everyone's hypersensitive about the least suggestion of anything whiffy. We're just copying the Americans in that, like we do in all things. Any over-zealous investigator out there is constantly looking for the next big scalp.'

'That man in America got a hundred and fifty years,' Simpson whispered, trying to choke back a sudden sob. 'A hundred and fifty!'

'Yes, well,' the Mayor replied, 'that won't happen here. I know that Joshua is as straight as they come.'

I wish I did, thought Simpson. 'Thank you.'

The noise in the background died away as Holyrod apparently sought out a quiet corner. 'I invested some money with him myself,' he mused.

Past tense, Simpson noted.

'He looked after me very nicely,' the Mayor continued.

So that's what you're worried about, Simpson thought; the idea that this could come back and bite you on the bum. 'That's good.'

'Yes, I was bit surprised when he decided to call it a day, but there's nothing wrong with quitting while you're ahead. More people should do so, in fact.'

'Yes.'

'Anyway, give him my best when you speak to him.'

'I will. Thank you.'

'And if there is anything I can do to help, let me know.'

'I will.'

There was a pause.

'There was one other thing that I wanted to talk to you about,' the Mayor said.

'Yes?'

'Mrs Agatha Mills.'

Given the day's events, Simpson took more than a moment to place the name.

'The lady who lived near the British Museum,' the Mayor prompted gently.

'The woman bludgeoned to death by her husband?'

'That's the one,' Holyrod said quickly. 'Where are you with that business? Has the investigation been completed? Is the case closed?'

Simpson didn't care to admit that she didn't know. She quickly focused on what she *did* know. 'The husband clearly did it. Then he walked out in front of a car – or rather, a van if I remember rightly.' As the words came out, she felt a chill. Joshua had to be under at least as much stress as Henry Mills had been. Could he react in a similar way? No, she reassured herself. Whatever else happened, he wasn't the kind of man to try and kill himself. She was sure of that. Fairly sure, at least.

She snapped out of her reverie. 'The case is closed.'

'Good,' the Mayor said cheerily. 'Would it be possible to see a copy of the final report?'

'Well . . .' The last thing Simpson needed right now was to be discovered playing fast and loose with official police files.

'Discretion assured, of course.'

She thought it through a little more. What the hell, it wasn't as if the hole she was already in could get any deeper. Maybe some goodwill in the Mayor's office could be helpful in the coming weeks. 'Of course. I'll get something sent over.'

'Thank you,' the Mayor replied. 'And be sure to give my best to Joshua.'

The line went dead before she could reply. Simpson carefully returned the handset to its cradle. Why was the Mayor so interested in the Mills case? And why hadn't she yet seen a copy of the final report herself? Getting up from the desk, she stepped out of her office, surprising her secretary who was engrossed in a copy of some wretched celebrity magazine. Simpson raised her eyebrows at the headline – *SUMMER LIPOSUCTION SPECIAL* – but didn't comment. The secretary dropped the magazine into her bag and looked up expectantly.

Simpson tried to summon up her usual authoritative tone. 'Get me Inspector Carlyle on the phone.'

THIRTY

Looking like a drowned rat, Carlyle had gone straight home from the cemetery. After a hot shower, some fresh clothes and lunch at Il Buffone, he felt much better, both mentally and physically, but without any real desire to venture towards the station. Ordering a second double macchiato to prolong his stay in the café, he felt his phone start to vibrate. Seeing that the call was from his sergeant, he answered.

'Have you seen the paper?' Joe began excitedly, sounding like a naughty schoolboy in possession of his first porn mag.

'Which one?'

'The *Standard*.'

'Hold on a second.' Carlyle turned to Marcello, the only other person still in the café at this late time. 'Have you got tonight's paper yet?'

'*Certo*.' Wiping his hands on a tea towel, Marcello stepped into the small alcove behind the counter, which served as both kitchen and storeroom, before returning immediately with a folded copy of the newspaper.

'Thanks.' Carlyle scanned the headline and brought the phone back to his ear.

'Spurs set for another good season?'

'No, you idiot,' Joe hissed. 'The *front* page!'

Carlyle flipped the paper over and felt his jaw drop to the floor. He stared at it all in disbelief for a couple of seconds: Simpson's wedding picture, the glaring headline, the mundane yet lurid details of her husband's arrest. 'Fucking hell!'

'Indeed,' Joe giggled. 'I spoke to a mate of mine in the Financial Crimes Unit, who says that Joshua Hunt, Mr Carole Simpson, is bang to rights.'

'Jesus.'

'The guy hasn't even tried to deny it. Have you ever met him?'

'Nah.' Carlyle thought about it for a moment. 'At least, not as far as I remember.'

'Well, it looks like he's going down for a long time.'

'Shit . . . what about Simpson herself?'

'The Met has already put out a statement saying that it is nothing to do with her.'

'But he's her husband!' Carlyle protested.

'Other people's marriages,' Joe remarked philosophically. 'Who knows what goes on behind closed doors. Maybe they were living separate lives.'

Carlyle looked back down at the story in front of him. 'In a six-million-pound North London mansion?'

'It's got to be big enough for the two of them to have their own living arrangements.'

'They were happily married, as far as I know,' the inspector mused.

'Who knows what was going on?' Joe continued. 'Even if everything was all hunky-dory between them, how much would you expect her to know about his financial dealings?'

'If she was anything like Helen,' Carlyle sighed, 'she would know everything.'

Joe laughed. 'That's *your* marriage.'

'Humph.'

'Seriously, though,' Joe added, 'whatever else we think about Simpson, she isn't flash and she works hard at her job – a proper job too. Maybe she didn't know anything about what he was up to.'

Carlyle scanned the article again. 'But all that cash . . .'

'Just numbers on a piece of paper,' Joe sniffed. 'And, anyway, you hear about lots of people making shedloads of cash. They can't all be crooks.'

'I don't know about that.'

'Even if he *is* bent, maybe she isn't – I could believe that.'

'I suppose I could too,' said Carlyle grudgingly. However much he disliked Simpson, ultimately, he didn't think that she was bent.

'Anyway,' said Joe, 'she's still at work. And she wants to speak to you.'

'Great.' Carlyle's heart sank. 'What about?'

'Agatha Mills. She wants to know why she hasn't seen the final report into the woman's murder.'

That's because I haven't written it, Carlyle thought. 'Shit. What did you tell her?'

'I haven't told her anything,' Joe said defensively. 'I just took the message from her secretary.'

'Okay.' Carlyle thought about it for a moment. 'Could you draft something for me, very factual, straight up and down, just the way she likes it?'

'All right,' said Joe, not sounding too happy about it.

'Good. I'll take a look at it in the morning. Thanks,' said Carlyle, pleased at having managed to exercise his power of delegation for once. 'See you, then.'

No sooner had he ended his call with Joe than the phone went again. This time it was Fiona Singleton from the Fulham station.

'Have you seen the news?' she asked, in a tone far more matter-of-fact than Joe's burbling call.

'Yes,' Carlyle replied. 'Amazing, isn't it?'

'Not that amazing really,' Singleton replied. 'Lovell has already confessed.'

'Sorry?' said Carlyle, confused.

'Simon Lovell,' Singleton explained, 'the saddo who was stalking Rosanna Snowdon. We picked him up last night and he was quite happy to admit that he'd done it. It was going to be in the paper today, but we've held it over because of all this . . . other stuff. I thought you might have heard anyway, but I just wanted to give you a heads-up.'

'Thanks.' Carlyle thought about it for a moment. 'Did he really kill her?'

'Lovell? I suppose so.' Singleton ran it through in her head one more time. 'Snowdon was dropped off outside the flat by her boss. Lovell admits he was waiting for her. He looks like a bit of a gentle giant, but he could have easily thrown her down those stairs, no problem at all.'

Justifying the easy win, Carlyle thought. 'She was drunk?'

Singleton grunted.

'Maybe it was an accident?' he suggested.

'We don't think so,' she said firmly.

'Is there any physical evidence?'

'I don't think so. It probably doesn't matter now.'

'Just make sure that this isn't another lame-brain going down for an easy win,' Carlyle said. 'It'll come back to haunt you, if it is.'

'Not your problem,' Singleton replied, sounding as if she was regretting having made the call.

'What about the boyfriend?' Carlyle asked, moving on.

'The rugby player? He's in New Zealand on a tour.'

'Good alibi.'

'Yes,' Singleton agreed. 'The colleague who spoke to him on the phone said he didn't seem particularly grief-stricken.'

'No?' If I'd just lost a girlfriend like Rosanna Snowdon, Carlyle thought, grief-stricken wouldn't be the half of it.

'No,' Singleton laughed. 'It may have something to do with a story in the tabloids yesterday about him groping a couple of groupies in a nightclub while watching a dwarf-throwing competition.'

'People deal with bereavement in different ways,' Carlyle reflected. 'Anyway, thanks for the call.'

'No problem.'

Carlyle studied the Simpson story once again, without finding out anything new. When he had finished, he looked at the clock behind the counter which told him that it was already almost four. No one had entered the café in the last twenty minutes and now Marcello was making a show of getting ready to close up. It was time for the inspector to take the hint and let the man get home.

After paying for his lunch, he decided to go back into Winter Garden House. Alice would be home from school soon. It would be nice to be there to meet her and find out how her day had been. Carlyle's own day was pretty much a write-off. A lot had happened but he'd achieved nothing. Sometimes you just had to quit while you were behind. Better now just to let things lie, then wait and see how they looked in the morning.

Stepping out of the café, Carlyle almost walked straight into a couple strolling arm-in-arm along Macklin Street. 'Sorry,' he mumbled, keeping his eyes on the pavement.

'Inspector!'

Carlyle looked up to see Harry Ripley – Heart Attack Harry – with a homely looking woman who appeared to be in her early sixties. 'Harry,' he said, 'how are you?' He nodded at the woman.

'This is Esther,' the old soldier beamed, 'Esther McGee. We met at a Residents' Association coffee morning not long after . . . er, you and I last met.'

Carlyle stuck out a hand. 'Nice to meet you, Esther,' he said. 'I'm John Carlyle, one of Harry's neighbours.'

'Oh, yes, Inspector,' the woman smiled. 'Harry has told me all about you.'

'I hope he's looking after you well,' Carlyle grinned, some of the couple's obvious good spirits now rubbing off on him.

'Oh, yes, he's a right gentleman.' A naughty twinkle appeared in Esther's eye, as she pulled Harry close. 'And still in such good shape,' she winked, 'if you know what I mean. There's still plenty of lead in his pencil.'

'Well, yes,' Carlyle coughed, feeling himself blush. But that was nothing compared to Harry, who had gone a bright beetroot red. The old dog, Carlyle thought. But at least we don't have to worry any more about him trying to top himself. Hoorah for the power of love, or whatever this is. 'Nice to run into you both,' he stammered. 'I'm glad things are going so well, Harry.'

It took the old man a few extra seconds to regain the power of speech. 'Nice to see you, too, Inspector,' he said finally. 'And give my best to Helen and Alice.'

'I will,' Carlyle replied. 'The pair of you must come round for tea some time soon.'

'Oh, yes,' Esther agreed, 'that would be lovely.'

'There you are, Harry,' Carlyle smiled. 'Speak to Helen and she can let you know when would be a good time.' With that, he scuttled across the road and quickly retreated inside Winter Garden House.

THIRTY-ONE

Carole Simpson sat morosely at her kitchen table in Highgate, holding a very large glass of Langoa Barton 2001, while waiting for her £800-an-hour lawyer to call. When the call finally came, she pounced on the handset lying in front of her.

'Hello?'

'Carole, it's John Lucas. I've just come out of Kentish Town police station.'

'Yes.' She could hear traffic noise in the background. Presumably the lawyer was walking along the road looking for a cab. Good luck to him, Simpson thought. Kentish Town was one of the neighbourhoods affected by the recent burst of rioting that had spread across the city before the Met had been able to react. Even at the best of times, it wasn't the kind of place a man in a suit should be wandering around alone at night. She hoped that Lucas would find a taxi before he got mugged.

As if to allay her fears, she heard Lucas suddenly bellow, 'TAXI!'

She waited as he clambered inside and told the driver to head for a restaurant in the West End, before restarting their conversation. 'You were in the station a long time,' she said, knowing what that must mean, waiting for the final confirmation of how completely her life had been demolished.

'Yes,' the lawyer said, sounding more chipper now that he was safely ensconced in the back of a black cab. 'More than eight hours, in fact.'

Simpson did the calculation in her head. Good God, she thought morosely, that's more than six grand. She wondered how much money she had in her purse. £50? All of their bank accounts had been frozen. Would they find the money to pay the legal bills?

'He's confessed, Carole. He's admitted to defrauding his investors.'

'You told him to do that?' she asked incredulously.

'No, no,' the lawyer said, shocked. 'Of course not. I'm not even completely sure what exactly he's confessing *to*, at this point. He was looking to wind the fund up, which isn't really what you would expect of someone in these circumstances.'

'What do you mean "*in these circumstances*"?' she asked sharply.

'Well . . .' Lucas chose his words carefully, 'in a so-called pyramid or ponzi scheme, things usually get to the point where the whole thing collapses as a result of too many people trying to take their money out at the same time. Here, it seems, Joshua was trying to give their money back to them – or at least part of it.'

'Doesn't that make him innocent?' She used the word in the narrowest, legal sense.

'By crystallising the losses,' Lucas continued, not caring to answer the question, 'he could have been hoping to share out the losses among everyone, rather than leaving the last ones left in holding the baby, and facing total financial ruin. If that was the thinking behind it, he would have known that there would still have been a big row about it, but the whole thing could have been represented as bad luck rather than actual fraud.'

That made his damn letter even more stupid, Simpson decided.

'At the moment,' Lucan continued, 'all this has to be argued over. We certainly don't know what the authorities have as yet, in terms of developing a case. Given where we are at this stage, I told him to say nothing. He chose to ignore me.'

'Not much use then, were you?' Simpson said bitterly.

The lawyer chose to ignore the barb. He'd been here many times before. One of his great strengths, so he liked to think, was an ability not to get wound up by clients who were, inevitably, having to operate under a great deal of pressure. 'That is always the client's prerogative,' he said gently. 'It may even be for the best, in the long run.'

'How so?' she asked, not prepared to believe it.

'Well,' the lawyer said, 'this way we can avoid a trial and can negotiate a lesser sentence.'

'So that's it?' she said, trying not to wail.

'Goodness, no,' said Lucas, trying to sound fatherly, even though he was at least five or six years younger than the woman struggling to hold it together on the other end of the line. 'Not at all. Whatever Joshua has said, it is still very early days here.'

'So what happens next?'

'He's going to be handed over to the City of London Police's Economic Crime Directorate. In due course, they will probably look to charge him under the Fraud Act of 2006. I expect that they will claim he is guilty of either false representation, failing to disclose information and or abuse of position. However, there's a long way to go yet. There are still various different possible outcomes, and we want to optimise the result for Joshua – and for you.'

'Should I go and see him?'

'Not yet,' the lawyer said firmly. 'Apart from anything else, they'll probably move him about a bit, depending on cell availability. You know what it's like.'

'Yes,' she said icily, 'I do.'

'You don't want to be rushing off on a wild-goose chase across London, especially if the media are on your tail.'

'No, you're right.' Simpson thought about taking a slug of wine, and decided against it. Putting the glass on the table, she cut to the chase. 'Will he go to jail?'

Definitely, thought Lucas. And for quite some time. There had never been a worse time to be caught out as a financial crook.

All it needed now was for the American authorities to get involved and the silly sod would have hit the jackpot. Those buggers would quite happily lock you up forever, with an extra hundred years on top, just to make them feel better. 'That is a possibility,' he replied cautiously, 'maybe even a probability. But that is not what you should be worrying about now.'

'No? What should I be worrying about?'

'We need to have a meeting in the morning. In the meantime, you should start thinking about the practicalities.'

'Such as?'

'Well, remember the good news here – the very good news – which is that there is no suggestion that you were party to any of this.'

'I wasn't.' Simpson picked up the wine glass and this time drank about half of its contents.

'No,' the lawyer said hastily, 'of course not. But you know what it's like in these situations.'

Simpson drained the remaining wine in the glass, and resisted the urge to smash it against the wall. 'No, I don't actually,' she bristled, all her desire to be rational, to be reasonable, slipping away.

'Well,' Lucas summoned up extra reserves of empathy and patience, 'as his wife, you will find that there will always be gossip and speculation. But *you* are not under investigation and there is not, as things stand, any . . . direct threat to your job. In the first instance, however, you need to consider various aspects of your relationship with your husband and in particular the distribution of your respective assets.'

After a day of feeling numb, Simpson suddenly recoiled as if she had been slapped in the face. 'Are you saying that I should divorce him?'

'Not at all,' Lucas said calmly. 'It is not my place to give any such advice. And, remember, technically, I am Joshua's lawyer, not yours. You should, of course, get your own representation. However, for the moment at least, there is a great commonality of interest here.'

'For the moment?'

Lucas gritted his teeth. He was getting increasingly irritated by Simpson's verbal tic of echoing what he said. But, once again, he ploughed on. 'Let us assume, for the moment, that the authorities will want to try and recover as much of Joshua's assets as possible. You will need to prove to them that anything you keep is not something that was gained as a result of his schemes.'

'Christ!' Simpson muttered as she grabbed the wine bottle and refilled her glass.

'Stop here!' Lucas told the cab driver. Before clambering out, he returned to his call: 'Remember, Carole, that you are a very successful professional in your own right. What's more, you have dedicated your entire career to public service. It should not be difficult to demonstrate that you have built up a reasonable portfolio of legitimately acquired assets over several decades. Draw up a list this evening, and we can discuss it in my office in the morning.'

'Fine,' Simpson sighed.

'Shall we say eleven?'

'I will see you there.'

'Good,' the lawyer replied. 'Until tomorrow then.'

With a click, the line went dead. Simpson tossed the phone back on the table. For the next few minutes she sat in silence, going over their conversation in her head. Then she pulled some paper and a pen from her bag, and began jotting down numbers.

Carlyle dropped his biography of the football manager Brian Clough on the coffee-table and glanced over at Helen, who was sitting on the other end of the sofa. A dispiriting sense of déjà vu overwhelmed him. His wife was still engrossed in her celebrities-in-the-jungle television show that seemed to have been running for months already. Carlyle was even more amazed to note that former Metropolitan Police Commissioner Luke Osgood was still hanging in there with a chance of winning. Osgood had made it down to the last three of the competition, along with a stripper (or, rather, 'burlesque performer') called Tizzy McDee and a nondescript-looking soap actor called Kevin. Carlyle tried to avert his eyes from the screen, particularly when Osgood appeared, but the sight of the pneumatic Tizzy, wearing a bikini that would have been too small even for young Alice, was predictably hypnotic.

Mercifully, a commercial break arrived. Helen pulled the remote out from under a cushion and muted the sound. 'Osgood's done well to get this far,' she said, 'but he's not going to win.'

'So it's between the soap star and the stripper?' Carlyle remarked, curious despite himself.

'Yes,' his wife replied, with all the seriousness appropriate to a discussion about a general election, 'but the actor is more likely to win. Once Osgood is out, he can combine the gay vote with the housewives' vote. There aren't enough teenage boys who can be bothered enough to ring in to vote for Tizzy over the line.'

'They've all got their hands full already, I expect,' Carlyle joked.

Helen shot him a sour look. 'Moving away from events in the jungle,' she said, 'I have some more news.'

'Oh, yes?' he said warily, expecting anything from a demand for money to an announcement that his mother-in-law would be paying them a visit.

'About Agatha Mills,' Helen said, rolling back on the sofa and pulling her knees up to her chest.

'What about her?'

'Well . . . Agatha and Sandra Groves *did* know each other.'

Carlyle yawned. 'You told me that already.'

Helen rose above the rebuke. 'They were both involved in a Daughters of Dismas campaign against the arms trade. Their particular interest was in British military aid to Chile. Apparently it was being used to finance mercenaries in Iraq.'

Carlyle let this new information sink in. 'Does this come from the woman that you spoke to before?'

'Yes.' Helen glanced at the television screen to make sure that the adverts were still running and that she wasn't missing any of her jungle fun. 'I spoke to Clara again this morning, and she put me on to a couple of other people she knows. They say that the two of them were quite active about it.'

'Was there anyone else involved?' Carlyle asked.

'Dunno,' Helen shrugged.

'Well, you'd better get your friend to check,' he chided her. 'These two have ended up dead, which means any of their chums could now be at risk. They need to get in touch with me straight away.'

'I will pass the message on,' Helen said coolly. She picked up some papers that were lying on the floor. 'They were targeting a company called LAHC.'

'Which stands for?'

Helen quickly scanned the text. 'I don't know. It was reportedly using men and equipment, paid for by British money, as so-called private security guards. Some of those guards are accused of human rights violations.'

'*I* get accused of human rights violations,' Carlyle snorted, 'on a fairly regular basis.'

'Not including murder,' Helen said bluntly. 'This isn't a laughing matter.'

'I was just—' Before he could finish his sentence, she dropped the sheaf of papers into his lap, restoring the television's sound just as her programme resumed.

If anything, the stripper's bikini seemed to have shrunk during the commercial break. Her nipples, meanwhile, seemed to have grown massively. Through great force of will, Carlyle managed to tear his eyes away from the screen and scan the documents that Helen had handed him. Much of the material was in Spanish, but one thing he could read was a Daughters of Dismas press release entitled *Time To Act Against Iraq Mercenaries*. Keeping one eye on the stripper's tits, Carlyle scanned the text. *Mercenary recruitment agencies are sending former soldiers to*

Iraq . . . human rights abuses . . . unauthorised use of Army weaponry . . . assault . . . murder. He read on: *American private security companies who recruit guards at the request of the US government to send into armed conflict zones, to protect strategic installations and military convoys, tend to subcontract to South American firms like LAHC Consulting. The owner of LAHC is Gomez Gori, a retired admiral of the Chilean navy who played a leading role in overthrowing the democratically elected Chilean government in 1973.*

Gomez Gori? Well, well, well. At that very moment, however, Tizzy McDee stepped into a shower. Her bikini became transparent and he completely lost his train of thought.

It took him several minutes to return to his reading. The only other item in English was a newspaper cutting from a year earlier:

IRAQ: CHILEAN MERCENARIES IN THE LINE OF FIRE
by Daniel Franklin

SANTIAGO, 9 March (CNW) *The 150 former members of the Chilean military who are working as private security personnel in Iraq are potential targets of the resistance there, as indicated by the gruesome murders of three security contractors a week ago.*

The former Chilean commandos are reported to work for the US Central Intelligence Agency (CIA). They are hired by private military firms that are benefiting from the lucrative contracts for the stabilisation and reconstruction of Iraq financed by the United States at an average monthly cost of four billion dollars.

Last November, a discreet ad was placed in the Chilean newspaper El Mercurio *inviting ex-commandos who could speak English, to sign up to provide security services abroad at the tempting pay of 18,000 dollars for just six months' work.*

The ad, placed by LAHC, awakened the interest of at least 400 Marines and 'Black Berets' – the Chilean army's special operations forces who retired early in the past few years.

The recruitment effort in Chile included a pre-selection of 400 men, who then participated in military exercises in San Bernardo, south of Santiago. That annoyed the Defence Ministry, which ordered an investigation into possible violations of Chile's law on weapons control.

LAHC finally selected 150 men who underwent training in the United States, after which they were sent to Kuwait, and from there to Iraq.

American media outlets have reported that the United States has hired retired members of the Chilean army who served under former dictator Augusto Pinochet (1973–90), as well as former henchmen of South Africa's apartheid regime to serve as soldiers of fortune in Iraq.

The private military industry is growing around the world, fed by local wars that are providing employment opportunities for former military personnel who found themselves out of a job, especially in Eastern Europe, when the Cold War came to an end. The 150 Chileans now in Iraq also form part of those displaced from active duty by a plan for the modernisation of the armed forces. Current army chiefs have carried out a discreet but effective purge, forcing into retirement officers and non-commissioned officers who played a role in the dictatorship's repression, in which some 3,000 people were killed or 'disappeared'.

At the top of the story was a photograph of three soldiers, standing in front of a battered jeep. They looked as if they were somewhere in a desert, but the location wasn't specified. Each was smiling while brandishing an automatic weapon that looked like something out of a *Terminator* movie.

Carlyle studied the photo carefully. None of these men was Matias Gori, but each of them was wearing what looked like a small badge. It was impossible to make it out clearly, but the motif could include a dagger, the same or similar to the one on the pin Matias had worn at the cemetery.

'I told you!' Helen punched the air in triumph.

'What?'

'He's off.' She pointed at the screen.

Carlyle turned back to the television. Fireworks were going off and Luke Osgood, dressed in a T-shirt and shorts, was walking across a swaying bridge and out of his jungle camp, after having been voted off the show.

'I told you he wouldn't win,' Helen grinned, giving him a gentle poke with her foot. 'Why don't you go and make me a cup of tea?'

When he returned a few minutes later with a cup of peppermint tea, the celebrity nonsense had ended, giving way to the late-evening news bulletin. Carlyle half-watched the end of a story about an earthquake in the Philippines or somewhere, and was just on his way to bed when an image of Rosanna Snowdon appeared on the screen.

He plonked himself back on the sofa, next to his wife as the newsreader solemnly delivered the commentary: '*Simon Lovell, the man accused of murdering television presenter Rosanna Snowdon, was freed today after a preliminary hearing at which the judge ruled that his confession had been obtained under duress.*'

The programme then cut to a clip of one of Lovell's lawyers, a hard-looking woman called Abigail Slater: '*My client is delighted by the decision made at today's hearing. The police have no evidence putting Mr Lovell at the scene of the alleged crime on the night in question, other than a forced confession which would never stand up at a full trial. All Mr Lovell wants to do now is to resume a normal, quiet life.*'

'Fat chance,' Carlyle muttered.

'Where does that leave the investigation into Rosanna's death?' Helen asked.

'Nowhere, as far as I know,' Carlyle sighed. 'They don't have anything else. Lovell was their only suspect.'

'So why did they pick on that poor guy?'

'They didn't pick on him,' Carlyle said testily, for some reason feeling the need to play Devil's Advocate. 'He confessed. What else were they supposed to do?'

'Do you think he did it?'

'No idea.'

'Will they find the killer?'

Carlyle finally found the strength to push himself off the sofa and head in the direction of his bed. 'I wouldn't bet on it,' he yawned.

'That poor woman,' Helen said. 'She deserved better.'

'Yes,' Carlyle agreed. 'She did.'

THIRTY-TWO

'Your dead friend is here.'

Carlyle had been lingering over lunch at Il Buffone when he took a call from Dave Prentice who had returned to his normal location behind the front desk at Charing Cross police station.

'Don't worry,' Prentice laughed, 'it looks like he's settling in for a nice long rest. Assuming he doesn't shit himself, I'll leave him in peace.'

'Thanks, Dave. I'll be about ten minutes.' The inspector returned to the story he had been reading from that morning's paper, entitled *SEX SWAP POLICE SCANDAL*. It was about public funding for the National Trans Police Association, which helped officers with 'gender identity issues'. Carlyle had never heard of it. Some rent-a-quote MP, whom he had never heard of either, complained: '*I don't care if a police officer is gay, straight, trans-gender or whatever. I just want them to catch criminals.*' Good luck with that, Carlyle chuckled to himself as he handed the paper back to Marcello and paid for his lunch.

Outside, it was a beautiful afternoon and he took his time sauntering back to work. Approaching Jubilee Hall, he felt a stab of guilt; it had been almost a week since he'd visited the gym, which wasn't good enough at his age. On Dennis Felix's old pitch, he passed a busker playing a dire rendition of Abba's 'Fernando', to a dozen or so bored-looking tourists. He wondered briefly what had happened to the poor sod and his anthrax-infested bongos. In the nearby snack van, a boy was handing over an ice cream to an expectant child. Of Kylie – the only person on the planet who had appeared upset at Dennis's demise – there was no sign. It's that kind of place, Carlyle thought. People come, people go.

When he got to the station, Walter Poonoosamy, aka 'Dog', was found in familiar pose, slumped in a corner of the waiting room, snoring loudly. Resplendent in a pair of tartan trousers and a newish-looking Prodigy T-shirt (the latter doubtless nicked from the local Oxfam shop on Drury Lane), he was cradling an almost empty vodka bottle in his arms, as if it was a baby. For once, he didn't seem to smell too bad, although he was still some way short of fragrant. Keeping a reasonable distance, Carlyle prodded him awake. Slowly, Dog opened his eyes. Sitting up slightly, he stared at the inspector. A flicker of recognition crept across his face and then he closed his eyes again. The snoring resumed immediately, if anything, louder than it had been before.

This time, Carlyle gave him a quick punch on the shoulder.

'Ouch!' Dog immediately sat bolt upright, rubbing his arm. 'What did you do that for?'

'Wakey, wakey.' Carlyle waved a hand in front of the drunk's face, making sure he had his full attention. 'Would you like a cup of tea?'

A kind of grin appeared on Dog's face. 'That would be nice.'

Squatting down, Carlyle fished a couple of pound coins out of his pocket and held them up for Dog to inspect. More than enough for a cup of tea. Even better, enough for a can of Special Brew from the newsagents round the corner – if the owner was up for a little haggling. 'Take a look at something for me first, and then I'll give you the cash.'

Dog gave a grunt of what Carlyle was happy to deem assent. The inspector quickly pulled a folded sheet of A4 paper from the inside pocket of his jacket. On it was printed a rather old and grainy picture of Matias Gori that Orb's office had emailed him. It wasn't great, but the key thing was that Gori still had his beard. 'Was this the man you saw hanging out at the back of Ridgemount Mansions?' he asked. 'The guy who gave you the dodgy note?'

Dog looked at the picture for a few seconds, eyes glazing over as he did his familiar impersonation of a man trying very hard to concentrate.

'Was that the man who gave you the thousand-peso note?'

Mock concentration gave way to genuine confusion on Dog's face. 'Huh?'

'The man who gave you the money that didn't work?'

There was a vague flicker of recognition in Dog's face. 'Maybe.'

Come on, Carlyle thought, frustration rising in his throat. Come on, you stupid bastard, think – just this once. He tried to hand the drunk the picture, but he wouldn't take it. 'Walter . . .'

'Excuse me.' The woman's voice, timid and polite, came from somewhere behind him. 'Are you Inspector Carlyle?'

Carlyle didn't look up. 'In a minute,' he replied rudely, still waving the picture at Dog.

The voice came a step closer. 'I was told that you wanted to see me.' Less timid now in the face of his rudeness.

'In a minute,' I said.

A hand appeared and took the picture from the inspector's hand. 'I know this man.'

Trying to keep his annoyance in check, Carlyle stood up and found himself in front of a tired-looking redhead in her thirties. 'Yes?'

Looking at least a few kilos light of healthy, the woman was conservatively dressed in a white blouse and a navy knee-length skirt. She held out a hand and he shook it. 'I'm Monica Hartson.'

He looked back at her blankly.

'Daughters of Dismas,' she added. 'I'm a friend of Agatha Mills and Sandra Groves.'

'Ah.'

She handed him back the picture. 'One of the people trying to finally bring Matias Gori to justice.'

'Mm.' Carlyle held out the two quid and dropped it into Dog's hand. 'How did you get my name?'

'After the episode on the bus,' Hartson explained, 'you are well known amongst the group.'

Fame at last, Carlyle thought.

'I got a message saying I should speak to you.'

'Thanks for coming.' Standing back, Carlyle watched the tramp struggle to his feet and shuffle towards the door. 'Not bad for a dead man,' he grinned.

'What?' Hartson eyed him quizzically.

'Nothing,' Carlyle said quickly. 'Thanks for coming in. Let's go and have a chat upstairs.'

For once, the air conditioning was working. The fourth-floor meeting room was decidedly chilly, just the way he liked it. Declining a cup of coffee, Hartson pulled a small bottle of water from her shoulder bag and took a delicate sip.

Carlyle toyed with his espresso but didn't take a drink. 'So,' he said casually, 'tell me your story.'

She thought about that for a second, then looked at him, nonplussed. 'Where do you want me to start?'

'How do you know Matias Gori?' he asked.

'I don't know him,' she said carefully, 'but I know *about* him.'

Great, thought Carlyle, a pedant zealot, just what I need. 'Okay, why are you interested in him?'

Once again, she thought about where to start. Normally, Carlyle thought, that means they're getting ready to lie to you. But in the case of Monica Hartson, he was sure she was just trying to be precise. 'We have a campaign . . .'

'The Daughters of Dismas?'

'Yes. We have been campaigning against the use of mercenaries in places like Iraq.' Rooting about in her bag, she pulled out a couple of flyers and pushed them across the table.

Carlyle let them lie there. 'Just tell me in your own words first.'

'Well, we have this campaign . . . we are particularly focusing on mercenaries who were being funded by British taxpayers' money.'

'LA . . . something . . .'

'LAHC, yes.' She seemed to relax slightly, buoyed by the hope that the policeman might be at least a little informed. 'The initials come from Luis Alberto Hurtado Cruchaga. Father Hurtardo was a Jesuit priest who was made a saint by the Pope a few years ago.'

'So,' Carlyle said, unable to resist teasing her gently, 'these people have a religious background, like you?'

'Not really,' she said evenly, not rising to the bait. 'LAHC has nothing to do with the Church, and it certainly has nothing to do with social reform. It is an American-registered company, but essentially owned and run by a group of rich Chileans with connections to the military. They take former commandoes and other special forces, and use British aid money to pay their wages.'

'And that's how you came across Gori?'

'Yes. Gori is former Chilean Special Forces, from the thirteenth Commando Group, known as the Scorpions. His uncle is also the founder of LAHC. After the Scorpions, Matias became,' she raised her fingers in the air to indicate quotation marks, 'a "diplomat". But he has very close ties to the mercenaries, some of whom he served with in the army.'

She glanced at Carlyle, who signalled for her to go on. 'He has even gone out on missions with them. One of these missions, to a town called Ishaqi, north of Baghdad, ended up with the massacre of more than fifty men, women and children. According to witness reports, Matias Gori killed as many as a dozen of them himself. When we found out that he was working in London, we tried to get him arrested so that he could be tried either here or in Iraq or maybe at the War Crimes Tribunal at The Hague.'

Carlyle took a sip of his espresso. 'And?'

Hartson looked angry. 'Our lawyers say we need more evidence. That is why we tried to confront him directly.'

Oh, oh, Carlyle thought, the Women's Institute takes on Rambo. Excellent idea. 'When was this?'

'Earlier this month there was a demonstration. We marched to the Embassy and lodged a petition with the Ambassador, asking for Gori to be handed over to the police for questioning.'

'And what did the Ambassador say?'

'We're still waiting for a reply.'

'And now two of you are dead.'

She looked at him blankly.

Shit, Carlyle thought, too late to sugar-coat the pill now. 'Agatha and Sandra were both murdered; didn't you know?'

The tears were already welling up in her eyes as she absorbed this shocking news. Carlyle made no attempt to comfort her, but gave her time to compose herself before he began running through a quick summary of the relevant events.

By the time he had finished, Hartson had largely regained her calm. 'I've been away for a while,' she explained. 'I only got back to London yesterday.'

That may well have saved your life, Carlyle reflected.

'Do you think,' her voice quivered a little, 'that Gori killed them?'

'Maybe.' Carlyle said. 'I think so.'

Monica looked at him carefully. 'Can you prove it?'

He smiled grimly. 'That's not the question.'

'Oh,' she said shakily. 'What is?'

'The question is – will I have to?'

'I'm not sure I understand.'

'Good.'

'Will he come after me?'

Yes. 'Maybe.'

She ran her hands through her hair and shivered. 'Will I be safe?'

Maybe. 'Yes.'

'Will you protect me?'

Don't promise what you can't deliver, he told himself. 'I will stop him.'

'What should I do?'

'Is there somewhere you can stay for a little while?' he asked. 'Out of the way, preferably somewhere outside of London.'

She thought about it for a moment. 'I've got some friends up in Glasgow.'

'Good, then this is what we'll do.' Carlyle programmed her mobile number into his private phone then took down the details of the people she would be staying with. 'I will call you once a day. If goes to voicemail, I'll leave a message.'

They walked back to the lifts in silence. Downstairs, by the front desk, Carlyle shook her hand again. 'Thank you for coming.'

Monica Hartson gave him a wan smile. 'I'm not sure whether I feel better for our conversation, or worse.'

'Don't worry,' he said. 'This is nearly over. Gori is a marked man. It will be done in a couple of days. Getting out of town is just an additional precaution.'

'I hope so.'

'One thing I was wondering, though . . .'

'Yes?'

'Why put yourself through all of this? Why go after someone like Gori?'

Hartson looked at him for a moment, as if deciding whether to tell him the whole story. 'I was there,' she said finally. 'I saw what he did.'

'What?'

'We arrived in Ishaqi the day after Gori and his comrades had blown through,' she said quietly. 'I set up a Red Cross office under a makeshift awning by the side of one of the houses that hadn't been burned out. I stood and watched a man in a black turban holding a hessian sack containing the remains of his son.' She swallowed. 'Only it wasn't his son, just random scraps that had been recovered from around the place. The elders had already given away all the bodies, and even the limbs, to mourners who had got there first. Identifying anybody or anything was almost impossible. All that they could do was try and give each family something approximating the right number of corpses.'

'Jesus.'

'By the time this man arrived there were just a few pieces left. But he had to have something to take home. He just scooped up what he could and put it in his sack.' Monica closed her eyes and stifled a sob. 'The man went home to tell his wife that this was their son, so the family had something to bury while they said their prayers.'

Carlyle mumbled something that he hoped sounded sympathetic.

'After that, I couldn't get home quickly enough.'

'I can understand.'

She was too polite to contradict him.

'But,' the inspector sighed, 'there have been lots of killings, and doubtless there will be lots more. Even if you finally get him, if you bring Matias Gori to justice, will it have been worth it?'

'Yes.'

'Despite the death of your friends?'

'The point is that they shouldn't have had to die; just like those poor people in Ishaqi shouldn't have had to die.' She looked at him with a fierceness in her eyes that had been absent before. 'If this was a decent country, something would have been done about Gori long before now. We wouldn't even have needed to get involved – *if* the police had done their job properly.'

She waited for a response, but Carlyle said nothing.

'But no one wanted to know,' Hartson continued, 'so we decided to take up the fight. All we wanted to do was bring one man – one *murderer* – to justice. We thought that was surely achievable – a small victory for decency. You're right, many people get away with terrible things, but that's no reason to give up. If everyone took your point of view, Inspector, the world would be an even worse place than it is now.'

Chastened, Carlyle held up a hand. 'I didn't say it was my point of view—' But it was too late. Hoisting her bag on to her shoulder, she was already slaloming through the small knots of supplicants in the waiting room, and had almost reached the door by the time his words had got out.

After she had left, the inspector went through what they had. It was probably not enough to get Hartson police protection and certainly not enough to arrest Gori. But at least now Carlyle should be able to persuade Carole Simpson to let him see this thing through. He hoped so, at any rate. The Commander's husband might still be making the news, but she remained at work. He rang her office and left a message with her PA, who promised to get Simpson to call him back as quickly as possible.

Ending the call, Carlyle looked around. What to do next? Scratching his head, he finally reached a decision; he would break his duck for the week and finally work up a sweat at Jubilee Hall.

THIRTY-THREE

Matias Gori stood in the shadows of the doorway of the long-since closed Zimbabwean High Commission, underneath a faded poster advertising trips to the Victoria Falls, and watched Monica Hartson as she walked down the front steps of Charing Cross police station and headed for the Strand. It was approaching rush-hour and the streets were crowded, so her progress was slow and Gori was able to stay close, no more than five or six yards behind her, without any danger of being detected.

Hartson then crossed the Strand, picked up a free newspaper and ducked inside Charing Cross train station. Dropping a little further behind, Gori watched her buy a coffee before heading down into the Tube. Realising that he didn't have a ticket, he followed her down the escalator and jogged over to the nearest machine. Grabbing a handful of change from his jacket pocket, he pushed in front of a group of Chinese tourists and dropped enough coins in the slot to get a standard single. He rushed through the barriers just in time to see the top of Hartson's head disappearing down another escalator, heading for the Northern Line. Skipping down into the bowels of the Tube station, he watched her turn right at the bottom of the escalator, stepping on to the platform for trains heading north. Slowly, he counted to five and followed.

The platform was full, but not packed, with sweaty, tired and frustrated-looking travellers. A voice on the tannoy was apologising about interruptions to the service, caused by signalling problems, and the electronic board was signalling a four-minute wait for the next train. Faced with a sea of blank faces, Gori made his way carefully down the platform, always moving, never making eye contact. He found her about three-quarters of the way along, standing just behind the yellow line, sipping her coffee and staring at a poster advertising Errazuriz Chardonnay. The board now showed two minutes until the next train. Over the tannoy came an announcement about planned engineering works on the Circle Line. Keeping out of her line of vision, Gori walked past Hartson, to the end of the platform, placing himself behind a pair of women intently studying a copy of the *A–Z*.

The next train was due. Gori walked cautiously back along the platform until he was standing about two feet behind Hartson and slightly to her left, on the opposite side of her from where the train would arrive. He could hear it now steadily getting closer, until there was a sudden blast of air and the harsh clatter of metal on metal as it emerged from the tunnel. As she looked up, Gori stepped forward. The train was halfway into the station now and he could see the driver yawning in his cab. Leaning forward, he gave her a firm shove in the small of the back as he walked past. Without making a sound, she involuntarily stepped over the yellow line and off the edge of the platform, disappearing under the front wheels with the gentlest of thuds.

It all happened so quickly. No one on the platform seemed to notice. Not breaking his stride, Gori thought he caught a whiff of burning meat, as if you were passing a kebab shop, but quickly dismissed the idea. Doubtless it was just his imagination.

By the time it came to a halt the train was fully inside the station. The doors opened as normal and he heard the usual recorded message: *Let passengers off the train first, please!* Keeping a bored, vaguely annoyed look on his face, he allowed himself to be swallowed up by the disembarking travellers heading for the exit. Somewhere behind him an alarm sounded. This being London, however, no one paid it any heed. Everyone kept shuffling forward. A couple of Tube workers in luminous orange jackets appeared on the platform, their walkie-talkie radios cracking with static. Gori watched as they passed to his left, fighting their way through the crowd towards the driver.

It took maybe another minute for Gori to get off the platform and move into a tunnel that connected the different underground lines. Finally, the crowd began to thin and he was able to resume a normal walking pace. At the bottom of a set of escalators, he checked a copy of the Tube map and came to a decision as to where he wanted to go next. As luck would have it, he reached the Bakerloo Line just in time to jump on a train for Willesden Junction.

Barely ten minutes later, Matias stepped out of Edgware Road station. The sun was still strong and he felt thirsty. Ignoring the man selling the *Big Issue* outside the station entrance, he turned right, heading north. Entering the first pub he came to, he ordered a bottle of Heineken Export. When it arrived, he drank more than half of it in one go. It tasted good.

THIRTY-FOUR

Who the fuck played darts, these days? Dominic Silver stood at the bar in the Endurance, watching Michael Hagger throw a trio of arrows towards random parts of the board, before sucking the head off his pint of fake German lager. Aside from Hagger's darts companion, Silver counted seven other men in the bar, plus the bartender. They were exactly the type of men you might expect to find in a bar in the middle of the afternoon on a working day: slackers and rejects of various descriptions. Everyone was busy minding his own business; no one was going to cause any trouble.

After managing to stay below the radar for longer than anyone imagined possible, Michael Hagger had finally reverted to type and turned up in a place where he was likely to find himself in the most amount of trouble in the shortest amount of time. The Endurance was located on Berwick Street, at the top end of the fruit and vegetable market. The pub was popular with an eclectic mix of media professionals, stallholders and the occasional hooker working in one of the walk-up brothels on the opposite side of the street. It was one of Hagger's favourite haunts, so Silver had made sure it was checked regularly as the hunt for him continued. When Hagger had turned up and settled in for a session, word had got back to Silver within the hour. Less than forty minutes later, his 'assistant', the ex-paratrooper Gideon Spanner, had parked the Range Rover outside, and they walked in.

Dominic took a sip from his glass of house rosé and winced. It was a long way short of the Etienne de Loury Sancerre he kept at home, and he now wished that he'd stuck to mineral water. No matter.

He turned to Gideon: 'Bring him over.'

'Sure thing.'

Dominic sighed to himself as he watched a familiar mix of shock and resignation spread across Hagger's face when Gideon tapped him on the shoulder. What did the idiot expect? The other player caught Gideon's eye and quickly dropped his darts on a nearby table, before scuttling outside with his drink.

'Dominic would like a word.' Gideon signalled back towards the bar.

Hagger looked round. Raising his pint to both men, he took another sip. Then he put it down carefully on the table and leaned closer to Spanner. 'Fuck off,' he hissed.

Gideon put his hands on his hips. 'No, Michael,' he said, keeping his voice bureaucratic-conversational, 'we will not fuck off. Please step over to the bar and talk to the man.'

Hagger threw back his shoulders to emphasise his physical advantage; he had a good couple of inches and quite a few pounds over the man in front of him. 'Fuck off!' he repeated, louder this time, before retrieving his pint and drinking deep.

Tutting to himself, Gideon stepped over to the table and picked up the three abandoned darts. 'Last chance . . .'

Hagger kept on drinking. He was about two-thirds of the way through his pint when Gideon fired a dart at the floor.

'Shit!' Hagger did a little jump, spilling some of the pint over his T-shirt as the arrow wedged itself firmly in the wooden floor, only an inch from his left foot. He scowled at Gideon. 'You could have hit me.'

'I was trying to hit you,' Gideon said, 'but I'm shit at darts.' Taking aim again, he swiftly sent a second arrow sinking deep into Michael Hagger's right foot.

This time Hagger jumped higher, his face turning red. 'Christ!

You bastard!' Grabbing the sole of his Converse trainers, he started hopping about.

'That was a lucky one – or maybe I'm just getting better at it.' Gideon lined up the third dart. Everyone else in the pub buried themselves deeper in their newspapers or stared harder at their betting slips.

'Okay, okay.' Hagger half-turned and slowly bounced in the direction of the bar like a drunken wallaby. Still holding the remainder of his pint to his chest, he made no effort to remove the arrow from his foot.

Gideon fired the last dart at the board, scoring a six. 'Like I said,' he mumbled to no one in particular, 'I'm shit at darts.'

Having safely placed his pint on the bar, Hagger looked at Silver.

'You've been hiding, Michael,' Dominic said eventually.

Hagger shrugged. 'Not really.'

'Where's the boy?'

'Jake is *my* kid.' Hagger looked at the glass but didn't take a drink. 'That's my business.'

'Not just *your* business,' Dominic Silver said gently. He felt a wave of infinite patience sweep over him. He was dealing with an idiot here, but for once, he had plenty of time. He almost felt serene. Not being in a rush was the greatest luxury of all.

'He's my boy,' Hagger said stubbornly.

'Michael, you are never going to be Parent of the Year. You stole your kid from his mother. Even she could do a better job of looking after him than you – which is *really* saying something. The Metropolitan Police are looking for you – at least, they're supposed to be. Your parental rights have been rescinded.'

'Huh?' This time Hagger reached for his glass.

'Is Jake still alive?'

'Yes!'

Dominic lowered his voice. 'Let's hope so, because if he's not, or if he's been damaged in any way, you are going to fucking die.'

Hagger took the threat in his stride. 'What's it to you, anyway?'

Dominic looked Hagger up and down once more and felt his wave of infinite patience retreat. While maintaining eye contact, he stomped one of his Timberlands down on the dart embedded in Hagger's foot.

The glass slipped from Hagger's hand, smashing on the floor. His face went white and he looked like he was going to vomit. 'Oh, Jesus!'

Dominic signalled to Gideon, who was hovering on the periphery. 'Put him in the car.' Leaving the remainder of his glass of rosé on the bar, he walked slowly out of the door.

THIRTY-FIVE

It took almost twenty minutes for Carlyle to find his 'private' mobile, the one on which he'd programmed Monica Hartson's number. Somehow, it was cunningly hidden under a pile of newspapers on the living-room floor. He had no recollection of leaving it there, but that was the way of these things: socks, keys, mobile phones – all designed to be regularly lost, and occasionally found. Letting out a small yelp of triumph at the phone's reappearance, he pulled up Hartson's number and hit the call button. After listening to it ring for what seemed like an eternity, he finally got a recorded message that simply said: *This number is not available. Please try later. Goodbye.*

Bemused by the lack of voicemail, Carlyle ended the call. That's not a good start, he thought, wondering what she might be up to. This kind of person was just so unreliable. Returning the phone to a prominent position by the television, he went off to make himself a cup of green tea.

In the kitchen he filled the kettle. While he was waiting for it to boil, his gaze settled on an oversized cream envelope propped up against the bread bin. It was addressed to *John Carlyle Esq.* He picked it up. On the back was a crest he didn't recognise. Helen must have left it there, he decided, picking it up and weighing it in his hand. It felt weighty. It also felt expensive.

He opened it carefully, pulling out an invitation, a piece of thick card, with a silver border and black inlaid script, requesting his attendance at a reception to be held at Number 10 Downing

Street for something called the Union of Social Givers. Where had that come from? Carlyle frowned. The kettle came to the boil. Placing the invite back in the envelope, he dropped a teabag into a mug and added water, counting to ten before removing the bag. Dropping it into the sink, he remembered his conversation with Rosanna Snowdon in Patisserie Valerie on Marylebone High Street. It seemed a long time ago now. Rosanna must have come through with her promise to get him invited to the Prime Minister's residence. He felt a frisson of embarrassment as he considered this last small act of kindness from a woman whose help he had never properly repaid and now never would.

Blowing on his tea, he took a cautious sip. It was still too hot. Should they go to the reception? It wasn't really his thing but, then again, he would only ever get the one chance. He smiled at the thought of walking past the police guards and through that black door. And, despite her liberal sensibilities, Helen might like it. He would let her decide.

Looking down at the traffic crawling round the square, Matias Gori stood on the roof of the Chilean Embassy. With one foot resting on the low parapet at the edge of the roof, he sucked greedily on a well-deserved cigarette. He felt a gentle breeze on his face and shivered. It was getting colder. Not for the first time, he cursed the type of country that made you stand outside for a smoke.

'I thought I'd find you here.'

Gori turned to find Claudio Orb stepping carefully towards him.

'Cold, isn't it?' the Ambassador smiled.

'Yes,' said Gori, taking a final drag of his Marlboro before flicking it over the side of the building. He caught Orb's eye and shrugged. 'This is the only place you are allowed to smoke these days.'

'And a good place for a quiet word.'

'If you want.' Gori stared at his immaculate John Lobb shoes.

What could the old fool want with him? To him, Orb was spineless, merely a straw in the wind. How could a man like this represent his country? For sure, he would have nothing interesting to say.

Orb stood by the parapet and gestured towards the city below. 'I really won't miss all this.'

'Neither will I,' Gori replied, 'when the time comes.'

'My time has already come.'

'You're going home?'

Orb nodded. 'I've decided that it is finally time for me to retire. My wife wants to see more of our grandchildren.'

'Is that a good enough reason?' Gori sniffed.

'Yes,' Orb ignored the younger man's bad humour, 'I think it is. Anyway, I've had enough. The Ministry of Foreign Affairs is already lining up my replacement, so there is no need for me to delay my decision.'

Gori nodded and lit another cigarette. 'I'm hoping to go back soon myself.'

'Oh?' said Orb casually. 'Is your work here done?'

Gori smirked. 'My work is never done. That's just the way it is.'

Orb looked up, to the skies, and listened to the sound of an airliner somewhere above the clouds. 'And what work would that be?'

'You know what they say . . .'

'No, Matias.' Orb's smile faded. 'I don't.'

Gori waved his cigarette in the air, as if he was writing on a blackboard. 'Never apologise, never explain, Mr Ambassador. Never apologise, never explain.'

'That wouldn't work for a diplomat.'

'I'm not a diplomat,' the younger man said sharply.

'What are you, Matias?'

'I'm a . . .' Gori's face broke into a broad smile, 'warrior.'

Orb looked at his colleague. 'How many more women were you thinking of killing?'

Gori let his gaze fall on a line of red tail-lights stretching all the way towards the Edgware Road, the city's most famous Arab neighbourhood. Gori spent a lot of time there. It reminded him of good times. He would head over there, to the Green Valley, his favourite Lebanese restaurant, for supper tonight.

'Well?' Orb asked quietly.

Gori turned and took a step closer to the old man, so that they were now only a couple of feet apart. Maybe the Ambassador wasn't as stupid as he had thought. Not that it mattered. 'Who told you?' he asked finally. 'Was it the policeman?'

'No, I don't think he knows quite what is going on here,' Orb replied. 'But he put me on the right track.'

'Maybe he knows, maybe he doesn't. Does it really matter?' Gori dropped his second cigarette on to the asphalt, and stubbed it out vigorously with his shoe. 'Are you going to tell him?'

'I don't think that would be very helpful.'

So why are we having this conversation? Gori wondered. 'And, anyway, even if he did find out, there's nothing he could do about it.'

'That is not the point, Matias.'

'Oh? And what *is* the point, then, Excellency?'

Orb threw his shoulders back and put on his most authoritative voice. 'This has to stop,' he said. 'It has to stop now.'

'It never stops,' Gori pouted.

'This isn't Iraq, Matias, or back home, circa 1973. You can't fight a dirty war here.'

Gori moved half a step backwards and took a good look at the old man in front of him. He estimated that he had the advantage of maybe three or four inches and at least as many kilos, not to mention more than thirty years. There was no guard rail, and no security cameras on the roof. A quick push and Orb would go straight over the edge. Easy, quick and clean. No one would ever know what had happened. He poked the cigarette butt with the toe of his shoe; he should remember to pick that up before he left the roof, otherwise there was no evidence to say that he had ever been there.

In the square below, there was the squeal of brakes, a clash of metal and someone angrily honking their horn. Gori looked down and saw a taxi driver get out of his cab and start shouting at a cyclist sitting in the road next to his mangled bike. After some extended finger-pointing, the driver gave the cyclist a sharp kick and stalked back to his taxi. Gori laughed and the spell was broken. He looked back at Orb. The old man would never know how close to death he had come in that moment.

Ultimately, however, killing the Ambassador wasn't necessary. Also, it would have been counter-productive, creating too much of a fuss. Orb would doubtless still have some allies, even if they were stuck in an office in Santiago. Not like the women. They had no connections; no influence. No one would ever bother about them, apart from maybe the dumb policeman.

And what about him?

Killing the policeman might be nice, but that wasn't really necessary either. He would go away soon enough. Matias had seen plenty like him in his time – not enough brains, not enough stamina, not enough *balls* – and more than enough to know that Carlyle was not a threat.

He stepped back towards Orb and smiled. 'We are just doing what is necessary.'

'Surely, Matias,' Orb said sadly, 'that is not for you to decide.' He straightened up and put a gentle hand on his young colleague's shoulder. 'I would counsel caution. People like this are no threat to you. For all its faults, this is a civilised country; a good friend of Chile. Relations are good. These people cannot spoil that relationship. They are allowed to make their protests, but they won't change anything. That is what democracy is all about. All you are doing is making a relatively harmless situation dangerous. London isn't Baghdad; murder here is an *event*. Human life means something. The police will investigate thoroughly. You will be found out. And, all the while, all you are doing is creating potential martyrs, boosting the very cause you are trying to defeat.'

‘I understand what you are saying,’ Gori conceded. He paused, knowing that he should leave it there, but unable to resist a final barb, he smiled maliciously and said: ‘But you have spent your whole life sitting on the fence, Excellency – you must have a very sore ass. It is good that you are retiring, because Chile needs stronger men than you for the battles ahead.’

Orb smiled weakly and removed his hand from Gori’s shoulder. ‘Maybe you are right, Matias. You have a point there. Certainly everyone’s time comes to an end.’ He took half a step backwards, away from the edge of the roof. ‘One thing, however, is guaranteed.’

‘Oh? What’s that?’

‘We will *both* be going home very soon.’ Placing his hand in the small of Gori’s back, Orb gave a firm push. Overcoming his initial surprise, the military attaché tried to keep his footing, but the parapet was in the way, causing him to fall forwards instead. Grunting, Orb pushed harder and Gori disappeared over the side of the building. For a second or two or three, Orb stood there, breathing heavily, listening to the sound of his beating heart. Then, without looking down, he walked away.

THIRYT-SIX

Staring into space, Gideon Spanner sat on the concrete floor, knees pulled up to his chest, his back resting against the metal wall. In his hand was the clipping he'd taken from yesterday's newspaper, reporting the deaths of another four British soldiers in Afghanistan, blown to bits by a roadside bomb while out on patrol. Gideon had known two of the dead well, they had spent three months on active service together before Gideon upped and left, and ended up working for Dominic Silver. Lee McCormack and Giles Smith were just boys like himself – they didn't want to stay on the front line, but they didn't want to come home either. They were soldiers who wanted to fight, but to fight for something they could understand.

As things turned out, the soldiers were merely the latest casualties in a campaign aimed at making Helmand Province secure for local elections to take place. In the end, only 110 people had felt safe enough to vote – 110 fucking people, Gideon thought. His mates had died for 110 votes. Funny kind of democracy, that.

How many such comrades did he know now? Fifteen? Sixteen? Something like that. Why had it not been him? he often wondered. Sometimes it made his eyes tear up, and his throat constrict until he couldn't breathe. Tonight he felt his heart beating strongly in his chest and a pain throbbing in his temples. His finger tickled the trigger of his Sig Sauer P226. All he had to do was flip the safety-catch and he would be good to go. One in the brain and it would all be over. Three seconds – one, two, three . . .

'Gideon! Come over here, please.'

Slowly getting to his feet, he headed towards Dominic Silver.

'Has he given you what you wanted, boss?' Gideon asked.

'Yes,' Silver nodded.

'And?' Gideon idly fingered the safety on the Sig.

'And now,' Dominic said in a conversational tone, 'it is time to get rid of him.'

'Okay.' Gideon stepped past Silver and stood in front of the man chained to the floor. There was nothing cocky about him now as he looked at his executioner with a mixture of resignation and pleading. Gideon finally flicked off the safety and stepped closer.

Hagger's eyes grew wide with fright. 'You can't!'

Gideon listened to Silver's receding footsteps and frowned. 'Why not?'

'It's . . . murder,' Hagger croaked.

'Yes,' Gideon nodded. 'Yes, it is.' He stepped closer, inhaling Hagger's stench, breathing in deeply, feeling that little bit more alive. 'But lots of good people, top blokes, get murdered all the time. So why not a useless little scumbag like you?'

'But—'

Before Hagger could say any more, Gideon raised the Sig and put two .357 rounds into his chest, instantly ending the debate.

THIRTY-SEVEN

It was a damp, grey morning and cold for the time of year. Desperate for a cup of hot, strong coffee, Carlyle stared morosely into the gloom. Looking out across the tops of the trees in the middle of the square, he imagined himself losing his balance and tipping over into the abyss. In reality, he made sure that he was a good two feet from the edge of the building before he cautiously leaned over and peered down at the body impaled on the railings below. From almost 100 feet up, Matias Gori looked like a speared fish that had gasped its last. Moreover, it looked as if he would be stuck there for a while yet. The technicians had yet to decide how best to remove him without leaving his guts all over the pavement.

Arriving at the Embassy, Carlyle had not stopped on the pavement to study Gori close-up. Rather, after a short chat with the stressed-looking DCI in charge, he had headed straight up to the roof. He didn't like it much up here either, but he felt that his fear of heights was less of a problem than his long-standing squeamishness around dead bodies.

Standing behind him, Joe Szyszkowski was, if anything, even more cautious than his boss. 'So,' Joe asked, staying well clear of the parapet, 'did he jump or was he pushed?'

'He didn't seem the suicidal kind to me,' said Carlyle gruffly. 'I met him – I dunno, a few days ago. He seemed like the kind of arrogant bastard who thought he was on a mission from God or something; thought he could live for ever.'

'It could have been an accident,' Joe suggested. 'Maybe he was pissed. What was he doing up here, anyway?'

'The DCI in charge downstairs said this is a no-smoking building, and apparently he liked to come up here for a crafty fag.'

'Did Forensics find anything?' Joe asked, looking vacantly at the asphalt.

'Just a cigarette butt – presumably Gori's.' Carlyle scanned the roof aimlessly. 'It's basically impossible to tell if he was up here on his own or not. There's no CCTV.'

'No chance of any witnesses?'

Carlyle shook his head. 'The Embassy was nearly empty at that time of night. The security guard was doing his rounds, but he doesn't come up here. Says he saw no one. None of the neighbouring buildings directly overlook this part of the roof.' He gestured at the Radisson Hotel, on the far side of the square, the only nearby building that was taller than the Embassy itself. 'Even someone over there probably wouldn't have seen anything, because it's too far away.'

Making sure he still didn't get too close to the edge, Carlyle gingerly leaned forward and took another quick glance down at the dead fish. 'You're not the first person to fall off a tall building recently, are you, matey?' he said quietly to himself. Thinking back to Jerome Sullivan and Michael Hagger, he felt a sharp pang of guilt. Since Hagger had appeared in the piazza, Carlyle had done nothing to try and track down young Jake. As far as he knew, Cutler, the officer leading the search, hadn't made any progress either. If there had been any hope, it had long since gone. The missing kid was doubtless beyond salvation now.

His stomach rumbled. Feeling a bit light-headed, Carlyle turned away from the edge of the building. 'Let's go.'

Joe nodded and they headed back inside.

'So where does this leave us?' Joe wondered, standing at the top of the stairs that led up to the roof.

'I think it leaves us in quite a good place,' Carlyle said. 'Gori's murder is not ours to worry about.'

'It'll probably get written up as an accident,' Joe sniffed.

'Quite,' Carlyle agreed. 'And if he was our killer, then it's case closed.'

'What about Groves?'

'She's not our problem either,' Carlyle said, yawning. 'I outlined my thinking to Chan and his sidekick at the hospital, and they pissed all over it, so let them work it out for themselves.' He thought about Monica Hartson – her Glasgow exile could come to a speedy end. Pulling out his mobile, he rang her number. Tapping his foot impatiently on the asphalt, he listened to the call this time go to voicemail. 'For fuck's sake!' he hissed. How was it that some people were just incapable of answering a bloody phone? Ending the call without leaving a message, he dropped the handset back into his jacket pocket. 'Did you write up the Mills report?'

Joe started down the stairs without looking up. 'No.'

'Don't worry about it,' Carlyle grinned. 'I'll sort it out after we've had breakfast.'

At the mention of food, Joe perked up considerably. 'Great.'

'And then I'll go and see Simpson.'

THIRTY-EIGHT

In conclusion, it appears that Mr Mills killed his wife for reasons unknown, and subsequently took his own life in a fit of remorse.

On that basis, we believe that no further investigation is required and that the case can be closed.

Carole Simpson reread the last sentence carefully. Try as she might, she couldn't find any double-meaning or hidden aside. She looked up at Carlyle, who was sitting in front of the desk with his hands clasped in his lap, an expression of Zen-like calm on his face. If there's been a worse impersonation of a choirboy in this office in the last decade then I wasn't around to see it, the Commander thought sourly.

Raising her eyebrows, she let the report drop on to the desk. 'And that's it?'

Sitting up straight in his chair, the inspector looked his boss directly in the eye. 'Yes, Commander,' he said stiffly.

'No Chilean hit men?'

Carlyle smiled. 'That was only ever one theory.'

'What about Sandra Groves and the . . .' she waved a hand impatiently in the air '. . . the Hartson woman?'

Carlyle felt his smile waver. You had to give it to Simpson, she was no mug. 'I haven't really kept up with the Groves case,' he said vaguely. 'As for Hartson, that has been listed as a suicide. Her GP confirmed that she had been suffering from post-traumatic stress disorder.'

I know the feeling, Simpson thought grimly.

'It seems that she had been unwell for some time—'

The Commander cut him off in mid-sentence. 'So she threw herself under a Tube train?'

Carlyle shrugged. When he finally managed to get through to Hartson's mobile, it had been answered by a brusque WPC. After establishing who he was, she unceremoniously declared that the phone's owner had 'topped herself in front of a Tube train'. There didn't seem any reason to argue the point.

'Just minutes after she'd had a meeting with your good self?'

'It looks like it all ended up getting too much for the poor woman.'

'You can have that effect on people,' Simpson mumbled to herself.

'What?'

'Nothing.' Despite her better judgement, Simpson persisted. 'It's all a bit of a coincidence, wouldn't you say?'

'The driver said she jumped,' Carlyle said evenly. 'No one who was on the platform at the time contradicted him.'

'Mmm.'

'And the CCTV was inconclusive.'

Well aware of her underling's ability to be exceedingly economical with the *actualité*, the Commander eyed Carlyle warily. 'But, Inspector, with your *theories*, didn't you think that Ms Hartson was in some kind of danger?'

'I was only guessing,' he said, showing some fake modesty in the face of the Commander's obvious bluff. 'But the poor woman had seen some truly terrible things. Some of her experiences in Iraq were horrific.'

'Yes, all right.' Simpson didn't want to hear the gory details.

'She was clearly in an unhappy place.'

'Okay.' The commander let out a long sigh. The inspector could stonewall all day if necessary and she had meetings to attend.

'So we're good?' Placing his hands on the arms of the chair, Carlyle made to get to his feet.

Simpson looked pained. 'I suppose so.' She tapped the report with her right index finger and he could see that the nail had been bitten down almost to the quick. 'But why did you feel the need to come here in person just to deliver this?'

'Well . . .' Carlyle cleared his throat, trying to get his tone of voice just right. 'I wanted to apologise for the delay in getting it to you, and – and to make sure that you were happy with the final findings.'

Something approximating a smile inched across the commander's face. 'Thank you, John,' she replied, 'but an email would have been perfectly acceptable. I know how busy you are, so you didn't have to take the time.'

'I know,' Carlyle replied, 'but under the circumstances . . .'

She shot him a look.

'. . . I felt,' he continued, lifting his gaze to the ceiling, 'that I should take the opportunity to come and say that, er, well . . .' he swallowed '. . . I know that this must be a difficult time for you, but that the view of everyone at Charing Cross is that you are a good copper, a respected colleague, and that if we can be of any help, please let us know.'

Where the hell had that come from? After all these years, it looked like he had found a new way to put a foot in his mouth. Feeling himself blushing slightly, he concentrated on trying to shut up.

When he finally felt able to look Simpson in the face, she seemed as bemused at his little speech as he was himself. 'Well, thank you, John.' Her cheeks reddening, she cleared her throat. 'Those are the first real words of support I've had since Joshua was arrested.'

He stared at a spot on the wall behind her head. 'The boys at the station thought it was important for it to be said.' Hopefully, 'the boys' wouldn't find out about his spontaneous, self-appointed role as their spokesman.

'And the sentiments are very much appreciated.' She stood up and waited for him to follow suit. 'And thank you for the report. It is good to know that the Mills case is closed.'

'Yes.'

'And how is the Royal Opera House investigation coming along?'

Carlyle's brow furrowed. The backlog of uncompleted interviews with the Puccini-loving alleged robbery victims had not even been touched. 'Slowly.'

'Ah well,' Simpson nodded as she moved round the desk. 'These things invariably proceed at their own pace.'

'Yes,' Carlyle replied, rather disconcerted by his boss's uncharacteristically laissez-faire attitude. Feeling a complete arse, he smiled awkwardly as he made swiftly for the door.

Leaving Simpson's office, he walked a short way along the corridor to the nearest gents, in order to compose himself and try to work out what he'd just done. And why he'd done it. At best, he had always found the commander a deeply unappealing and flawed colleague. Now the selfish careerist had come a cropper, so where was the Schadenfreude? Being supportive was so far removed from his usual style that he wondered if he might not be coming down with something. Failing to find any instant answers, he splashed some water on his face and retraced his steps, before heading out into the bustle of the West London afternoon.

THIRTY-NINE

Christian Holyrod was momentarily distracted by the small passenger jet passing in front of the ground-to-ceiling windows of his office as it climbed away from City airport, on its way to some European destination. Once it had had disappeared from view, he returned his gaze to the three sheets of A4-sized paper laid out on the desk in front of him, and gave a low murmur of satisfaction. As if on cue, a butler appeared with a glass of Talisker on a silver salver. The man placed the drink on the table, gave a small nod, and disappeared without saying a word.

Once he had left, Holyrod picked up the sheet of paper to his left and scanned it while sniffing his Scotch. The summary of the police report into Agatha Mills's death was short, to the point and, most importantly, came to exactly the conclusion the Mayor wanted to see. 'Who would have thought it?' Holyrod murmured to himself. 'That idiot Carlyle gets something right for once.' On second thoughts, it was doubtless down to his boss. About to ring Simpson and congratulate her on a job well done, he remembered her toxic husband and thought better of it. The whole fraud thing was a crying shame, it really was, but these things happened and when they did one had to keep one's distance.

Tearing the report into small pieces, he assembled the bits into a small pile on his desk, contemplating them with satisfaction as he took a first sip of his Scotch. Returning the tumbler to the desk, he scooped up his handiwork, carefully placing the rubbish in a locked bin marked *CONFIDENTIAL SHREDDING ONLY*.

After a little more whisky, the Mayor felt his cheeks begin to flush and a gentle warmth filled his belly. With a satisfied sigh, he lifted a second sheet of paper from his desk. This was an email from the Company Secretary at Pierrepoint Aerospace, confirming that the final signed contract from the Chilean defence contractor LAHC Consulting had been received. As a result, Pierrepoint had effectively subcontracted large parts of its contract to manage British military bases in Afghanistan to the South Americans, at a fraction of the rate that it was charging the Ministry of Defence. The effect on the company's earnings would be considerable. So too would be the effect on his year-end bonus. As he contemplated his windfall, it dawned on Holyrod that this must have been one of the last things poor Matias Gori had attended to before his unfortunate death. The Mayor lifted his glass to absent friends. 'Jolly good show,' he grinned. 'Well done indeed.'

'Would you like a drink, Inspector?'

'Why not?' Carlyle settled into his soft leather armchair and smiled. 'I'll have a whisky, thank you.' Watching Claudio Orb shuffle off to get their drinks, the inspector gazed out across Heathrow's new Terminal 5. This was the first time he had ever set foot in an Executive Lounge. On the few times he'd ever travelled through the airport on holiday, Carlyle had been stuck with the unwashed masses milling round the fast-food restaurants and duty-free shops on the main concourse. It didn't make for a happy experience. This, on the other hand, was really quiet and pleasant. Peace and quiet were what you paid for; that and the free booze. Carlyle turned away from the window and contemplated the scattering of rich-looking types casually getting blasted while, at the same time, taking a last few hits on their crackberrys before take-off. 'How the other half live,' he said quietly to himself. The other half a per cent, more like.

'There you are.' Orb handed him a tumbler half-full of indeterminate Scotch and kept a tall glass half-filled with a red liquid for himself. 'Just a cranberry juice for me,' he grinned, sinking slowly into the chair opposite. 'It's a long flight. Cheers!'

Carlyle raised his glass slightly. 'Cheers.' He took a sip. Smooth. And, again, better than he was used to.

Orb placed his glass on the low table between them. 'So, I take it that you have come to see me quietly off the premises?'

'No, not really,' Carlyle replied. 'I just wanted to see you before you left to say thank you for all your help with my investigation.'

'Come now, Inspector,' Orb grinned, 'I do not get the impression that you are the type of man to come all the way to the airport just to fulfil a minor social pleasantry.'

Carlyle took another mouthful of Scotch, letting it sit under his tongue before it slipped down his throat. 'Well, maybe I'm not just here to say thank you. I hoped you might be able to clear up a few things for me – some loose ends.'

Orb raised an eyebrow. 'There are loose ends?'

'Not officially. My case – the murder of Agatha Mills – is closed.'

'Good.'

'The final verdict was that her husband did it.'

'I see.'

'But . . .'

The Ambassador smiled. 'But you do not think this was a simple case of a man killing his wife?'

Carlyle shrugged. 'Things are often more complicated than they might seem.'

'Inspector, I am – I *was* a diplomat – I know that things are *always* more complicated than they seem. Or, if not, then we make them so.' Orb chuckled. 'What do *you* think happened here?'

'I think that Matias Gori killed Agatha Mills,' Carlyle said softly, 'along with another woman, Sandra Groves and probably a third, Monica Hartson.'

Orb looked at the inspector, giving nothing away. 'Why?'

'Because they wanted to have him arrested and tried for war crimes. They think he murdered a whole family in Iraq.'

A soothing female voice with a perfect Home Counties accent came over the tannoy: '*Passengers are now invited to begin boarding BA flight 93 to Toronto and Santiago*.'

Placing his juice on the table, Orb shifted in his seat.

'I assume that you knew about all this,' Carlyle continued, 'because those women wrote to you, asking for action to be taken against Gori.'

'You should never assume, Inspector, said Orb, holding his gaze. 'Assumptions can be misleading – dangerous even.'

'Only if they're wrong.' Carlyle shrugged. 'My job is all about making assumptions. The facts either fit them or they don't. If they don't, I make some new ones.'

'It's an approach, I suppose.'

'Did you know about the accusations against Gori?'

'Lots of people write to the Embassy, Inspector. The Ambassador gets to read hardly any of this correspondence. If any of those ladies ever wrote to me, I am sure that I did not see it. For that I apologise.'

'Sir.' Carlyle pushed himself to the edge of his seat and leaned forward. 'I am not here in any official capacity. I am certainly not looking to cause you any trouble. Nothing that we say will go any further.'

Orb stared into his drink.

'I just want to know what happened.'

'Why?' Orb asked. 'We both know that this . . . mess has been dealt with. It's over now.'

Good question. The inspector sipped his whisky. 'Agatha Mills spent forty years fighting on behalf of her brother. She, and the others, fought for what they believed in.'

The Ambassador smiled. 'And you think they deserve answers?'

'I suppose so,' Carlyle mumbled into his glass.

'Then I fear that you will be disappointed,' Orb sighed. 'You see, I made some enquiries of my own. It seems that there are a number of cases relating to the 1973 coup that are in the process of being dropped. The Pettigrew case is one of them. There will therefore be no trial.'

Finishing his drink, Carlyle thought about the empty space in the family mausoleum in North London that would never be filled. 'That is a shame.'

'That is life, Inspector.'

'Yes, I suppose it is. But the Pettigrew trial was not what was concerning Gori.'

'That was the other thing I checked,' Orb said. 'Matias has never been cited in any of the various investigations, either concluded or ongoing, into the Ishaqi massacre in Iraq.' Carlyle made to say something, but the Ambassador held up a hand. 'He didn't even get a mention. Whatever these ladies, or indeed Matias himself, might have thought, no one else was paying any attention.'

'Maybe they should have done.'

Orb raised an eyebrow. 'For a policeman, that sounds a little *limp*, if you don't mind me saying so.'

Carlyle sucked down a little more of the Scotch. 'Not at all.'

'*This is a second call for BA flight 93 to Toronto and Santiago.*'

The Ambassador pulled a boarding card from his jacket pocket and started playing with it. 'We both know,' he said quietly, 'that there was something wrong with Matias. The wiring in his brain wasn't quite right. He was the kind of man who would have been very much at home in the Chile of 1973.' He looked at Carlyle. 'In the London of today, he did not fit in so well.'

'So he *did* kill those women?'

Orb stood up. 'Really,' he said, 'I don't know. I assume so, but I don't know.'

The inspector placed his empty glass on a nearby table and got to his feet. 'What about his death?' he asked.

Orb picked up a small tan leather case from beside his chair and weighed it in his hand. 'That was a surprise, for Matias to step off the roof like that.' He gazed up at the monitor above his head telling him to go to Gate 72. 'Maybe he was overcome with remorse.'

Carlyle laughed. 'Maybe.'

Orb extended a hand. 'Remorse can be a good thing.'

Carlyle shook his hand. 'Indeed it can. I hope you have a safe journey home, sir, and good luck with your retirement.'

'Thank you, Inspector. My wife has plenty of plans to keep me busy, so I'm not sure that I'll even notice being retired!'

'I know the feeling,' Carlyle said. 'My wife doesn't like to see me idle either.'

'Good luck to both of us, then.' Orb smiled as he turned away, heading for the terminal and his departure gate.

Watching him go, Carlyle looked up the time on the screen listing upcoming departures. The day was ebbing away; by the time he managed to get back into the city, the working day would be over. Settling back into his seat, he thought that he might just enjoy his luxurious surroundings here for a little while longer.

He had just finished his second whisky – a sixteen-year-old Lagavulin – and was contemplating a third, when his private phone rang. That'll be Helen, he thought. I shouldn't have made that quip about her keeping me busy. Answering, he tried to assume his most sober voice. 'Yes?'

The voice on the other end of the line wasn't his wife's, but was immediately recognisable all the same. Not bothering with any pleasantries, Dominic Silver got straight to the point.

'I've found the boy.'

FORTY

Carlyle looked along the empty road and wondered quite how he had ended up here. Behind him was a two-storey, steel-framed warehouse on the edge of an industrial estate near the M25. Standing under an orange street light, he looked up at the seemingly deserted offices on the first floor. Ferociously tired, he hopped from foot to foot to try and keep himself alert while he waited.

Eventually, Dominic Silver appeared out of a side door and strolled across the car park. As he approached Carlyle, Silver pointed at a car parked on the other side of the road. It was some kind of Toyota hatchback. Without saying a word, Dominic walked past him and over to the vehicle. Popping the trunk, he beckoned the policeman over to take a look.

Carlyle stuck his head closer to the bundle inside, and watched the covering blanket move up and down with the child's breathing. Jake Hagger was asleep. The inspector realised he had been holding his breath and now let out a long sigh. Reaching into the trunk, he was careful to get a good hold on both boy and blanket before carefully lifting them out into the cold night air. Jake groaned but he did not wake. He felt light in Carlyle's arms, somewhat less than the inspector imagined a boy of his age ought to weigh. They would have to check him thoroughly at the hospital. Dominic opened the door and Carlyle laid Jake gently across the back seat before stepping away and easing the door shut as quietly as he could.

The two men stood in silence for several moments, unwilling to look at each other. The inspector knew better than to ask how the boy was found. Out of the corner of his eye, he saw something emerge from the bushes about twenty yards away. The fox sauntered right into the middle of the road, eyed the pair of them briefly, then trotted off in the opposite direction.

Dominic let out a low whistle. 'First time I've seen that!' He stuck a hand in his trouser pocket and pulled out a car key. 'Here you go,' he said, tossing it to Carlyle. 'Now get the kid out of here.'

'What about . . . ?' Carlyle made the vaguest of gestures towards the doomed men inside the warehouse.

'That's my business,' said Dominic firmly. 'Just go.'

Carlyle stared at the key as he turned it around in his hand. 'I can't drive.'

'What?' Dominic said, somewhat dumbfounded.

'I never learned to drive.' Carlyle shrugged. 'In London you don't really need to.'

Dominic put his hands on his hips and stared into the night. 'For God's sake.'

'Half the people in London don't have a car,' Carlyle protested.

'I'm sure most of them can fucking drive, though.' Dominic shook his head. 'You really are a useless tosser.'

'Sorry.'

'Get in.'

Carlyle headed for the passenger side.

Dominic grabbed his arm. 'Get in the driver's side, before I fucking thump you.'

Over the next few minutes, Dominic showed Carlyle the basics. Fortunately for the inspector, the vehicle was an automatic. Once it was switched on, all he really had to worry about was the accelerator and the brake.

'Take him to A and E at UCH,' Dominic said, once the tutorial was over. Slipping out of the passenger seat, he pointed at a small box on the dashboard. 'Use the SatNav.'

'What?'

'For fuck's sake.' Dom did a little dance on the tarmac, fists clenched, as if he was getting ready to clock the inspector. 'Just follow the bloody signs for Central London.'

'Okay.' Carlyle thought he could manage that. Probably.

'Take it slow. Nothing above thirty miles an hour. Even at that pace, it shouldn't take you much more than an hour. There's no traffic at this time of night anyway. When you get there, leave the keys in the ignition. Maybe someone will nick it. If not, it will get towed. It's clean anyway.'

'What about a licence?' Carlyle asked.

'If anybody stops you, just show them your Warrant Card.' Dominic grinned widely. 'Don't worry, there are no coppers about this late – I should know. As long as you don't hit anything, or go so slow that you might be mistaken for a kerb crawler or a cruising car bomber, you'll be fine.'

Carlyle looked doubtful.

'Even if you get stopped, so what? You're a hero,' Dom went on. 'Socially inept when it comes to motors, but a hero nonetheless. Just remember your story.'

Carlyle nodded obediently.

'It was an anonymous tip. You picked the car up half a mile down the road. Don't bring anyone back here, at least for a while.' Slamming the passenger door shut, Dom stuck his hand through the open window and they shook.

'Thanks,' said Carlyle.

'No problem,' said Dominic, eyeing the inspector carefully. 'Do we have a deal?'

'Yes,' Carlyle said, 'we have a deal.' Taking his foot off the brake, he pressed tentatively on the accelerator. The engine squealed and they moved slowly forward. Looking in the rear-view mirror, he saw Dominic head back towards the warehouse and out of sight.

In the back, the boy was still sleeping peacefully. Carlyle's heart rose and sank at the same time. They were heading for home, wherever that might be.